IRISH GANGS AND
STICK-FIGHTING

IRISH GANGS AND STICK-FIGHTING

In The Works Of
William Carleton

John W. Hurley

Caravat Press
Philadelphia, PA.

CONTENTS

This book is dedicated to Liam O'Cathalain, who preserved for all time, the stories of his people. His work remains a poignant memorial to their way of life and a tribute to Carleton himself: *Molann an obair an fear*.

This book is also dedicated to the millions of Carleton's countrymen who lived these lives, fought the good fight and in An Gorta Mór, were brutally silenced.
May their lives and fighting spirit always be remembered, honored and emulated by their descendants.

ACKNOWLEDGMENTS

This book might never have come about had my Irish-born father not instilled in me a love of Irish culture and Irish fighting traditions—thanks Dad for everything. I have to thank my brother Matthew, who shares my interests and constantly helped with advice and encouragement, even while on assignment overseas. My sister Mary Lou and my other brother Joseph also provided much needed encouragement and support with this book. I also have to thank my friends Heather Smyth Heinzmann and Jennifer Holt for their contributions.

Without the patience, kindness, understanding and support of my best friend and wife Julie, whose contributions are too numerous to mention, this project might never have come to fruition. Thank you Julie for everything.

William Carleton, (1794-1869).

John W. Hurley

INTRODUCTION

When I first came across an old copy of Carleton's *The Party Fight and Funeral*, I never could have imagined the effect it would have on my life. *The Party Fight* lead me to the other works of William Carleton, and these in turn have provided not only hours of entertaining reading, but deep and meaningful insights into Irish history and culture, the Irish character and the Irish way of life in the nineteenth century and today. Reading Carleton also confirmed my life-long belief that Irish fighting styles or "martial arts" of the eighteenth and nineteenth centuries were developed, and consisted of much more than just the drunken brawling often depicted in modern literature and film. This confirmation alone affected the course of my life, by encouraging me to continue to explore and research Irish fighting arts. While exploring other sources of information, I also made a thorough study of all of Carleton's works. Eventually, I committed myself to getting all of his stories about Irish stick-fighters reprinted in a single volume, so that others who share my interest could have easier access to them. This volume is the fruit of that work. Putting it together has been a long and difficult process, but the process of reading, editing and finally publishing these works of William Carleton has brought me great satisfaction.

Carleton's Life

Readers unfamiliar with him may ask who William Carleton was, and how these stick-fighting stories of his came about. William Carleton was Ireland's first great short story writer and novelist of international repute, although today he is mostly forgotten. His works have been largely overshadowed by subsequent generations of Irish writers. Today, William Butler Yeats, James Joyce, and scores of other Irish writers dominate the Irish literature courses offered at most universities. This is ironic given that it could be argued that the Irish literary movement which began in the 1890's, was largely initiated by Carleton, however unintentionally, as far back as the 1820's.

Carleton was actually born "Liam O'Cathalain" on Shrove Tuesday in 1794, at Prillisk, near the town of Clogher in County Tyrone. He was the youngest of fourteen children born to a small farmer endowed with a considerable memory for stories and lore, and a mother who could perform the old Irish songs with great emotional pathos and beauty. The O'Cathalain's were native Irish speakers, and Liam's father was in fact a seanchaí, while his mother was a gifted sean-nós singer. In O'Cathalain's time, "folk-positions" (as I call them), such as these were actually very professional in nature. By today's standards, performances of songs and stories by seanchaís and sean-nós singers would have been of high caliber. It was probably professional performers like the O'Cathalain's who were largely responsible for the Irish contribution to the performing arts of nineteenth century American popular culture. The children of such performers, newly emigrated to America, were able to translate their skills over into the new mediums of the vaudeville culture being performed in the song and dance halls of America. In a similar way, Liam O'Cathalain was able to translate his own native Irish "show business" background into the English-language, pop culture medium of fiction writing.

From his father, Liam inherited a virtually photographic memory, and an endless supply of history and lore; from his mother, he seems to have inherited an extraordinary ability to present this material creatively and in an entertaining and theatrical way.

O'Cathalain's classical education consisted of attending the local hedgeschool, traveling (and teaching) as a "poor scholar", and feeding his literary appetite by reading all the books he could lay his hands on. In his lifetime, Catholic boys and young adults of his intelligence and learning were destined for the priesthood, but Liam O'Cathalain's entry into the seminary was delayed both by his father's death, and by an ever daunting loss of faith, first in Roman Catholicism, and then in Protestantism. This loss of faith haunted him for the rest of his life, and his continuing struggle between faith and the loss of it, seems to have echoed multiple struggles over the numerous layers of dualism extant in the lives of so many generations of Irish people. Irish civilization continues to grapple with the dichotomies of country and city life, tradition and innovation, Gaelic and English language and culture, Christian idealism and worldly secularism, and Catholic and Protestant traditions. The choices—often contradictory and tragic—which the very existence of these opposing cultural elements requires each individual in Irish society to make, and the req-

John W. Hurley

uisite debates and struggles over those decisions, provided the basic elements underlying all of Carleton's stories. They are constant themes and they have continued to be the central themes throughout most of Irish, English-language literature.

O'Cathalain eventually gained some genuine classical knowledge at the school of a Dr. Keenan, a parish priest in the diocese of Down, and later he became tutor to the children of a farmer in County Louth. A reading of the novel *Gil Blas* created in him a desire to see more of the world, and quitting his job as tutor, the restless O'Cathalain walked across the country from Tyrone to Dublin.

Penniless, and without any real plans, he took any sort of work he could find. In desperation, he eventually decided to enlist in the British army, and wrote a letter—in Latin—stating his intentions to a colonel of a regiment. Impressed by his intelligence, the colonel dissuaded O'Cathalain from enlisting, and not long after this, O'Cathalain met the protestant minister, Rev. Caesar Otway. Otway was an eccentric character, a mix of antiquarian and missionary zealot, but he was quick to recognize O'Cathalain's intelligence and talent. Otway urged O'Cathalain to try writing stories about Irish peasant life for his Protestant newspaper, the *Christian Examiner*, to which O'Cathalain enthusiastically agreed, and "William Carleton's" career as a writer was launched. From the start, Otway's missionary agenda and sectarian beliefs influenced the editing of the stories, and this bothered Carleton greatly; eventually they parted ways. For Roman Catholic readers who might find aspects of the stories offensive (as I first did), it should be remembered that when Carleton wrote for Otway, he was in a very desperate situation economically. Carleton may have been an initially enthusiastic convert, but he seems to have also been choosing between severe poverty and destitution on the one hand, and being paid to help further the Protestant missionary agenda of Otway on the other. Like many artists, Carleton was a social critic, and his writing provided him with a chance to use his substantial talents while trying to change what he felt were the less positive aspects of Irish culture. While Carleton was critical of many aspects of Roman Catholicism, it is not known how much Otway interfered with and edited the stories, and some of the more sectarian comments may be attributed to him. Eventually, Carleton distanced himself from Otway and his conversion to the Church of Ireland faltered as well.

When Carleton was about thirty, the stories he had written for the *Christian Examiner* were printed in one collection, *Traits and Stories of the Irish Peasantry*, considered by some to be his best work. His next work was his first novel, *The Dead Boxer*, and he subsequently wrote nineteen more novels. The amazing ease and speed with which Carleton could write was demonstrated in 1845 when he agreed to fill in for the great nationalist writer Thomas Davis, a regular contributor to the newspaper publications of James Duffy. Davis died suddenly, and Duffy's newspaper was left unprepared and unable to fill the enormous gap in copy left as a result of his death. Carleton was asked to help and in just six days he presented Duffy with another novel, *Paddy-Go-Easy (or Parra Sastha; or The History of Paddy-Go-Easy And His Wife Nancy)*, which was serialized in Duffy's newspaper with great success. Throughout his life, Carleton continued to write for an ever growing number of readers. Later in his life, he lived at Woodville, Sandford, near Dublin, where he died on 30th January, 1869, aged seventy years, and was buried at Mount Jerome. Although not popular with many academics, time has shown that Carleton was the undisputed master of depicting nineteenth century Irish peasant life and traditions in the English language. Many Irish authors who have come after him have acknowledged his greatness. Although Carleton was really Ireland's first great international novelist in the English language, it could also be argued that he was an insightful social historian and anthropologist as well. Through his stories Carleton consciously documented and forever preserved, the disappearing traditions of nineteenth century Gaelic Irish culture.

Liam O'Cathalain the Stick-fighter

In addition to his considerable literary and artistic talents, Liam O'Cathalain was also a gifted athlete. In the early years of his life, he achieved local fame for his ability at playing the many sports and games in which the Gaelic Irish peasantry took part. These sports included what in today's terms would be considered martial arts such as Irish wrestling and boxing, and from his early youth O'Cathalain seems to have been especially trained as a stick fighter. For the stu-

John W. Hurley

dent of Irish stick-fighting, his works provide an incredible amount of information about Irish stick-fighting, from terminology and traditions, to first-hand, autobiographical accounts of battles. Much of this information in effect, instructs the reader in the rudiments of Ireland's stick-fighting culture. And although the stories are not manuals on self-defense, they do describe some of the techniques used.

It should be emphasized that O'Cathalain himself was an Irish speaking stick-fighter, who trained and fought as a stick-fighter for much of his early life. That his neighbors, friends and family members continued to do so long after his move to Dublin seems evident from *The Party Fight and Funeral*. Since O'Cathalain almost always wrote from autobiographical material, the historical accuracy of the Irish stick-fighting traditions documented in his works must be considered authentic and reliable.

The Stories

Although many of Carleton's stories make mention of factions, faction fighting and stick-fighting, the stories in this collection all focus specifically on faction gangs or individual stick-fighters. *The Battle Of The Factions* tells the story of two feuding Irish clans, the O'Callaghans and the O'Hallaghans, as related by a member of the O'Callaghan family; it has a Romeo and Juliet sub-plot. *Neal Malone*, the tailor of the O'Callaghan faction in *The Battle Of The Factions*, is the main character in the comedic, Neal Malone, the story of a diminutive and heroic fighting tailor. Neal—who wants nothing more than to fight and prove his mettle—is forced to solve the conundrum of getting himself involved in a fight when he is so well liked, even by his enemies, that he cannot find anyone who will accommodate him. In *The Party Fight And Funeral*, the narrator of the tale, Toby D'Arcy, returns to the village of his youth, only to find that one of his childhood friends has recently been killed in one of the huge Party Fights which were common in early nineteenth century Ireland. This sets the stage for various anecdotes, some amusing, some incredibly tragic, and many of which still reflect very real aspects of life in Ulster.

Carleton's Language

All of the tales in this book contained some footnotes by Carleton explaining Irish words, Hiberno-Irish expressions, or elements of the stories. These footnotes were minimal and I felt that much of Carleton's language was too obscure for the modern reader to understand. Many other words and expressions needed to be defined if the stories were to be fully understood, so wherever possible I have expanded on Carleton's notes or added my own. Deciding which terms, phrases and explanations to include proved difficult, because of Carleton's impressive use of language. Carleton had a genius for making easily expressed thoughts and ideas more complicated than they need be and he often used phrases from more than one language when doing so. He did this deliberately in order to flaunt his intellectual abilities, vast vocabulary and for comedic effect. But above all he did it in order to bring realism to his stories, for it was common practice for Irish people of the nineteenth century to constantly flaunt their verbal skills, whether in Irish or a newly acquired English. Impressing, entertaining and competing with each other verbally in English, was a continuation of Irish language traditions, and as Carleton himself says in a footnote from the story *Shane Fadh's Wedding*, "...the (Irish) peasantry are often extremely fond of hard and long words, which they call tall English". Carleton's own "tall English" comes out repeatedly in the stories: two factions who may unite through a marriage would become "penultimately amalgamated", while kilt wearing men who wore no underwear "eschewed inexpressibles".

The Irish peasant's fondness for "tall English" has resulted in some of the most imaginative, creative and entertaining literature ever written in the English language. Ireland has produced four winners of the Nobel Prize for Literature, remarkable for such a small country, and in Carleton's writings we find the real beginnings of that great literary tradition. As we can see in his writings, that tradition and the worldview of Irish culture which it expresses, has its roots in the Irish language and in Gaelic culture, the oldest culture in Western Europe.

The language of Carleton is in fact a mixture of Gaelic Irish, Elizabethan English and nineteenth century English, referred to by scholars as "Hiberno-English". Many of Carleton's expressions are pho-

John W. Hurley

netically spelt Hiberno-English pronunciations of English language words: "sated" for "seated", "bade" for "bead", etc. In cases such as these where the word is a slight Hiberno-English variation from English, I have not provided endnotes because I felt the meaning of the word was relatively clear. Where I felt the pronunciation and the context of a word left no hints at its meaning, I have provided endnotes. More complex or rarely used English language words were the most difficult to decide on and again, I made endnotes where I felt the context of the word left little or no hint at its meaning. Trying to gloss every word that a reader might not understand would have been impossible.

Wherever possible I have also tried to give modern Irish spellings and translations from Carleton's Irish language expressions. For some cases these are clearly given by Carleton, but for most I have had to come up with my own explanations. My endnotes are the result of much research and an ongoing attempt to familiarize myself with nineteenth century Irish literature. I feel confident about most, but I am not a professional linguist or philologist and a few of my explanations—in particular for "Tunder-an'-ouns", "tarean-ounty", "Murther-an-age", "Blur-an'-agers", "Tare-an'-ounze" and "Big tarean'-ouns"—are purely theoretical reconstructions. These expressions may be rooted in Irish or they may simply be obscure English language exclamations that I have over interpreted. Readers will notice that there is some repetition in the endnotes. My intention in designing the book this way was to make every story and its endnotes stand completely on their own, giving readers the freedom to start the book wherever they wanted while still being able to refer to the endnotes for that specific story quickly and easily. Because of Carleton's variations in spelling, some readers might not have realized that "shillely", "shillelah" and "shillelagh" are all the same word, and yet because of their variations in spelling, I felt that all needed to be individually noted.

Carleton and Bataireacht

While in the course of writing this book, I have often wondered if Carleton the cantankerous social critic would have chafed at the idea that future generations of readers would use his works to learn more about Irish stick-fighting or "bataireacht". At first it would seem that he would object, after all, part of Carleton's whole purpose in writing these stories was to expose some of the more negative aspects of Irish society which had affected his life and the lives of his family and friends. But Carleton had diverse reasons for writing and he spent a lifetime verbally attempting to slay those dragons which confronted the downtrodden Irish peasantry: the social ostracization, superstitious fears, secret conspiracies, alcoholism and violence which they often seemed to impose upon themselves and the grinding poverty, sectarianism, injustice and social and political inequality imposed on them by others. He may at times seem too harsh in condemning his countrymen but ultimately, despite all the protestations, Carleton was a man of his people, one who cared deeply about those people, a mixture of the raconteur seanchaí and the taciturn Irish schoolmaster.

Carleton seems to have been a bit of a thrill-seeker and a risk taker as well, who never really lost his love of excitement and the chance to relate the experience of excitement in a good story. Athletics was one subject which provided him with many good memories and anecdotes, and from his stories, I can't help but think that had the Irish stick-fighting of his day been less brutal and less identified with grudges, para-militarism, etc. Carleton would not have objected to it. In Carleton's youth he, like most Irish Catholics of the nineteenth century, would have heard many times the Fenian Lays and other native Irish martial arts lore. Through their practice of Irish martial arts and their involvement in Irish military and para-military organizations, many Irishmen tried to emulate the exploits of their childhood heroes, and in this Carleton was at first no different from other boys. Instruction through story is an ancient Irish tradition, and even in Carleton's own stories, this paradigm of instruction through story is often at work. But in Carleton's day the ancient, aristocratic and once scientific art of Irish stick-fighting had degenerated in many parts of Ireland into little more than bouts of no holds barred gang warfare. For Carleton the reverie of violence instilled in him by the traditional tales of ancestral martial glory did not survive the brutal realities of nineteenth century faction combat. Like many of his contemporaries, Carleton was quick to see the futility in what appeared to be a tradition of routinely attempting to beat his neighbors sense-

John W. Hurley

less, all for the sake of honor, glory or sport. Carleton's generation questioned the old wisdom of stick-fighting which was done, as one Irish peasant of the time had said, "because our ancestors had always fought this way". Carleton's generation asked itself why Irishmen were fighting each other in increasingly larger and more deadly battles, while important social and political issues which affected Irish life, were being left unresolved. They began to ask themselves how the Irish could ever claim the right to govern themselves when the countryside was regularly erupting in what amounted to outbreaks of chaotic civil war.

Many Irishmen of the nineteenth century came to the conclusion that while the practice of martial arts was positive, the practice of faction fighting was a tradition which had outlived its usefulness and which needed to be eliminated from Irish society. Faction fights had become the major public venues where Irish martial artists could display their considerable skills. By the 1820's these fights seem to have come under the total control of the local factions or gangs in many regions of Ireland. A small, anonymous and unaffiliated group of men seemed to wield complete control over these gangs, and many in Ireland felt that if Irish society was to evolve in a more positive direction, the power of these gangs needed to be broken, and their considerable energies, re-directed. Factionalism needed to be replaced by patriotic nationalism, gangs needed to be replaced by disciplined Irish regiments (and an Irish revolutionary army), and the stick and sword needed to be replaced by the gun.

Led by Irish nationalists, this transformation in Irish society did in fact occur although the factions have never disappeared completely. Many Irish nationalists, (both Catholic and Protestant alike), were "reformed" faction fighters and retained their martial arts skills after abandoning the practice of faction fighting. But despite this, the decline in faction fighting seems to have witnessed an overall decline in the practice of Irish stick-fighting. The new social taboo against faction fighting discouraged future generations from becoming professional stick-fighters and encouraged them to train instead to become professional soldiers. The futility of, and blind adherence to, faction fighting—which had kept the Irish divided—seems to have tainted the practice of Irish stick fighting.

As faction fighting became socially unacceptable, interest in learning stick-fighting waned and the resulting decline in students meant that fewer and fewer Irish stick-fighters were able to pass their skills on to others. In succeeding generations, the energies once devoted to factionism and stick-fighting, were channeled instead into the Fenian movement, the political struggles of the Land League and the sports programs of the Gaelic Athletic Association. The Irish martial arts of wrestling and boxing did not die out—if anything the practice of these arts seems to have actually increased at first—but stick-fighting seems to have lost the central place that it had held in Irish society for centuries. What had once been a traditional, rural martial art, which combined the use of athletic skills with the impassioned pursuit of the political, economic and regional objectives of the local community, was broken up and divided into its component parts. The once unified "Shillelagh Culture" as I call it, endured a cultural revolution as Ireland's traditional, peasant culture was slowly replaced with all the trappings of an aspiring Victorian pseudo-state. Organizations and associations built on a national scale and dominated publicly by the Church and the Catholic middle-class (and dominated secretly by the Fenian movement), classified, divided and fragmented various interests or pursuits—sports, politics, the Irish language—into specialized areas of activity or study. The exciting sport violence of faction fighting was replaced with the exciting sport violence of hurling; the economic objectives of faction fighting were replaced by membership in the Land League; the political violence of faction fighting was replaced by membership in the Fenian organization. This re-organization of Irish society did have the desired effect of uniting people across the island in many ways, but at the loss of many local customs and traditions as Irish culture itself became more unified, homogenous and "modern". Modernization was of course, the whole point of this process, with many people in Ireland feeling that this change was a necessary step if Irish society was ever to regain its ancient traditions of independent nationhood. Desperate times call for desperate measures and in post-Famine Ireland, the extinction of Irish civilization still loomed on the horizon as a genuine possibility. It was felt by many that if the Irish did not unite, all could be lost.

Prior to the nineteenth century Irish martial arts had consisted of

John W. Hurley

more disciplined training for self-defense and warfare and Irish nationalists of the era did promote this fact. Carleton was aware of this as well and admired the ideal of disciplined, controlled martial arts training which enables a person to defend themselves while promoting healthy habits and behaviors. It would be fair to say that Carleton did not object at all to the practice of wrestling, boxing or stick-fencing; the heroes of many of his stories are actually enthusiastically described by Carleton as being expert practitioners of these martial arts. But what Carleton did object to were the social effects of factionism itself, which warped the lives of many of the practitioners of these martial arts. Carleton felt that membership in the factions was misguided as faction fighting itself forced Irish martial artists to misuse and waste their martial arts abilities in senseless and often lethal violence. Making matters worse (Carleton felt), was that this violence often had no clear objective beyond the petty machinations of invisible (and hence unaccountable) leaders. Carleton's own philosophy towards the practice of martial arts actually coincides with the modern ideal of the ethical use of martial arts skills which we find promoted in popular culture today.

Carleton had a long list of things which he wanted to change in Irish society; his success in effecting change and his place in Irish history has yet to be determined. But he clearly pointed the way to what in the nineteenth century amounted to an alternative Irish identity, one that was traditional and Gaelic in nature, but one which sought to free itself of the negative cultural baggage which had come to ruin the lives of so many. Like many Irish innovators, Carleton was never able to witness Irish society's escape from the social conditions which he hoped would change. Yet with hindsight, we can see today that his writings must have articulated the spirit of a whole segment of Irish society which was traditionally Irish, yet which was independent minded and innovative enough to refuse to be victimized by either the pitfalls of Irish history or the status quo of Irish society. Proof of this is to be found in the fact that many of the changes which Carleton once called for have actually since come about.

Yet Carleton with all his high-minded ideals knew—perhaps better than anyone else—that he could never have been who he had become if he had not first been the "sportin' lad" from Clogher. For all his complaints, mistakes and contradictions, the fact remains that William Carleton was the product of the sum experiences of his Irish peasant youth. The battle hardened boy faction fighter who, by his teen years, had faced potential death hundreds of times on the faction field, grew into the man who routinely challenged virtually every symbol of authority in Ireland from the hierarchy of the Catholic Church, to the administrators of the British government. Men have been killed for much less in Ireland, and whatever his original purpose under Otway, Carleton's continued actions afterwards were actually quite courageous in his day. The personal code of honor which Carleton adhered to was without a doubt first formed on the faction fields of Ulster, and Carleton knew this. But like many of his era, Carleton had evolved beyond his youth, and grown into a thinking-man's martial artist. He encouraged Irishmen to empower themselves both through education and by rejecting debasing images of themselves (and the debasing behaviors such images invoked), which Carleton felt were ultimately the product of certain anti-Irish elements found in English culture. To Carleton, the darker side of Irish life was ultimately the result not of some Darwinian concept of an alleged Irish inferiority, but rather of the unseen forces which governed the lives of the people: the conditions of unnatural ignorance and poverty forced upon many Irishmen by English Penal Laws. Carleton knew that the persecution of the Irish people had created a poverty stricken culture in which many of the basic components for a healthy culture were lacking. Yet he also knew that despite society's messages to the contrary, what really lay at the heart of his nineteenth century Irish identity was the resilient and indomitable spirit of the Gaelic Irish people.

In stories such as *Willy Reilly*, and *Redmond Count O'Hanlon, The Irish Rapparee*, Carleton reveals how that spirit of the people is a direct continuation of the old Irish warrior tradition. This spirit is an inheritance from Ireland's warrior aristocracy, an aristocracy which since the sixteenth century, had succeeded in the relentless struggle to maintain the traditions and identity of its civilization despite what must be the most sustained and ruthless campaign of ethnocide in human history. Carleton knew his history and he would have known that this spirit of "the fighting race" had been the product of a culture which was once whole and complete. That culture existed when the structures and institutions of Gaelic society had been intact, and it would have included the original forms of highly developed Irish stick-fighting and other martial arts which I feel Carleton would have also approved of. I believe that Carleton would have seen the value in modern martial arts practices and the values they promote, and I think that he would have identified these values as Irish ones. I think he would be glad to know that he had succeeded in documenting some of the Irish martial arts traditions of his day—both positive and negative—so that future generations could profit from the lessons of history. (Readers interested in obtaining more information about these Irish martial arts can contact the author via his website at www.johnwhurley.com). *Irish Gangs and Stick-Fighting In The Works of William Carleton*, is part of a series of books on Irish stick-fighting and other Irish fighting styles which I hope to publish, and I think it fitting that the works of William Carleton—as authentic and genuine an authority on 19th century Irish stick fighting as we may ever find—should start this series.

John W. Hurley

Chapter 1: The Battle Of The Factions

Accordingly, the next evening found them all present, when it was determined unanimously that Pat Frayne, the hedge schoolmaster, should furnish them with the intellectual portion of the entertainment for that night, their object being, each to tell a story in his turn. "Very well," said, Pat, " I am quite simultaneous to the wishes of the company ; but you will plaise to observe, that there is clay which *is* moist, and clay which is *not* moist. Now, under certain circumstances, the clay which is not moist, ought to be made moist, and one of those circumstances is that in which any larned person becomes loquacious, and indulges in narrative. The philosophical raison, as decided on by Socrates, and the great Phelim M'Poteen, two of the most celebrated liquorary characters that ever graced the sunny side of a plantation, is, that when a man commences a narration with his clay not moist, the said narration is found, by all larned experience, to be a very dry one—ehem!"

"Very right, Mr. Frayne," replied Andy Morrow; "So in order to avoid a dhry narrative, Nancy, give the masther a jug of your goutest to wet his whistle, and keep him in wind(1) as he goes along."

"Thank you, Mr. Morrow—and in requital for your kindness, I will elucidate you such a sample of unadulterated Ciceronian(2) eloquence, as would not be found originating from every chimney-corner in this Province, anyhow. I am not bright, however, at oral relation.—I have accordingly composed into narrative the following tale, which is appellated 'The Battle of the Factions:'—

"My grandfather, Connor O'Callaghan, though a tall, erect man, with white cowing hair, like snow, that falls profusely about his broad shoulders, is now in his eighty-third year: an amazing age, considhering his former habits. His countenance is still marked with honesty and traces of hard fighting, and his cheeks ruddy and cudgel-worn; his eyes, though not as black as they often used to be, have lost very little of that nate fire which characterises the eyes of the

O'Callaghans, and for which I myself have been—but my modesty won't allow me to allude to that: let it be sufficient for the present to say, that there never was remembered so handsome a man in his native parish, and that I am as like him as one Cork-red phatie(3) is to another. Indeed, it has been often said, that it would be hard to meet an O'Callaghan without a black eye in his head. He has lost his fore-teeth, however, a point in which, unfortunately, I, though his grandson, have a strong resemblance to him. The truth is, they were knocked out of him in rows, before he had reached his thirty-fifth year—a circumstance which the kind reader will be pleased to receive in extenuation for the same defect in myself. That, however, is but a trifle, which never gave either of us much trouble.

"It pleased Providence to bring us through many hair-breadth escapes, with our craniums uncracked; and when we considher that he, on taking a retrogradation of his past life, can indulge in the plasing recollection of having broken two skulls in his fighting days, and myself one, without either of us getting a fracture in return, I think we have both rasen to be thankful. He was a powerful bulliah battha(4) in his day, and never met a man able to fight him, except big Mucklemurray, who stood before him the greater part of an hour and a half, in the fair of Knockimdowney, on the day that the first great fight took place—twenty years afther the hard frost(5)—between the O'Callaghans and the O'Hallaghans. The two men fought single hands—for both factions were willing to let them try the engagement out, that they might see what side could boast of having the best man. They began where you enter the north side of Knockimdowney, and fought successively up to the other end, then back again to the spot where they commenced, and afterwards up to the middle of the town, right opposite to the market-place, where my grandfather, by the same a-token, lost a grinder;(6) but he soon took satisfaction for that, by giving Mucklemurray a tip(7) above the eye with the end of an oak stick, decently loaded with lead, which made the poor man feel very quare entirely, for the few days that he survived it.

"Faith, if an Irishman happened to be born in Scotland, he would find it mighty inconvenient—afther losing two or three grinders in a row—to manage the hard oaten bread that they use there; for which rason, God be good to his sowl that first invented the phaties,(8)

John W. Hurley

anyhow, because a man can masticate them without a tooth, at all at all. I'll engage, if larned books were consulted, it would be found out that he was an Irishman. I wonder that neither Pastorini nor Columbkill(9) mentions anything about him in their prophecies consarning the church; for my own part, I'm strongly inclinated to believe that it must have been Saint Patrick himself; and I think that his driving all kinds of venomous reptiles out of the kingdom is, according to the Socrastic method of argument, an undeniable proof of it. The subject, to a dead certainty, is not touched upon in the Brehon Code,(10) nor by any of the three Psalters,(11) which is extremely odd, seeing that the earth never produced a root equal to it in the multiplying force of prolification. It is, indeed, the root of prosperity to a fighting people: and many a time my grandfather boasts to this day, that the first bit of bread he ever ett was a phatie.

"In mentioning my grandfather's fight with Mucklemurray, I happened to name them blackguards, the O'Hallaghans: hard fortune to the same set, for they have no more discretion in their quarrels, than so many Egyptian mummies, African buffoons, or any other uncivilised animals. It was one of them, he that's married to my own fourth cousin, Biddy O'Callaghan, that knocked two of my grinders out, for which piece of civility I had the satisfaction of breaking a splinter or two in his carcase, being always honestly disposed to pay my debts.

"With respect to the O'Hallaghans, they and our family have been next neighbours since before the Flood(12)—and that's as good as two hundred years; for I believe it's 198, anyhow, since my great grandfather's grand uncle's ould mare was swept out of the 'Island,' in the dead of the night, about half an hour after the whole country had been ris out of their beds by the thunder and lightning. Many a field of oats and many a life, both of beast and Christian, was lost in it, especially of those that lived on the bottoms about the edge of the river: and it was true for them that said it came before something; for the next year was one of the hottest summers ever remembered in Ireland.

"These O'Hallaghan's couldn't be at peace with a saint. Before they and our faction began to quarrel, it's said that the O'Donnells, or Donnells, and they had been at it,—and a blackguard set the same

O'Donnells were, at all times—in fair and market, dance, wake, and berrin,(13) setting the country on fire. Whenever they met, it was heads cracked and bones broken; till by degrees the O'Donnells fell away, one after another, from fighting, accidents, and hanging; so that at last there was hardly the name of one of them in the neighbourhood. The O'Hallaghans, after this, had the country under themselves—were the cocks of the walk entirely;—who but they? A man darn't look crooked at them, or he was certain of getting his head in his fist. And when they'd get drunk in a fair, it was nothing but 'Whoo! for the O'Hallaghans!' and leaping yards high off the pavement, brandishing their cudgels over their heads, striking their heels against their hams,(14) tossing up their hats; and when all would fail, they'd strip off their coats, and trail them up and down the street, shouting, 'Who dare touch the coat of an O'Hallaghan? Where's the blackguard Donnells now?'—and so on, till flesh and blood couldn't stand it.

"In the course of time, the whole country was turned against them; for no crowd could get together in which they didn't kick up a row, nor a bit of stray fighting couldn't be, but they'd pick it up first; and if a man would venture to give them a contrairy answer, he was sure to get the crame of a good welting for his pains. The very landlord was timourous(15) of them; for when they'd get behind in their rint, hard fortune to the bailiff, or proctor, or steward, he could find, that would have anything to say to them. And the more wise they; for maybe, a month would hardly pass till all belonging to them in the world would be in a heap of ashes: and who could say who did it? For they were as cunning as foxes.

"If one of them wanted a wife, it was nothing but find out the purtiest and the richest farmer's daughter in the neighbourhood, and next march into her father's house, at the dead hour of night, tie and gag every mortal in it, and off with her to some friend's place in another part of the country. Then what could be done? If the girl's parents didn't like to give in, their daughter's name was sure to be ruined; at all events, no other man would think of marrying her, and the only plan was, to make the best of a bad bargain; and God he knows, it was making a bad bargain for a girl to have any matrimonial concatenation(16) with the same O'Hallaghans; for they always had the bad

John W. Hurley

drop(17) in them, from first to last, from big to little—the black-guards! But wait, it's not over with them yet.

"The bone of contintion that got between them and our faction was this circumstance: their lands and ours were divided by a river that ran down from the high mountains of Sliev Boglish, and, after a coorse of eight or ten miles, disembogued(18) itself, first into Georgo Duffy's mill-dam, and afterwards into that superb stream, the Black-water, that might be well and appropriately appellated the Irish Niger. This river, which, though small at first, occasionally inflated itself to such a gigantic altitude, that it swept away cows, corn, and cottages, or whatever else happened to be in the way, was the march ditch, or merin(19) between our farms. Perhaps it is worth while remarking, as a solution for natural philosophers, that these inundations were much more frequent in winter than in summer; though, when they did occur in summer, they were truly terrific.

"God be with the days, when I and half a dozen gorsoons(20) used to go out, of a warm Sunday in summer, the bed of the river nothing but a line of white meandering stones, so hot that you could hardly stand upon them, with a small obscure thread of water creeping in-visibly among them, hiding itself, as it were, from the scorching sun; except here and there, that you might find a small crystal pool where the streams had accumulated. Our plan was to bring a pocketful of roche lime with us, and put it into the pool, when all the fish used to rise on the instant to the surface, gasping with open mouth for fresh air, and we had only to lift them out of the water; a nate plan, which, perhaps, might be adopted successfully, on a more extensive scale, by the Irish fisheries. Indeed, I almost regret that I did not remain in that station of life, for I was much happier then than ever I was since I began to study and practice larning. But this is vagating(21) from the subject.

"Well, then, I have said that them O'Hallaghans lived beside us, and that this stream divided our lands. About half a quarter—i. e. to accommodate myself to the vulgar phraseology—or, to speak more scientifically, one-eighth of a mile from our house, was as purty a hazel glen as you'd wish to see, near half a mile long—its develop-ments and proportions were truly classical. In the bottom of this glen was a small green island, about twelve yards, diametrically, of Irish admeasurement, that is to say, be the same more or less; at all events, it lay in the way of the river, which, however, ran towards the O'Hallaghan side, and, consequently, the island was our property.

"Now, you'll observe, that this river had been, for ages, the merin between the two farms, for they both belonged to separate landlords, and so long as it kept the O'Hallaghan side of the little peninsula in question there could be no dispute about it, for all was clear. One wet winter, however, it seemed to change its mind upon the subject; for it wrought and wore away a passage for itself on our side of the island, and by that means took part, as it were, with the O'Hallaghans, leaving the territory which had been our property for centhries, in their possession. This was a vexatious change to us, and, indeed, eventually produced very feudal consequences. No sooner had the stream changed sides, than the O'Hallaghans claimed the island as theirs, according to their tenement; and we, having had it for such length of time in our possession, could not break ourselves of the habitude of occupying it. They incarcerated our cattle, and we incarcerated theirs. They summoned us to their landlord, who was a magistrate; and we summoned them to ours, who was another. The verdicts were north and south. Their landlord gave it in favour of them, and ours in favour of us. The one said he had law on his side; the other, that he had proscription and possession, length of time and usage.

"The two squires then fought a challenge upon the head of it, and what was more singular, upon the disputed spot itself; the one standing on their side, the other on ours; for it was just twelve paces every way. Their friend was a small, light man, with legs like drumsticks; the other was a large, able-bodied gentleman, with a red face and hooked nose. They exchanged two shots, one only of which—the second—took effect. It pastured(22) upon their landlord's spindle leg, on which he held it out, exclaiming, that while he lived he would never fight another challenge with his antagonist, 'because,' said he, holding out his own spindle shank, 'the man who could hit that could hit anything.'

"We then were advised, by an attorney, to go to law with them; and they were advised by another attorney to go to law with us: accordingly, we did so, and in the course of eight or nine years it might have been decided, but just as the legal term approximated in which the decision was to be announced, the river divided itself with mathematical exactitude on each side of the island. This altered the state and law of the question in toto; but, in the mean time, both we and the O'Hallaghans were nearly fractured by the expenses. Now during the law-suit we usually houghed and mutilated each other's cattle,(23) according as they trespassed the premises. This brought on the usual concomitants of various battles, fought and won by both sides, and occasioned the law-suit to be dropped; for we found it a mighty inconvanient matter to fight it out both ways; by the same atoken that I think it a proof of stultity(24) to go to law at all at all, as long as a person is able to take it into his own management. For the only incongruity in the matter is this: that, in the one case, a set of lawyers have the law in their hands, and, in the other, that you have it in your own; that's the only difference, and 'tis easy knowing where the advantage lies.

"We, however, paid the most of the expenses, and would have ped them all with the greatest integrity, were it not that our attorney, when about to issue an execution against our property, happened somehow to be shot, one evening, as he returned home from a dinner which was given by him that was attorney for the O'Hallaghans. Many a boast the O'Hallaghans made, before the quarrelling between us and them commenced, that they'd sweep the streets with the fighting O'Callaghans, which was an epithet that was occasionally applied to our family. We differed, however, materially from them; for we were honourable; never starting out in dozens on a single man or two, and beating him into insignificance. A couple, or maybe, when irritated, three, were the most we ever set at a single enemy; and if we left him lying in a state of imperception, it was the most we ever did, except in a regular confliction, when a man is justified in saving his own skull by breaking one of an opposite faction. For the truth of the business is, that he who breaks the skull of him who endeavours to break his own is safest; and, surely, when a man is driven to such an alternative, the choice is unhesitating.

"O'Hallaghans' attorney, however, had better luck: they were, it is true, rather in the retrograde(25) with him touching the law charges, and, of coorse, it was only candid in him to look for his own. One morning, he found that two of his horses had been executed by some incendiary unknown, in the coorse of the night; and, on going to look at them, he found a taste of a notice posted on the inside of the stable-door, giving him intelligence that if he did not find a horpus corpus(26) whereby to transfer his body out of the country, he would experience a fate parallel to that of his brother lawyer or the horses. And, undoubtedly, if honest people never perpetrated worse than banishing such varmin, along with proctors, and drivers of all kinds, out of a civilised country, they would not be so very culpable or atrocious.

"After this, the lawyer went to reside in Dublin; and the only bodily injury he received was the death of a land-agent and a bailiff, who lost their lives faithfully in driving for rent. They died, however, successfully; the bailiff having been provided for nearly a year before the agent was sent to give an account of his stewardship—as the Authorised Version has it.

"The occasion on which the first rencountor between us and the O'Hallaghans took place, was a peaceable one. Several of our respective friends undertook to produce a friendly and oblivious potation(27) between us—it was at a berrin belonging to a corpse who was related to us both; and, certainly, in the beginning we were all as thick as whigged milk. But there is no use now in dwelling too long upon that circumstance: let it be sufficient to assert that the accommodation was effectuated by fists and cudgels, on both sides—the first man that struck a blow being one of the friends that wished to bring about the tranquillity. From that out the play commenced, and God he knows when it may end; for no dacent faction could give in to another faction without losing their character, and being kicked, and cuffed, and kilt, every week in the year.

"It is the great battle, however, which I am after going to describe: that in which we and the O'Hallaghans had contrived, one way or other, to have the parish divided—one-half for them, and the other for us; and, upon my credibility, it is no exaggeration to declare that the whole parish, though ten miles by six, assembled itself in the town of Knockimdowny, upon this interesting occasion. In thruth, Ireland ought to be a land of mathemathitians; for I am sure her population is well trained, at all events, in the two sciences of multiplication and division. Before I adventure, however, upon the narration, I

John W. Hurley

must wax pathetic a little, and then proceed with the main body of the story.

"Poor Rose O'Hallaghan!—or, as she was designated—Rose Galh, or Fair Rose, and sometimes simply, Rose Hallaghan, because the detention of the big O often produces an afflatus(28) in the pronunciation, that is sometimes mighty inconvenient to such as do not understand oratory—besides, that the Irish are rather fond of sending the liquids in a gutthural direction—Poor Rose! that faction fight was a black day to her, the sweet innocent! When it was well known that there wasn't a man, woman, or child, on either side, that wouldn't lay their hands under her feet. However, in order to insense the reader better into her character, I will commence a small sub-narration, which will afterwards emerge into the parent stream of the story.

"The chapel of Knockimdowny is a slated house, without any ornament, except a set of wooden cuts, painted red and blue, that are placed seriatim(29) around the square of the building in the internal side. Fourteen(30) of these suspind at equal distances on the walls, each set in a painted frame; these constitute a certain species of country devotion. It is usual, on Sundays, for such of the congregation as are most inclined to piety, to genuflect at the first of these pictures, and commence a certain number of prayers to it; after the repetition of which, they travel on their knees along the bare earth to the second, where they repate another prayer peculiar to that, and so on, till they finish the grand tower of the interior. Such, however, as are not especially addictated to this kind of locomotive prayer, collect together in various knots through the chapel, and amuse themselves by auditing or narrating anccdotes, discussing policy, or detraction; and in case it be summer, and the day of a fine texture, they scatter themselves into little crowds on the chapel-green, or lie at their length upon the grass in listless groups, giving way to chat and laughter. In this mode, laired on the sunny side of the ditches and hedges, or collected in rings round that respectable character, the Academician of the village, or some other well-known Senachie, or storyteller, they amuse themselves till the priest's arrival. Perhaps, too, some walking geographer of a pilgrim may happen to be present; and if there be, he is sure to draw a crowd about him, in spite of all the efforts of the learned Academician to the contrary. It is no unusual thing to see such a vagrant, in all the vanity of conscious sanctimony, standing in the middle of the attentive peasants, like the nave and felloes of a cart-wheel—if I may be permitted the loan of an apt similitude—repeating some piece of unfathomable and labyrinthine devotion, or perhaps warbling, from Stentorian lungs, some melodia sacra,(31) in an untranslateable tongue; or, it may be, exhibiting the mysterious power of an amber bade, fastened as a Decade to his paudareens,(32) lifting a chaff or light bit of straw by the force of its attraction. This is an exploit which causes many an eye to turn from the bades to his own bearded face, with a hope, as it were, of being able to catch a glimpse of the lurking sanctimony by which the knave hoaxes them in the miraculous.

"The amusements of the females are also nearly such as I have drafted out. Nosegays(33) of the darlings might be seen sated on green banks, or sauntering about with a sly intention of coming in compact with their sweethearts, or, like bachelors' buttons in smiling rows, criticising the young men as they pass. Others of them might be seen screened behind a hedge, with their backs to the spectators, taking the papers off their curls before a small bit of looking-glass placed against the ditch; or perhaps putting on their shoes and stockings—which phrase can be used only by authority of the figure heusteron proteron(34)—inasmuch as if they put on the shoes first, you persave,(35) it would be a scientific job to get on the stockings after; but it's an idiomatical expression, and therefore justifiable. However, it's a general custom in the country, which I dare to say has not yet spread into large cities, for the young women to walk bare-footed to the chapel, or within a short distance of it, that they may exhibit their bleached thread stockings and well-greased slippers to the best advantage, not pretermitting a well-turned ankle and neat leg, which, I may fearlessly assert, my fair countrywomen can show against any other nation living or dead.

"One sunny Sabbath, the congregation of Knockimdowney were thus assimilated, amusing themselves in the manner I have just outlined: a series of country girls sat on a little green mount, called the Rabbit Bank, from the circumstance of its having been formerly an open burrow, though of late years it has been closed. It was near twelve o'clock, the hour at which Father Luke O'Shaughran was generally seen topping the rise of the hill at Larry Mulligan's public-house, jogging on trig bay hack at something between a walk and a trot—that is to say, his horse moved his fore and hind legs on the off side at one motion, and the fore and hind legs of the near side in another, going at a kind of dog's trot, like the pace of an idiot with sore feet in a shower—a pace, indeed, to which the animal had been set for the last sixteen years, but beyond which, no force, or entreaty, or science, or power, either divine or human, of his Reverence could drive him. As yet, however, he had not become apparent; and the girls already mentioned were discussing the pretensions which several of their acquaintances had to dress or beauty.

"'Peggy,' said Katty Carroll to her companion, Peggy Donohoe, 'were you out(36) last Sunday?'

"'No, in troth,(37) Katty, I was disappointed in getting my shoes from Paddy Mellon(38) though I left him the measure of my foot three weeks agone, and gave him a thousand warnings to make them duck-nebs;(39) but, instead of that,' said she, holding out a very purty foot, 'he has made them as sharp in the toe as a pick-axe, and a full mile too short for me. But why do ye ax was I out, Katty?'

"'Oh, nothing,' responded Katty, 'only that you missed a sight, any way.'

"'What was it, Kitty, a-hagur?'(40) asked her companion with mighty great curiosity.

"'Why, nothing less, indeed, nor Rose Cullenan decked out in a white muslin gown, and a black sprush bonnet, tied under her chin wid a silk ribbon, no less; but what killed us out and out was—you wouldn't guess?'

"'Arrah,(41) how could I guess, woman alive? A silk handkerchy, maybe; for I wouldn't doubt the same Rose but she would be setting herself up for the likes of such a thing.'

"'It's herself that had, as red as scarlet, about her neck; but that's not it.'

"'Arrah, Katty, tell it to us at wanst; out with it, a-hagur; sure there's no treason in it, anyhow.'

"'Why, thin, nothing less nor a crass-bar red-and-white pockethandkerchy, to wipe her purty complexion wid!'

"To this Peggy replied by a loud laugh, in which it was difficult to say whether there was more of sathir than astonishment.

"'A pocket-handkerchy!' she exclaimed; 'musha,(42) are we alive afther that, at all at all! Why, that bates Molly M'Cullagh and her red mantle entirely. I'm sure, but it's well come up for the likes of her, a poor, imperint crathur, that sprung from nothing, to give herself sich airs.'

"'Molly M'Cullagh, indeed,' said Katty; 'why, they oughtn't to be mintioned in the one day, woman. Molly's come of a dacent ould stock, and kind mother for her to keep herself in genteel ordher at all times: she sees nothing else, and can afford it, not all as one as the other flipe,(43) that would go to the world's end for a bit of dress.'

"'Sure she thinks she's a beauty, too, if you plase,' said Peggy, tossing her head with an air of disdain; 'but tell us, Katty, how did the muslin sit upon her at all, the upsetting crathur?'

"'Why, for all the world like a shift on a Maypowl,(44) or a stocking on a body's nose: only nothing killed us outright but the pockethand kerchy!'

"'Hut!' said the other, 'what could we expect from a proud piece like her, that brings a Manwill(45) to mass every Sunday, purtending she can read in it, and Jem Finigan saw the wrong side of the book toards her, the Sunday of the Purcession!'(46)

"At this hit they both formed another risible junction, quite as sarcastic as the former—in the midst of which the innocent object of their censure, dressed in all her obnoxious finery, came up and joined them. She was scarcely sated—I blush to the very point of my pen during the manuscription—when the confabulation(47) assumed a character directly antipodial(48) to that which marked the precedent dialogue.

"'My gracious, Rose, but that's a purty thing you have got in your gown!—where did you buy it?'

"'Och, thin, not a one of myself likes it over much. I'm sorry I didn't buy a gingham:(49) I could have got a beautiful patthern, all out, for two shillings less; but they don't wash so well as this. I bought it in Paddy McGartland's, Peggy.'

"'Troth, it's nothing else but a great beauty; I didn't see anything on you this long time that becomes you so well, and I've remarked that you always look best in white.'

John W. Hurley

"'Who made it, Rose?' inquired Katty; 'for it sits illegant.'

"'Indeed,' replied Rose, 'for the differ of the price, I thought it better to bring it to Peggy Boyle, and be sartin of not having it spoiled. Nelly Keenan made the last; and although there was a full breadth more in it nor this, bad cess(50) to the one of her but spoiled it on me; it was ever so much too short in the body, and too tight in the sleeves, and then I had no step at all at all.'

"'The sprush bonnet is exactly the fit for the gown,' observed Katty; 'the black and the white's jist the cut—how many yards had you, Rose?'

"'Jist ten and a half; but the half-yard was for the tucks.'

"'Ay, faix!(51) and brave full tucks she left in it; ten would do me, Rose?'

"'Ten!—no, nor ten and a half; you're a size bigger nor me at the laste, Peggy; but you'd be asy fitted, you're so well made.'

"'Rose, darling,' said Peggy, 'that's a great beauty, and shows off your complexion all to pieces: you have no notion how well you look in it and the sprush.'

"In a few minutes after this her namesake, Rose Galh O'Hallaghan, came towards the chapel, in society with her father, mother, and her two sisters. The eldest, Mary, was about twentyone; Rose, who was the second, about nineteen, or scarcely that; and Nancy, the junior of the three, about twice seven.

"'There's the O'Hallaghans,' says Rose.

"'Ay,' replied Katty; 'you may talk of beauty, now; did you ever lay your two eyes on the likes of Rose for downright—musha, if myself knows what to call it—but, anyhow, she's the lovely crathur to look at.'

"Kind reader, without a single disrespectful insinuation against any portion of the fair sex, you may judge what Rose O'Hallaghan must have been, when even these three were necessitated to praise her in her absence!

"'I'll warrant,' observed Katty, 'we'll soon be after seeing John O'Callaghan,'—(he was my own cousin)— 'sthrolling afther them, at his ase.'

"'Why,' asked Rose, 'what makes you say that?'

"'Bekase,' replied the other, 'I've a rason for it.'

"'Sure John O'Callaghan wouldn't be thinking of her,' observed Rose, 'and their families would see other shot: their factions would never have a crass-marriage, anyhow.'

"'Well,' said Peggy, 'it's the thousand pities that the same two couldn't go together; for fair and handsome as Rose is, you'll not deny but John comes up to her: but, faix! sure enough it's they that's the proud people on both sides, and dangerous to make or meddle with, not saying that ever there was the likes of the same two for dacency and peaceableness among either of the factions.'

"'Didn't I tell yez?' cried Katty; 'look at him now, staling after her: and it'll be the same thing going home again; and, if Rose is not much belied, it's not a bit displasing to her.'

"'Between ourselves; observed Peggy, 'it would be no wondher the darling young crathur would fall in love with him; for you might thravel the counthry afore you'd meet with his fellow for face and figure.'

"'There's Father Ned,' remarked Katty; 'we had betther get into the chapel before the scroodgin(52) comes an, or your bonnet and gown, Rose, won't be the betther for it.'

"They now proceeded to the chapel, and those who had been amusing themselves after the same mode, followed their exemplar. In a short time the hedges and ditches adjoining the chapel were quite in solitude, with the exception of a few persons from the extreme parts of the parish, who might be seen running with all possible velocity 'to overtake mass,' as the phrase on that point expresses itself.

"The chapel of Knockimdowney was situated at the foot of a range of lofty mountains; a bye-road went past the very door, which had under subjection a beautiful extent of cultivated country, diversificated by hill and dale, or rather by hill and hollow; for, as far as my own geographical knowledge goes, I have uniformly found them insepar-able. It was also ornamented with the waving verdure of rich corn-fields and meadows, not pretermitting phatie-fields in full blossom—a part of rural landscape which, to my utter astonishment, has es-caped the pen of poet, and the brush of painter; although I will risk my reputation as a man of pure and categorical taste, if a finer ingre-dient in the composition of a landscape could be found than a field of Cork-red phaties or Moroky blacks(53) in full bloom, allowing a man to judge by the pleasure they confer upon the eye, and therefore to the heart. About a mile up from the chapel, towards the south, a mountain-stream—not the one already intimated—over which there was no bridge, crossed the road.

But in lieu of a bridge, there was a long double plank laid over it, from bank to bank; and as the river was broad, and not sufficiently incarcerated within its channel, the neighbours were necessitated to throw these planks across the narrowest part they could find in the contiguity of the road. This part was consequently the deepest, and, in floods, the most dangerous; for the banks were elevated as far as they went, and quite tortuositous.

"Shortly after the priest had entered the chapel, it was observed that the hemisphere became, of a sudden, unusually obscure, though the preceding part of the day had not only been uncloudously bright, but hot in a most especial manner. The obscurity, however, increased rapidly, accompanied by that gloomy stillness which always takes precedence of a storm, and fills the mind with vague and interminable terror. But this ominous silence was not long unfractured; for soon after the first appearance of the gloom, a flash of lightning quivered through the chapel, followed by an extravagantly loud clap of thunder, which shook the very glass in the windows, and filled the congregation to the brim with terror. Their dismay, however, would have been infinitely greater, only for the presence of his Reverence, and the confidence which might be traced to the solemn occasion on which they were assimilated.

"From this moment the storm became progressive in dreadful magnitude, and the thunder, in concomitance with the most vivid flashes of lightning, pealed through the sky, with an awful grandeur and magnificence, that were exalted and even rendered more sublime by the still solemnity of religious worship. Every heart now prayed fervently—every spirit shrunk into a deep sense of its own guilt and helplessness—and every conscience was terrorstricken, as the voice of an angry God thundered out of his temple of storms through the heavens; for truly, as the Authorised Version(54) has it, 'darkness was under his feet, and his pavilion round about was dark waters, and thick clouds of the skies, because he was wroth.'

"The rain now condescended in even-down torrents, and thunder succeeded thunder in deep and terrific peals, whilst the roar of the gigantic echoes that deepened and reverberated among the glens and hollows, 'laughing in their mountain mirth,'—hard fortune to me, but they made the flesh creep on my bones!

"This lasted for an hour, when the thunder slackened: but the rain still continued. As soon as mass was over, and the storm had elapsed, except an odd peal which might be heard rolling at a distance behind the hills, the people began gradually to recover their spirits, and enter into confabulation; but to venture out was still impracticable. For about another hour it rained incessantly, after which it ceased; the hemisphere became lighter—and the sun shone out once more upon the countenance of nature with his former brightness. The congregation then decanted itself out of the chapel—the spirits of the people dancing with that remarkable buoyancy or juvenility which is felt after a thunderstorm, when the air is calm, soople, and balmy—and all nature garmented with glittering verdure and light. The crowd next began to commingle on their way home, and to make the usual observations upon the extraordinary storm which had just passed, and the probable effect it would produce on the fruit and agriculture of the neighbourhood.

"When the three young women whom we have already introduced to our respectable readers had evacuated the chapel, they determined to substantiate a certitude, as far as their observation could reach, as to the truth of what Kitty Carroll had hinted at, in reference to John O'Callaghan's attachment to Rose Galh O'Hallaghan, and her taciturn approval of it. For this purpose they kept their eye upon John, who certainly seemed in no especial hurry home, but lingered upon the chapel green in a very careless method. Rose Galh, however, soon made her appearance, and, after going up the chapel-road a short space, John slyly walked at some distance behind, without seeming to pay her any particular notice, whilst a person up to the secret might observe Rose's bright eye sometimes peeping back to see if he was after her. In this manner they procceded until they came to the river, which, to their great alarm, was almost fluctuating over its highest banks.

"A crowd was now assembled, consulting as to the safest method of crossing the planks, under which the red boiling current ran, with less violence, it is true, but much deeper than in any other part of the

John W. Hurley

stream. The final decision was, that the very young and the old, and such as were feeble, should proceed by a circuit of some miles to a bridge that crossed it, and that the young men should place themselves on their knees along the planks, their hands locked in each other, thus forming a support on one side, upon which such as had courage to venture across might lean, in case of accident or megrim.(55) Indeed, anybody that had able nerves might have crossed the planks without this precaution, had they been dry; but, in consequence of the rain, and the frequent attrition of feet, they were quite slippery; and, besides, the flood rolled terrifically two or three yards below them, which might be apt to beget a megrim that would not be felt if there was no flood.

"When this expedient had been hit upon, several young men volunteered themselves to put it in practice; and in a short time a considerable number of both sexuals crossed over, without the occurrence of any unpleasant accident. Paddy O'Hallaghan and his family had been stationed for some time on the bank, watching the success of the plan; and as it appeared not to be attended with any particular danger, they also determined to make the attempt. About a perch below the planks stood John O'Callagllan, watching the progress of those who were crossing them, but taking no part in what was going forward. The river under the planks, and for some perches above and below them, might be about ten feet deep; but to those who could swim it was less perilous, should any accident befal them, than those parts where the current was more rapid, but shallower. The water here boiled, and bubbled, and whirled about; but it was slow, and its yellow surface unbroken by rocks or fords.

"The first of the O'Hallaghans that ventured over it was the youngest, who, being captured by the hand, was encouraged by many cheerful expressions from the young men who were clinging to the planks. She got safe over, however; and when she came to the end, one who was stationed on the bank gave her a joyous pull, that translated her several yards upon terra firma.(56)

"'Well, Nancy,' he observed, 'you're safe, anyhow; and if I don't dance at your wedding for this, I'll never say you're dacent.'

"To this Nancy gave a jocular promise, and he resumed his station, that he might be ready to render similar assistance to her next sister.

Rose Galh then went to the edge of the plank several times, but her courage as often refused to be forthcoming. During her hesitation, John O'Callaghan stooped down, and privately untied his shoes, then unbuttoned his waistcoat, and very gently, being unwilling to excite notice, slipped the knot of his cravat.(57) At long last, by the encouragement of those who were on the plank, Rose attempted the passage, and had advanced as far as the middle of it, when a fit of dizziness and alarm seized her with such violence, that she lost all consciousness—a circumstance of which those who handed her along were ignorant. The consequence, as might be expected, was dreadful; for as one of the young men was receiving her hand, that he might pass her to the next, she lost her momentum, and was instantaneously precipitated into the boiling current.

"The wild and fearful cry of horror that succeeded this cannot be laid on paper. The eldest sister fell into strong convulsions, and several of the other females fainted on the spot. The mother did not faint; but, like Lot's wife, she seemed to be translated into stone: her hands became clenched convulsively, her teeth locked, her nostrils dilated, and her eyes shot half way out of her head. There she stood, looking upon her daughter struggling in the flood, with a fixed gaze of wild and impotent frenzy, that, for fearfulness, beat the thunderstorm all to nothing. The father rushed to the edge of the river, oblivious of his incapability to swim, determined to save her or lose his own life, which latter would have been a dead certainty, had he ventured; but he was prevented by the crowd, who pointed out to him the madness of such a project.

"'For God's sake, Paddy, don't attimpt it,' they exclaimed, 'except you wish to lose your own life, without being able to save hers: no man could swim in that flood, and it upwards of ten feet deep.'
"Their arguments, however, were lost upon him; for, in fact, he was insensible to everything but his child's preservation. He, therefore, only answered their remonstrances by attempting to make another plunge into the river.

"'Let me alone, will yez,' said he— 'let me alone! I'll either save my child, Rose, or die along with her! How could I live after her? Merciful God, any of them but her! Oh! Rose, darling,' he exclaimed, 'the favourite of my heart—will no one save you?' All this passed in less than a minute.

"Just as these words were uttered, a plunge was heard a few yards below the bridge, and a man appeared in the flood, making his way with rapid strokes to the drowning girl. Another cry now arose from the spectators: 'It's John O'Callaghan,' they shouted—'it's John O'Callaghan, and they'll be both lost.' 'No,' exclaimed others; 'if it's in the power of man to save her, he will!' 'O, blessed father, she's lost!' now burst from all present; for, after having struggled and been kept floating for some time by her garments, she at length sunk, apparently exhausted and senseless, and the thief of a flood flowed over her, as if she had not been under its surface.

"When O'Callaghan saw that she went down, he raised himself up in the water, and cast his eye towards that part of the bank opposite which she disappeared, evidently, as it proved, that he might have a mark to guide him in fixing on the proper spot where to plunge after her. When he came to the place, he raised himself again in the stream, and, calculating that she must by this time have been borne some distance from the spot where she sank, he gave a stroke or two down the river, and disappeared after her. This was followed by another cry of horror and despair; for, somehow, the idea of desolation which marks, at all times, a deep, over-swollen torrent, heightened by the bleak mountain scenery around them, and the dark, angry voracity of the river where they had sunk, might have impressed the spectators with utter hopelessness as to the fate of those now engulphed(58) in its vortex. This, however, I leave to those who are deeper read in philosophy than I am.

"An awful silence succeeded the last shrill exclamation, broken only by the hoarse rushing of the waters, whose wild, continuous roar, booming hollowly and dismally in the ear, might be heard at a great distance over all the country. But a new sensation soon invaded the multitude; for after the lapse of about half a minute, John O'Callaghan emerged from the flood, bearing in his sinister hand, the body of his own Rose Galh—for it's he that loved her tenderly. A peal of joy congratulated them from the assembled crowd; hundreds of directions were given to him how to act to the best advantage. Two young men in especial, who were both dying about the lovely creature that he held, were quite anxious to give advice.

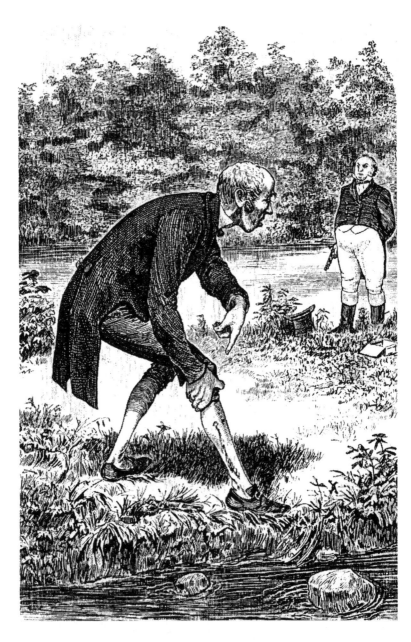

The pistol duel.

44   John W. Hurley

"Where's the O'Callaghan will place his toe on this frieze?"

Neal Malone "annigulating" Frank Farrell the miller.

John W. Hurley

Rose Galh avenging her lovers death.

"'Bring her to the other side, John, ma bouchal;(59) it's the safest,' said Larry Carty.

"'Will you let him alone, Carty?' said Simon Tracy, who was the other, 'you'll only put him in a perplexity.'

"But Carty should order in spite of every thing. He kept bawling out, however, so loud, that John raised his eye to see what he meant, and was near losing hold of Rose. This was too much for Tracy, who ups with his fist, and downs him—so they both at it; for no one there could take themselves off those that were in danger, to interfere between them. But at all events, no earthly thing can happen among Irishmen without a fight.

"The father, during this, stood breathless, his hands clasped, and his eyes turned to heaven, praying in anguish for the delivery of his darling. The mother's look was still wild and fixed, her eyes glazed, and her muscles hard and stiff; evidently she was insensible to all that was going forward; while large drops of paralytic agony hung upon her cold brow. Neither of the sisters had yet recovered, nor could those who supported them turn their eyes from the more imminent danger, to pay them any particular attention. Many, also, of the other females, whose feelings were too much wound up when the accident occurred, now fainted, when they saw she was likely to be rescued; but most of them were weeping with delight and gratitude.

"When John brought her to the surface, he paused a moment to recover breath and collectedness; he then caught her by the left arm, near the shoulder, and cut, in a slanting direction, down the stream, to a watering-place, where a slope had been formed in the bank. But he was already too far down to be able to work across the stream to this point; for it was here much stronger and more rapid than under the planks. Instead, therefore, of reaching the slope, he found himself, in spite of every effort to the contrary, about a perch below it; and except he could gain this point, against the strong rush of the flood, there was very little hope of being able to save either her or himself—for he was now much exhausted.

"Hitherto, therefore, all was still doubtful, whilst strength was fast failing him. In this trying and almost hopeless situation, with an admirable presence of mind, he adopted the only expedient which could possibly enable him to reach the bank. On finding himself receding

John W. Hurley

down, instead of advancing up the current, he approached the bank, which was here very deep and perpendicular; he then sank his fingers into and pressed his right foot against the firm blue clay with which it was stratified, and by this means advanced, bit by bit, up the stream, having no other force by which to propel himself against it. After this mode did he breast the current with all his strength—which must have been prodigious, or he never could have borne it out—until he reached the slope, and got from the influence of the tide, into dead water. On arriving here, his hand was caught by one of the young men present, who stood up to the neck, waiting his approach. A second man stood behind him, holding his other hand, a link being thus formed, that reached out to the firm bank; and a good pull now brought them both to the edge of the river. On finding bottom, John took his Colleen Galh(60) in his own arms, carried her out, and pressing his lips to hers, laid her in the bosom of her father; then, after taking another kiss of the young drowned flower, he burst into tears, and fell powerless beside her. The truth is, the spirit that had kept him firm was now exhausted; both his legs and arms having become nerveless by the exertion.

"Hitherto her father took no notice of John, for how could he? seeing that he was entirely wrapped up in his daughter; and the question was, though rescued from the flood, if life was in her. The sisters were by this time recovered, and weeping over her, along with the father—and, indeed, with all present; but the mother could not be made to comprehend what they were about, at all, at all. The country people used every means with which they were intimate, to recover Rose; she was brought instantly to a farmer's house beside the spot, put into a warm bed, covered over with hot salt, wrapped in half-scorched blankets, and made subject to every other mode of treatment that could possibly revoke the functions of life. John had now got a decent draught of whiskey, which revived him. He stood over her, when he could be admitted, watching for the symptomatics of her revival; all, however, was vain. He now determined to try another course: by-and-by he stooped, put his mouth to her mouth, and, drawing in his breath, respired with all his force from the bottom of his very heart into hers; this he did several times rapidly—faith, a tender and agreeable operation, any how. But mark the consequence: in less than a minute her white bosom heaved—her breath returned—her pulse began to play—she opened her eyes, and felt his tears of love raining warmly on her pale cheek!

"For years before this, no two of these opposite factions had spoken, nor up to this minute had John and they, even upon this occasion, exchanged a monosyllable. The father now looked at him—the tears stood afresh in his eyes; he came forward stretched out his hand—it was received; and the next moment he fell upon John's neck, and cried like an infant.

"When Rose recovered, she seemed as if striving to recordate what had happened; and, after two or three minutes, inquired from her sister, in a weak but sweet voice, 'Who saved me?'

"''Twas John O'Callaghan, Rose darling replied the sister, in tears, 'that ventured his own life into the boiling flood, to save yours—and did save it, jewel!'

"Rose's eye glanced at John—and I only wish, as I am a bachelor not further than my forty-fourth, that I may ever have the happiness to get such a glance from two blue eyes, as she gave him that moment—a faint smile played about her mouth, and a slight blush lit up her fair cheek, like the evening sunbeams on the virgin snow, as the poets have said for the five-hundredth time, to my own personal knowledge. She then extended her hand, which John, you may be sure, was no way backward in receiving, and the tears of love and gratitude ran silently down her cheeks.

"It is not necessary to detail the circumstances of this day farther; let it be sufficient to say, that a reconciliation took place between those two branches of the O'Hallaghan and O'Callaghan families, in consequence of John's heroism and Roses soft persuasion, and that there was, also, every perspective of the two factions being penultimately amalgamated.(61) For nearly a century they had been pell-mell(62) at it, whenever and where-ever they could meet. Their forefathers, who had been engaged in the lawsuit about the island which I have mentioned, were dead and petrified in their graves; and the little peninsula in the glen was gradationally worn away by the river, till nothing remained but a desert, upon a small scale, of sand and gravel. Even the ruddy, able-bodied Squire, with the longitudinal nose, projecting out of his face like a broken arch, and the small,

John W. Hurley

fiery magistrate—both of whom had fought the duel, for the purpose of setting forth a good example, and bringing the dispute to a peaceable conclusion—were also dead. The very memory of the original contention had been lost (except that it was preserved along with the cranium of my grandfather), or became so indistinct that the parties fastened themselves on some more modern provocation, which they kept in view until another fresh motive would start up, and so on. I know not, however, whether it was fair to expect them to give up at once the agreeable recreation of fighting. It's not easy to abolish old customs, particularly diversions; and every one knows that this is our national amusement.

"There were, it is true, many among both factions who saw the matter in this reasonable light, and who wished rather, if it were to cease, that it should die away by degrees, from the battle of the whole parish, equally divided between the factions, to the subordinate row between certain members of them—from that to the faint broil of certain families, and so on to the single-handed play between individuals. At all events, one-half of them were for peace, and two-thirds of them equally divided between peace and war.

"For three months after the accident which befell Rose Galh O'Hallaghan, both factions had been tolerantly quiet—that is to say, they had no general engagement. Some slight skirmishes certainly did take place on market-nights, when the drop was in, and the spirits up;(63) but in those neither John nor Rose's immediate families took any part. The fact was that John and Rose were on the evening of matrimony; the match had been made—the day appointed, and every other necessary stipulation ratified. Now, John was as fine a young man as you would meet in a day's travelling; and as for Rose her name went far and near for beauty: and with justice, for the sun never shone on a fairer, meeker, or modester virgin than Rose Galh O'Hallaghan.

"It might be, indeed, that there were those on both sides who thought that, if the marriage was obstructed, their own sons and daughters would have a better chance. Rose had many admirers: they might have envied John his happiness; many fathers, on the other side, might have wished their sons to succeed with Rose. Whether I am sinister in this conjecture is more than I can say. I grant, indeed, that a great portion of it is speculation on my part. The wedding-day, however, was arranged; but, unfortunately, the fair-day of Knockimdowney occurred, in the rotation of natural time, precisely one week before it. I know not from what motive it proceeded, but the factions on both sides were never known to make a more light-hearted preparation for battle. Cudgels of all sorts and sizes (and some of them, to my own knowledge, great beauties) were provided.

"I believe I may as well take this opportunity of saying that real Irish cudgels must be root-growing, either oak, black-thorn, or crab-tree—although crab-tree, by the way, is apt to fly.(64) They should not be too long—three feet and a few inches is an accommodating length. They must be naturally top-heavy, and have around the end that is to make acquaintance with the cranium three or four natural lumps, calculated to divide the flesh in the natest manner, and to leave, if possible, the smallest taste in life of pit in the skull. But if a good root-growing kippeen(65) be light at the fighting-end, or possess not the proper number of knobs, a hole, a few inches deep, is to be bored in the end, which must be filled with melted lead. This gives it a widow-and-orphan-making quality, a child-bereaving touch, altogether very desirable. If, however, the top splits in the boring—which, in awkward hands, is not uncommon—the defect may be remediated by putting on an iron ferrule, and driving two or three strong nails into it, simply to preserve it from flying off; not that an Irishman is ever at a loss for weapons when in a fight, for so long as a scythe, flail, spade,(66) pitchfork, or stone is at hand, he feels quite contented with the lot of war. No man, as they say of great statesmen, is more fertile in expedients during a row; which, by the way, I take to be a good quality, at all events.

"I remember the fair-day of Knockimdowney well: it has kept me from griddle-bread and tough nutriment ever since. Hard fortune to Jack Roe O'Hallaghan! No man had better teeth than I had till I met with him that day. He fought stoutly on his own side; but he was ped then for the same basting that fell to me, though not by my hands, if to get his jaw decently divided into three halves could be called a fair liquidation of an old debt—it was equal to twenty shillings in the pound, any how.

"There had not been a larger fair in the town of Knockimdowney

John W. Hurley

for years. The day was dark and sunless, but sultry. On looking through the crowd, I could see no man without a cudgel; yet, what was strange, there was no certainty of any sport. Several desultory skrimmages(67) had locality, but they were altogether sequestered from the great factions of the O's. Except that it was pleasant, and stirred one's blood to look at them, or occasioned the cudgels to be grasped more firmly, there was no personal interest felt by any of us in them; they therefore began and ended, here and there, through the fair, like mere flashes in the pan, dying in their own smoke.

"The blood of every prolific nation is naturally hot; but when that hot blood is inflamed by ardent spirits, it is not to be supposed that men should be cool; and, God he knows, there is not on the level surface of this habitable globe, a nation that has been so thoroughly inflamed by ardent spirits of all kinds as Ireland.

"Up till four o'clock that day, the factions were quiet. Several relations on both sides had been invited to drink by John and Rose's families, for the purpose of establishing a good feeling between them. But this was, after all, hardly to be expected, for they hated one another with an ardency much too good-humoured and buoyant; and, between ourselves, to bring Paddy over a bottle is a very equivocal mode of giving him an anti-cudgelling disposition. After the hour of four, several of the factions were getting very friendly, which I knew at the time to be a bad sign. Many of them nodded to each other, which I knew to be a worse one; and some of them shook hands with the greatest cordiality, which I no sooner saw than I slipped the knot of my cravat, and held myself in preparation for the sport.

"I have often had occasion to remark—and few men, let me tell you, had finer opportunities of doing so—the differential symptomatics between, a Party Fight, that is, a battle between Orangemen and Ribbonmen,(68) and one between two Roman Catholic Factions. There is something infinitely more anxious, silent, and deadly, in the compressed vengeance, and the hope of slaughter, which characterise a party fight, than is to be seen in a battle between factions. The truth is, the enmity is not so deep and well grounded in the latter as in the former. The feeling is not political nor religious between the factions; whereas, in the other, it is both, which is a mighty great advantage; for when this is adjuncted to an intense personal hatred, and a sense of wrong, probably arising from a too intimate recollection of the leaded black-thorn, or the awkward death of some relative, by the musket or the bayonet,(69) it is apt to produce very purty fighting, and much respectable retribution.

"In a party fight, a prophetic sense of danger hangs, as it were, over the crowd—the very air is loaded with apprehension; and the vengeance burst is proceeded by a close, thick darkness, almost sulphury, that is more terrifical than the conflict itself, though clearly less dangerous and fatal. The scowl of the opposing parties, the blanched cheeks, the knit brows, and the grinding teeth, not pretermitting the deadly gleams that shoot from their kindled eyes, are ornaments which a plain battle between factions cannot boast, but which, notwithstanding, are very suitable to the fierce and gloomy silence of that premeditated vengeance which burns with such intensity in the heart, and scorches up the vitals into such a thirst for blood. Not but that they come by different means to the same conclusion; because it is the feeling, and not altogether the manner of operation, that is different.

"Now a faction fight doesn't resemble this, at all, at all. Paddy's at home here; all song, dance, good-humour, and affection. His cheek is flushed with delight, which, indeed, may derive assistance from the consciousness of having no bayonets or loaded carabines to contend with: but, any how, he's at home—his eye is lit with real glee—he tosses his hat in the air, in the height of mirth—and leaps, like a mountebank, two yards from the ground. Then, with what a gracious dexterity he brandishes his cudgel! what a joyous spirit is heard in his shout at the face of a friend from another faction! His very 'whoo!' is contagious, and would make a man, that had settled on running away, return and join the sport with an appetite truly Irish. He is, in fact, while under the influence of this heavenly afflatus, in love with every one, man, woman, and child. If he meet his sweetheart, he will give her a kiss and a hug, and that with double kindness, because he is on his way to thrash her father or brother. It is the acumen(70) of his enjoyment; and woe be to him who will adventure to go between him and his amusements. To be sure, skulls and bones are broken, and lives lost; but they are lost in pleasant fighting—they are the consequences of the sport, the beauty of which consists in breaking

John W. Hurley

as many heads and necks as you can; and certainly when a man enters into the spirit of any exercise, there is nothing like elevating himself to the point of excellence. Then a man ought never to be disheartened. If you lose this game, or get your head goodhumouredly beaten to pieces, why you may win another, or your friends may mollify(71) two or three skulls as a set-off to yours; but that is nothing.

"When the evening became more advanced, maybe, considering the poor look up there was for anything like decent sport—maybe, in the early part of the day, it wasn't the delightful sight to see the boys on each side of the two great factions, beginning to get frolicksome. Maybe the songs and the shouting,(72) when they began, hadn't melody and music in them, any how! People may talk about harmony; but what harmony is equal to that in which five or six hundred men sing and shout, and leap and caper at each other, as a prelude to neighbourly fighting, where they beat time upon the drums of each other's ears and heads with oak drum-sticks? That's an Irishman's music; and hard fortune to the garran(73) that wouldn't have friendship and kindness in him to join and play a stave(74) along with them! 'Whoo! your sowl! Hurroo! Success to our side! Hi for the O'Callaghans! Where's the blackguard to——', I beg pardon, decent reader; I forgot myself for a moment, or rather I got new life in me, for I am nothing at all at all for the last five months—a kind of nonentity I may say, ever since that vagabond Burgess occasioned me to pay a visit to my distant relations, till my friends get that last matter of the collarbone settled.

"The impulse which faction fighting gives to trade and business in Ireland is truly surprising; whereas party fighting depreciates both. As soon as it is perceived that a party fight is to be expected, all buying and selling are nearly suspended for the day; and those who are not up,(75) and even many who are, take themselves and their property home as quickly as may be convenient. But in a faction fight, as soon as there is any perspective of a row, depend upon it, there is quick work at all kinds of negotiation; and truly there is nothing like brevity and decision in buying and selling; for which reason faction fighting, at all events, if only for the sake of national prosperity, should be encouraged and kept up.

"Towards five o'clock, if a man was placed on an exalted station, so that he could look at the crowd, and wasn't able to fight, he could have seen much that a man might envy him for. Here a hat went up, or maybe a dozen of them; then followed a general huzza.(76) On the other side, two dozen caubeens(77) sought the sky, like so many scaldy crows attempting their own element for the first time, only they were not so black. Then another shout, which was answered by that of their friends on the opposite side; so that you would hardly know which side huzzaed loudest, the blending of both was so truly symphonious. Now there was a shout for the face of an O'Callaghan; this was prosecuted on the very heels by another for the face of an O'Hallaghan. Immediately a man of the O'Hallaghan side doffed his tattered frieze,(78) and catching it by the very extremity of the sleeve, drew it with a tact, known only by an initiation of half-a-dozen street days, up the pavement after him. On the instant, a blade from the O'Callaghan side peeled with equal alacrity, and stretching his home-made(79) at full length after him, proceeded triumphantly up the street, to meet the other.

"Thundher-an-ages, what's this for, at all, at all! I wish I hadn't begun to manuscript an account of it, any how; 'tis like a hungry man dreaming of a good dinner at a feast, and afterwards awaking and finding his front ribs and back-bone on the point of union. Reader, is that a black-thorn you carry—tut, where is my imagination bound for?—to meet the other, I say.

"Where's the rascally O'Callaghan that will place his toe or his shillely(80) on this frieze?' 'Is there no blackguard O'Hallaghan jist to look crucked at the coat of an O'Callaghan, or say black's the white of his eye?'

"'Throth and there is, Ned, avourneen,(81) that same on the sod here.'

"'Is that Barney?'

"'The same, Ned, ma bouchal; and how is your mother's son, Ned?'

"'In good health at the present time, thank God and you; how is yourself, Barney?'

"'Can't complain as time goes; only take this, any how, to mend your health, ma bouchal.' (Whack.)

"'Success, Barney, and here's at your service, avick,(82) not making little of what I got, any way.' (Crack.)

John W. Hurley

"About five o'clock on a May evening, in the fair of Knockimdowney, was the ice thus broken, with all possible civility, by Ned and Barney. The next moment a general rush took place towards the scene of action, and ere you could bless yourself, Barney and Ned were both down, weltering in their own and each other's blood. I scarcely know, indeed, though with a mighty respectable quota of experimentality myself, how to describe what followed. For the first twenty minutes the general harmony of this fine row might be set to music, according to a scale something like this:—Whick whack—crick crack—whick whack—crick crack—&c. &c. &c. 'Here yer sowl—(crack)—there yer sowl—(whack.) Whoo for the O'Hallaghans!'—(crack, crack, crack.) 'Hurroo for the O'Callaghans!—(whack, whack, whack.) The O'Callaghans for ever!'—(whack) 'The O'Hallaghans for ever!'—(crack.) 'Murther! murther! (crick, crack)—foul! foul!—(whick, whack.) Blood and turf!—(whack, whick)—tunther-an-ouns'—(crack, crick.) 'Hurroo! my darlings! handle your kippeens—(crack, crack)—the O'Hallagans are going!'—(whack, whack.)

"You are to suppose them here to have been at it for about half an hour.

"Whack, crack— 'oh—oh—oh! have mercy upon me, boys (crack—a shriek of murther! murther—crack, crack, whack)—my life—my life—(crack, crack—whack, whack)—oh! for the sake of the living Father!—for the sake of my wife and childher, Ned Hallaghan, spare my life.'

"'So we will, but take this, any how'—(whack, crack, whack, crack.)

"'Oh! for the love of God don't kill—(whack, crack, whack.) Oh!'—(crack, crack, whack—dies.)

"'Huzza! huzza! huzza!' fram the O'Hallaghans. 'Bravo, boys! there's one of them done for: whoo! my darlings! hurroo! The O'Hallahans for ever!'

"The scene now changes to the O'Callaghan side.

"'Jack—oh, Jack, avourneen—hell to their sowls for murdherers—Paddy's killed—his skull's smashed! Revenge, boys, Paddy O'Callaghan's killed! On with you, O'Callaghans—on with you—on with you, Paddy O'Callaghan's murdhered—take to the stones—

that's it—keep it up—down with him! Success!—he's the bloody villain that didn't show him mercy—that's it. Tunder-an'-ouns,(83) is it laving him that way you are afther—let me at him!'

"'Here's a stone, Tom!'

"'No, no, this stick has the lead in it.(84) It'll do him, never fear!'

"'Let him alone, Barney, he's got enough.'
mother's son that's in it—(crack, crack, a general huzza:) (Mickey and Larry) huzza! huzza! huzza for the O'Hallaghans! What have you got, Larry?'—(crack, crack.)

"'Only the bone of my arm, God be praised for it, very purtily snapt across!'—(whack, whack).

"'Is that all? Well, some people have luck!'—(crack, crack, crack).

"'Why I've no reason to complain, thank God—(whack, crack!)—purty play that, any way—Paddy O'Callaghan's settled—did you hear it?—(whack, whack, another shout)—That's it, boys—handle the shilleleys!—Success O'Hallaghans—down with the bloody O'Callaghans!'

"'I did hear it: so is Jem O'Hallaghan—(crack, whack, whack, crack)—you're not able to get up, I see—tare-an-ounty,(86) isn't it a pleasure to hear that play?—What ails you?'

"'Oh, Larry, I'm in great pain, and getting very weak, entirely'—(faints).

"'Faix, and he's settled too, I'm thinking.'

"'Oh, murdher, my arm!' (One of the O'Callaghans attacks him—crack, crack)—

"'Take that, you bagabone!'—(whack, whack).

"'Murdher, murdher, is it strikin' a down man you're after?—foul, foul, and my arm broke!'—(crack, crack).

"'Take that, with what you got before, and it'll ase you, maybe.'

"(A party of the O'Hallaghans attack the man who is beating him).

"'Murdher, murdher!'—(crack, whack, whack, crack, crack, whack).

"'Lay on him, your sowls to pirdition—lay on him, hot and heavy—give it to him! He sthruck me and me down wid my broken arm!'

"'Foul, ye thieves of the world!—(from the O'Callagllan)—foul! five against one—give me fair play!—(crack, crack, crack)—Oh!—(whack)—Oh, oh, oh!'—(falls senseless, covered with blood).

"'Ha, hell's cure to you, you bloody thief; you didn't spare me with my arm broke.'—(Another general shout). 'Bad end to it, isn't it a poor case entirely, that I can't even throw up my caubeen, let alone join in the diversion.'

"Both parties now rallied, and ranged themselves along the street, exhibiting a firm compact phalanx, wedged close against each other, almost foot to foot. The mass was thick and dense, and the tug of conflict stiff, wild, and savage. Much natural skill and dexterity were displayed in their mutual efforts to preserve their respective ranks unbroken, and as the sallies and charges were made on both sides, the temporary rush, the indentation of the multitudinous body, and the rebound into its original posititition, gave an undulating appearance to the compact mass—reeking, dragging, groaning, and huzzaing as it was, that resembled the serpentine motion of a rushing waterspout in the clouds.

"The women now began to take part with their brothers and sweethearts. Those who had no bachelors among the opposite factions, fought along with their brothers; others did not scruple even to assist in giving their enamoured swains the father of a good beating. Many, however, were more faithful to love than to natural affection, and these sallied out, like heroines, under the banners of their sweethearts, fighting with amazing prowess against their friends and relations; nor was it at all extraordinary to see two sisters engaged on opposite sides—perhaps tearing each other as, with dishevelled hair, they screamed with a fury that was truly exemplary. Indeed it is no untruth to assert that the women do much valuable execution. Their manner of fighting is this   as soon as the fair one decides upon taking a part in the row, she instantly takes off her apron or her stocking, stoops down, and lifting the first four pounder(87) she can get, puts it in the corner of her apron, or the foot of her stocking, if it has a foot, and marching into the scene of action, lays about her right and left. Upon my credibility, they are extremely useful and handy, and can give mighty nate knockdowns—inasmuch as no guard that a man is acquainted with can ward off their blows. Nay, what is more, it often happens, when a son-in-law is in a faction against his father in-law and his wife's people generally, that if he and his wife's brother meet, the wife will clink him with the pet in her apron, downing her own husband with great skill, for it is not always that marriage extinguishes the hatred of factions; and very often 'tis the brother that is humiliated.

"Up to the death of these two men, John O'Callaghan and Rose's father, together with a large party of their friends on both sides, were drinking in a public-house, determined to take no portion in the fight, at all, at all. Poor Rose, when she heard the shouting and terrible strokes, got as pale as death, and sat close to John, whose hand she captured in hers, beseeching him, and looking up in his face with the most imploring sincerity as she spoke, not to go out among them; the tears falling all the time from her fine eyes, the mellow flashes of which, when John's pleasantry in soothing her would seduce a smile, went into his very heart. But when, on looking out of the window where they sat, two of the opposing factions heard that a man on each side was killed; and when on ascertaining the names of the individuals, and of those who murdered them, it turned out that one of the murdered men was brother to a person in the room, and his murderer uncle to one of those in the window, it was not in the power of man or woman to keep them asunder, particularly as they were all rather advanced in liquor. In an instant the friends of the murdered man made a rush at the window, before any pacifiers had time to get between them, and catching the nephew of him who had committed the murder, hurled him head-foremost upon the stone pavement, where his skull was dashed to pieces, and his brains scattered about the flags!

"A general attack instantly took place in the room, between the two factions; but the apartment was too low and crowded to permit of proper fighting, so they rushed out to the street, shouting and yelling, as they do when the battle comes to the real point of doing business. As soon as it was seen that the heads of the O'Callaghans and O'Hallaghans were at work as well as the rest, the fight was re-commenced with retrebled spirit; but when the mutilated body of the man who had been flung from the window, was observed lying in a pool of his own proper brains and blood, such a cry arose among his friends, as would cake(88) the vital fluid in the veins of any one not a party in the quarrel. Now was the work—the moment of interest—men and women groaning, staggering, and lying insensible; others shouting, leaping, and huzzaing; some singing, and not a few able-bodied

John W. Hurley

spalpeens(89) blurting, like overgrown children, on seeing their own blood; many raging and roaring about like bulls;—all this formed such a group as a faction fight, and nothing else, could represent.

"The battle now blazed out afresh; and all kinds of instruments were pressed into the service. Some got flails, some spades, some shovels, and one man got his hands upon a scythe, with which, unquestionably, he would have taken more lives than one; but, very fortunately, as he sallied out to join the crowd, he was politely visited in the back of the head by a brick-bat,(90) which had a mighty convincing way with it of giving him a peaceable disposition, for he instantly lay down, and did not seem at all anxious as to the result of the battle. The O'Hallaghans were now compelled to give way, owing principally to the introvention of John O'Callaghan, who, although he was as good as sworn to take no part in the contest, was compelled to fight merely to protect himself. But, blood-and-turf! when he did begin, he was dreadful. As soon as his party saw him engaged, they took fresh courage, and in a short time made the O'Hallaghans retreat up the churchyard. I never saw any thing equal to John; he absolutely sent them down in dozens: and when a man would give him any inconvenience with the stick, he wonld down him with the fist, for right and left were all alike to him. Poor Rose's brother and he met, both roused like two lions; but when John saw who it was, he held back his hand:—

"'No, Tom,' says he, 'I'll not strike you, for Rose's sake. I'm not fighting through ill will to you or your family; so take another direction, for I can't strike you.'

"The blood, however, was unfortunately up in Tom.

"'We'll decide it now,' said he. 'I'm as good a man as you, O'Callaghan; and let me whisper this in your ear—you'll never warm the one bed with Rose, while's God's in heaven—it's past that now—there can be nothing but blood between us!'

"At this juncture two of the O'Callaghans ran with their shillelaghs(91) up, to beat down Tom on the spot.

"'Stop, boys!' said John, 'you musn't touch him; he had no hand in the quarrel. Go, boys, if you respect me; lave him to myself.'

"The boys withdrew to another part of the fight; and the next instant Tom struck the very man that interfered to save him, across the temple, and cut him severely. John put his hand up and staggered.

"'I'm sorry for this,' he observed; 'but it's now self-defence with me;' and, at the same moment, with one blow, he left Tom O'Hallaghan stretched insensible on the street.

"On the O'Hallaghans being driven to the church-yard, they were at a mighty great inconvenience for weapons. Most of them had lost their sticks, it being a usage in fights of this kind, to twist the cudgels from the grasp of the beaten men, to prevent them from rallying. They soon, however, furnished themselves with the best they could find, videlicet,(92) the skull, leg, thigh, and arm bones, which they found lying about the grave-yard. This was a new species of weapon, for which the majority of the O'Callaghans were scarcely prepared. Out they sallied in a body—some with these, others with stones, and, making fierce assault upon their enemies, absolutely druv them back— not so much by the damage they were doing, as by the alarm and terror which these unexpected species of missiles excited.

"At this moment, notwithstanding the fatality that had taken place, nothing could be more truly comical and facetious than the appearance of the field of battle. Skulls were flying in every direction—so thick, indeed, that it might with truth be asseverated,(93) that many who were petrified in the dust, had their skulls broken in this great battle between the factions.—God help poor Ireland! when its inhabitants are so pugnacious, that even the grave is no security against getting their crowns cracked, and their bones fractured! Well, any how, skulls and bones flew in every direction; stones and brick-bats were also put in motion; spades, shovels, loaded whips, pot-sticks, churn-staffs, flails, and all kinds of available weapons were in hot employment.

"But, perhaps, there was nothing more truly felicitous or original in its way than the mode of warfare adopted by little Neal Malone,(94) was tailor for the O'Callaghan side: for every tradesman is obliged to fight on behalf of his own faction. Big Frank Farrell, the miller, being on the O'Hallaghan side, had been sent for, and came up from his mill behind the town, quite fresh. He was never what could be called a good man,(95) though it was said that be could lift ten hundred-weight. He puffed forward with a great cudgel, determined to commit slaughter out of the face, and the first man he met was the

John W. Hurley

weeshy(96) fraction of a tailor, as nimble as a hare. He immediately attacked him, and would probably have taken his measure for life had not the tailor's activity protected him. Farrell was in a rage, and Neal, taking advantage of his blind fury, slips round him, and, with a short run, sprung upon the miller's back, and planted a foot upon the threshold of each coat pocket, holding by the mealy collar of his waist-coat.(97) In this position he belaboured the miller's face and eyes with his little hard fist to such purpose, that he had him in the course of a few minutes nearly as blind as a mill-horse. The miller roared for assistance, but the pell-mell was going on too warmly for his cries to be available. In fact, he resembled an elephant with a monkey on his back.

"'How do you like that, Farrell?' Neal would say, giving him a cuff—'and that, and that; but that is best of all. Take it again, gud-geon(98) (two cuffs more)—here's grist for you (half a dozen addi-tional)—Hard fortune to you! (crack, crack.) What! going to lie down!—by all that's terrible, if you do, I'll annigulate(99) you! Here's a dhuragh,(100) (another half dozen)—long measure, you savage!—the baker's dozen, you baste!—there's five-an'-twenty to the score, Sampson! and one or two in' (crack, whack).

"'Oh! murther sheery!'(101) shouted the miller. 'Murtheran-age,(102) I'm kilt! Foul play!—foul play!'

"'You lie, big Nebuchodonosor!(103) it's not—this in all fair play, you big baste! Fair play, Sampson!(104)—by the same atoken, here's to jog your memory that it's the Fair day of Knockimdowney! Irish Fair play, you whale! But I'll whale you' (crack, crack, whack).

"'Oh! oh!' shouted the miller.

"'Oh! oh! is it? Oh, if I had my scissors here till I'd clip your ears off—wouldn't I be the happy man, any how, you swab, you?' (whack, whack, crack.)

"'Murther! murther! murther!' shouted the miller. 'Is there no help?'

"'Help is it?—you may say that (crack crack): there's a trifle—a small taste in the milling style,(105) you know; and here goes to dis-lodge a grinder. Did ye ever hear of the tailor on horseback, Sampson? eh? (whack, whack.) Did you ever expect to see a tailor o' horseback of yourself, you baste? (crack.) I tell you, if you offer to lie down, I'll annigulate you out o' the face.'

"Never, indeed, was a miller before or since so well dusted,(106) and, I dare say, Neal would have rode him long enough, but for an O'Hallaghan, who had gone into one of the houses to procure a weapon. This man was nearly as original in his choice of one as the tailor in the position which he selected for beating the miller. On entering the kitchen, he found that he had been anticipated: there was neither tongs, poker, nor churn-staff, nor, in fact, anything wherewith he could assault his enemies: all had been carried off by others. There was, however, a goose, in the action of being roasted on a spit at the fire: this was enough; Honest O'Hallaghan saw nothing but the spit, which he accordingly seized, goose and all, making the best of his way, so armed, to the scene of battle. He just came out of an entry as the miller was once more roaring for assistance, and, to a dead certainty, would have spitted the tailor like a cock-sparrow against the miller's carcase, had not his activity once more saved him. Unluckily, the unfortunate miller got the thrust behind which was intended for Neal, and roared like a bull. He was beginning to shout 'Foul play!' again, when, on turning round, he perceived that the thrust had not been intended for him, but for the tailor.

"'Give me that spit,' said he; 'by all the mills that ever were turned, I'll spit the tailor this blessed minute beside the goose, and we'll roast them both together.'

"The other refused to part with the spit; but the miller, seizing the goose, flung it with all his force after the tailor, who stooped, however, and avoided the blow.

"'No man has a better right to the goose than the tailor,' said Neal, as he took it up, and, disappearing, neither he nor the goose could be seen for the remainder of the day.

"The battle was now somewhat abated. Skulls, and bones, and bricks, and stones, were, however, still flying; so that it might be truly said, the bones of contention were numerous. The streets presented a woeful spectacle: men were lying with their bones broken—others, though not so seriously injured, lappered in their blood—some were crawling up, but were instantly knocked down by their enemies—some were leaning against the walls, or groping their way silently along them, endeavouring to escape observation, lest they might be smashed down and altogether murdered. Wives were sitting with the

64   John W. Hurley

bloody heads of their husbands in their laps, tearing their hair, weeping, and cursing, in all the gall of wrath, those who left them in such a state. Daughters performed the said offices to their fathers, and sisters to their brothers; not pretermitting(107) those who did not neglect their broken-paled(108) bachelors to whom they paid equal attention. Yet was the scene not without abundance of mirth. Many a hat was thrown up by the O'Callaghan side, who certainly gained the day. Many a song was raised by those who tottered about with trickling sconces,(109) half drunk with whiskey, and half stupid with beating. Many a 'whoo,' and 'hurroo,' and 'huzza,' was sent forth by the triumphanters; but truth to tell, they were miser ably feeble and faint, compared to what they had been in the beginning of the amusement; sufficiently evincing that, although they might boast of the name of victory, they had got a bellyful of beating; still there was hard fighting.

"I mentioned, some time ago, that a man bad adopted a scythe. I wish from my heart there had been no such bloody instrument there that day; but truth must be told. John O'Callaghan was now engaged against a set of the other O's, who had rallied for the third time, and attacked him and his party. Another brother of Rose Galh's was in this engagement, and him did John O'Callaghan not only knock down, but cut desperately across the temple. A man, stripped, and covered with blood and dust, at that moment made his appearance, his hand bearing the blade of the aforesaid scythe. His approach was at once furious and rapid, and I may as well add, fatal; for before John O'Callaghan had time to be forewarned of his danger, he was cut down, the artery of his neck laid open, and he died without a groan. It was truly dreadful, even to the oldest fighter present, to see the strong rush of red blood that curveted about his neck, until it gurgled, gurgled, gurgled, and lappered, and bubbled out, ending in small red spouts, blackening and blackening, as they became fainter and more faint. At this criticality, every eye was turned from the corpse to the murderer; but he had been instantly struck down, and a female, with a large stone in her apron, stood over him, her arms stretched out, her face horribly distorted with agony, and her eyes turned backwards, as it were, into her head. In a few seconds she fell into strong convulsions, and was immediately taken away. Alas! alas! it was Rose Galh; and when we looked at the man she had struck down, he was found to be her brother! flesh of her flesh, and blood of her blood! On examining him more closely, we discovered that his underjaw hung loose, that his limbs were supple; we tried to make him speak, but in vain—he too was a corpse.

The fact was, that in consequence of his being stripped, and covered by so much blood and dust, she knew him not; and, impelled by her feelings to avenge herself on the murderer of her lover, to whom she doubly owed her life, she struck him a deadly blow, without knowing him to be her brother. The shock produced by seeing her lover murdered, and the horror of finding that she herself, in avenging him, had taken her brother's life, was too much for a heart so tender as hers. On recovering from her convulsions, her senses were found to be gone for ever! Poor girl! she is still living; but from that moment to this, she has never opened her lips to mortal. She is, indeed, a fair ruin, but silent, melancholy, and beautiful as the moon in the summer heaven. Poor Rose Galh! you and many a mother, and father, and wife, and orphan, have had reason to maledict the bloody Battles of the Factions.

"With regard to my grandfather, he says that he didn't see purtier fighting within his own memory; not since the fight between himself and Big Mucklemurray took place in the same town. But, to do him justice, be condemns the scythe and every other weapon except tbe cudgels; because, he says, that if they continue to be resorted to, nate fighting will be altogether forgotten in the country."

[It was the original intention of the author to have made every man in the humble group about Ned M'Keown's hearth narrate a story illustrating Irish life, feeling, and manners; but on looking into the matter more closely, he had reason to think that such a plan, however agreeable for a time, would ultimately narrow the sphere of his work, and perhaps fatigue the reader by a superfluity of Irish dialogue and its peculiarities of phraseology. He resolved therefore, at the close of the Battle of the Factions, to abandon his original design, and leave himself more room for description and observation.]

John W. Hurley

Cork-red "phaties," or potatoes.

John W. Hurley

Chapter 2:
Neal Malone

There never was a greater souled or doughtier tailor than little Neal Malone. Though but four feet four in height, he paced the earth with the courage and confidence of a giant; nay, one would have imagined that he walked as if he feared the world itself was about to give way under him. Let no one dare to say in future that a tailor is but the ninth part of a man. That reproach has been gloriously taken away from the character of the cross-legged corporation(1) by Neal Malone. He has wiped it off like a stain from the collar of a second-hand coat; he has pressed this wrinkle out of the lying front of antiquity; he has drawn together this rent in the respectability of his profession. No. By him who was breechesmaker(2) to the gods—that is, except, like Highlanders, they eschewed inexpressibles(3)—by him who cut Jupiter's frieze jocks(4) for winter, and eke by the bottom of his thimble, we swear, that Neal Malone was more than the ninth part of a man! Setting, aside the Patagonians,(5) we maintain that two-thirds of mortal humanity were comprised in Neal; and, perhaps, we might venture to assert, that two-thirds of Neal's humanity were equal to six-thirds of another man's. It is right well known that Alexander the Great was a little man, and we doubt whether, had Alexander the Great been bred to the tailoring business, he would have exhibited so much of the hero as Neal Malone. Neal was descended from a fighting family, who had signalised themselves in as many battles as ever any single hero of antiquity fought. His father, his grandfather, and his great grandfather, were all fighting men, and his ancestors in general, up, probably, to Con of the Hundred Battles(6) himself. No wonder, therefore, that Neal's blood should cry out against the cowardice of his calling; no wonder that he should be an epitome of all that was valorous and heroic in a peaceable man, for we neglected to inform the reader that Neal, though "bearing no base mind," never fought any man in his own person. That, however, deducted nothing from his courage. If he did not fight, it was simply because he found cowardice universal. No man would engage him; his spirit blazed in vain: his thirst for battle was doomed to remain unquenched, except by whiskey, and this only increased it. In short, he could find no foe. He has often been known to challenge the first cudgel-players and pugilists of the parish;(7) to provoke men of fourteen stone weight;(8) and to bid mortal defiance to faction heroes of all grades—but in vain. There was that in him which told them that an encounter with Neal would strip them of their laurels. Neal saw all this with a lofty indignation; he deplored the degeneracy of the times, and thought it hard that the descendant of such a fighting family should be doomed to pass through life peaceably, whilst so many excellent rows and riots took place around him. It was a calamity to see every man's head broken but his own; a dismal thing to observe his neighbours go about with their bones in bandages, yet his untouched; and his friends beat black and blue, whilst his own cuticle remained undiscoloured.(9) "Blur-an'-agers!"(10) exclaimed Neal one day, when half-tipsy in the fair, "am I never to get a bit of fightin'? Is there no cowardly spalpeen(11) to stand afore Neal Malone? Be this an' be that, I'm blue-mowlded for want of a batin'!(12) I'm disgracin' my relations by the life I'm ladin'! Will none o' ye fight me aither for love, money, or whiskey—frind or inimy, an' bad luck to ye? I don't care a traneen(13) which, only out o' pure frindship, let us have a morsel o' the rale kick-up, 'tany rate. Frind or inimy, I say agin, if you regard me; sure that makes no differ, only let us have the fight."

"This excellent heroism was all wasted; Neal could not find a single adversary. Except he divided himself like Hotspur, and went to buffets one hand against the other,(14) there was no chance of a fight; no person to be found sufficiently magnanimous to encounter the tailor. On the contrary, every one of his friends—or, in other words, every man in the parish—was ready to support him.(15) He was clapped on the back, until his bones were nearly dislocated in his body; and his hand shaken, until his arm lost its cunning at the needle for half a week afterwards. This, to be sure, was a bitter business—a state of being past endurance. Every man was his friend—no man was his enemy. A desperate position for any person to find himself in, but doubly calamitous to a martial tailor.(16) Many a dolorous complaint did Neal make upon the misfortune of having none to wish him ill; and what rendered this hardship doubly oppressive, was the unlucky

John W. Hurley

fact that no exertions of his, however offensive, could procure him a single foe. In vain did he insult, abuse, and malign all his acquaintances. In vain did he father upon them all the rascality and villany he could think of; he lied against them with a force and originality that would have made many a modern novelist blush for want of invention—but all to no purpose. The world for once became astonishingly Christian; it paid back all his efforts to excite its resentment with the purest of charity; when Neal struck it on the one cheek, it meekly turned unto him the other. It could scarcely be expected that Neal would bear this. To have the whole world in friendship with a man is beyond doubt rather an affliction. Not to have the face of a single enemy to look upon, would decidedly be considered a deprivation of many agreeable sensations by most people, as well as by Neal Malone. Let who might sustain a loss, or experience a calamity, it was a matter of indifference to Neal. They were only his friends, and he troubled neither his head nor his heart about them. Heaven help us! There is no man without his trials; and Neal, the reader perceives, was not exempt from his. What did it avail him that he carried a cudgel ready for all hostile contingencies? Or knit his brows and shook his kippeen(17) at the fiercest of his fighting friends? The moment he appeared, they softened into downright cordiality. His presence was the signal of peace; for, notwithstanding his unconquerable propensity to warfare, he went abroad as the genius of unanimity, though carrying in his bosom the redoubtable disposition of a warrior;(18) just as the sun, though the source of light himself, is said to be dark enough at bottom.

It could not be expected that Neal, with whatever fortitude he might bear his other afflictions, could bear such tranquillity like a hero. To say that he bore it as one, would be to basely surrender his character; for what hero ever bore a state of tranquillity with courage? It affected his cutting out!(19) It produced what Burton calls "a windie melancholie," which was nothing else than an accumulation of courage that had no means of escaping, if courage can without indignity be ever said to escape. He sat uneasy on his lapboard.(20) Instead of cutting out soberly, he flourished his scissors as if he were heading a faction; he wasted much chalk by scoring his cloth in wrong places, and even caught his hot goose(21) without a holder. These symptoms alarmed his friends, who persuaded him to go to a doctor. Neal went, to satisfy them; but he knew that no prescription could drive the courage out of him—that he was too far gone in heroism to be made a coward of by apothecary stuff. Nothing in the pharmacopoeia could physic him into a pacific state.(22) His disease was simply the want of an enemy, and an unaccountable superabundance of friendship on the part of his acquaintances. How could a doctor remedy this by a prescription? Impossible. The doctor, indeed, recommended blood-letting;(23) but to lose blood in a peaceable manner was not only cowardly, but a bad cure for courage. Neal declined it: he would lose no blood for any man until he could not help it; which was giving the character of a hero at a single touch. His blood was not to be thrown away in this manner; the only lancet ever applied to his relations was the cudgel, and Neal scorned to abandon the principles of his family. His friends finding that he reserved his blood for more heroic purposes than dastardly phlebotomy,(24) knew not what to do with him. His perpetual exclamation was, as we have already stated, "I'm blue-mowlded for want of a batin'!" They did everything in their power to cheer him with the hope of a drubbing; told him he lived in an excellent country for a man afflicted with his malady; and promised, if it were at all possible, to create him a private enemy or two, who, they hoped in heaven, might trounce him to some purpose. This sustained him for a while; but as day after day passed, and no appearance of action presented itself, he could not choose but increase in courage. His soul, like a sword blade too long in the scabbard, was beginning to get fuliginous by inactivity. He looked upon the point of his own needle, and the bright edge of his scissors, with a bitter pang, when he thought of the spirit rusting within him: he meditated fresh insults, studied new plans, and hunted out cunning devices for provoking his acquaintances to battle, until by degrees he began to confound his own brain, and to commit more grievous oversights in his business than ever. Sometimes he sent home to one person a coat, with the legs of a pair of trousers attached to it for sleeves, and dispatched to another the arms of the aforesaid coat tacked together as a pair of trousers. Sometimes the coat was made to button behind instead of before, and he frequently placed the pockets in the lower part of the skirts, as if he had been in league with cut-purses. This was a melan-

John W. Hurley

choly situation, and his friends pitied him accordingly.

"Don't be cast down, Neal," said they, "your friends feel for you, poor fellow."

"Divil carry my frinds," replied Neal, "sure there's not one o' yez frindly enough to be my inimy, Tare-an'-ounze!(25) what'll I do? I'm blue-mowldled for want of a batin'!" Seeing that their consolation was thrown away upon him, they resolved to leave him to his fate; which they had no sooner done than Neal had thoughts of taking to the Skiomachia(26) as a last remedy. In this mood he looked with considerable antipathy at his own shadow for several nights; and it is not to be questioned, but that some hard battles would have taken place between them, were it not for the cunning of the shadow, which declined to fight him in any other position than with its back to the wall. This occasioned him to pause, for the wall was a fearful antagonist, inasmuch that it knew not when it was beaten; but there was still an alternative left. He went to the garden one clear day about noon, and hoped to have a bout with the shade, free from interruption. Both approached, apparently eager for the combat, and resolved to conquer or die, when a villanous cloud happening to intercept the light, gave the shadow an opportunity of disappearing; and Neal found himself once more without an opponent.

"It's aisy known," said Neal, "you haven't the blood in you, or you'd come to the scratch(27) like a man." He now saw that fate was against him, and that any further hostility towards the shadow was only a tempting of Providence. He lost his health, spirits, and everything but his courage. His countenance became pale and peaceful looking; the bluster departed from him; his body shrunk up like a withered parsnip. Thrice was he compelled to take in his clothes, and thrice did he ascertain that much of his time would be necessarily spent in pursuing his retreating person through the solitude of his almost deserted garments. God knows it is difficult to form a correct opinion upon a situation so paradoxical as Neal's was. To be reduced to skin and bone by the downright friendship of the world, was, as the sagacious reader will admit, next to a miracle. We appeal to the conscience of any man who finds himself without an enemy, whether he be not a greater skeleton than the tailor; we will give him fifty guineas provided he can show a calf to his leg. We know he could not; for the tailor had none, and that was because he had not an enemy. No man in friendship with the world ever has calves to his legs. To sum up all in a paradox of our own invention, for which we claim the full credit of originality, we now assert, that more men have risen in the world by the injury of their enemies, than have risen by the kindness of their friends. You may take this, reader, in any sense; apply it to hanging if you like, it is still immutably and immovably true. One day Neal sat cross-legged, as tailors usually sit, in the act of pressing a pair of breeches; his hands were placed, backs up, upon the handle of his goose, and his chin rested upon the back of his hands. To judge from his sorrowful complexion one would suppose that he sat rather to be sketched as a picture of misery, or of heroism in distress, than for the industrious purpose of pressing the seams of a garment. There was a great deal of New Burlingtonstreet pathos(28) in his countenance; his face, like the times, was rather out of joint; "the sun was just setting, and his golden beams fell, with a saddened splendour, athwart the tailor's"—the reader may fill up the picture.

In this position sat Neal, when Mr. O'Connor, the schoolmaster, whose inexpressibles he was turning for the third time, entered the workshop. Mr. O'Connor, himself, was as finished a picture of misery as the tailor. There was a patient subdued kind of expression in his face, which indicated a very fair portion of calamity; his eye seemed charged with affliction of the first water;(29) on each side of his nose might be traced two dry channels which, no doubt, were full enough while the tropical rains of his countenance lasted. Altogether, to conclude from appearances, it was a dead match in affliction between him and the tailor; both seemed sad, fleshless, and unthriving.

"Misther O'Connor," said the tailor, when the schoolmaster entered, "won't you be pleased to sit down?"

Mr. O'Connor sat; and, after wiping his forehead, laid his hat upon the lap-board, put his half handkerchief in his pocket, and looked upon the tailor. The tailor, in return, looked upon Mr. O'Connor; but neither of them spoke for some minutes. Neal, in fact, appeared to be wrapped up in his own misery, and Mr. O'Connor in his; or, as we often have much gratuitous sympathy for the distresses of our friends, we question but the tailor was wrapped up in Mr. O'Connor's misery, and Mr. O'Connor in the tailor's. Mr. O'Connor at length said—"Neal, are my inexpressibles finished?"

"I am now pressin' your inexpressibles," replied Neal; "but, be my sowl, Mr. O'Connor, it's not your inexpressibles I'm thinkin' of. I'm not the ninth part of what I was. I'd hardly make paddin' for a collar now."

"Are you able to carry a staff still, Neal?"(30)

"I've a light hazel one that's handy," said the tailor; "but where's the use of carryin' it, whin I can get no one to fight wid. Sure I'm disgracing my relations by the life I'm leadin'. I'll go to my grave widout ever batin' a man, or bein' bate myself; that's the vexation. Divil the row ever I was able to kick up in my life; so that I'm fairly bluemowlded for want of a batin'. But if you have patience—',

"Patience!" said Mr. O'Connor, with a shake of the head, that was perfectly disastrous even to look at; "patience, did you say, Neal?"

"Ay," said Neal, "an,' be my sowl, if you deny that I said patience, I'll break your head!"

"Ah, Neal," returned the other, "I don't deny it—for though I am teaching philosophy, knowledge, and mathematics, every day in my life, yet I'm learning patience myself both night and day. No, Neal; I have forgotten to deny any thing. I have not been guilty of a contradiction, out of my own school, for the last fourteen years. I once expressed the shadow of a doubt about twelve years ago, but ever since I have abandoned even doubting. That doubt was the last expiring effort at maintaining my domestic authority—but I suffered for it."

"Well," said Neal, "if you have patience, I'll tell you what afflicts me from beginnin' to endin'."

"I will have patience," said Mr. O'Connor, and he accordingly heard a dismal and indignant tale from the tailor.

"You have told me that fifty times over," said Mr. O'Connor, after hearing the story. "Your spirit is too martial for a pacific life. If you follow my advice, I will teach you how to ripple the calm current of your existence to some purpose. Marry a wife. For twentyfive years I have given instructions in three branches, viz.—philosophy, knowledge, and mathematics—I am also well versed in matrimony, and I declare that, upon my misery, and by the contents of all my afflictions, it is my solemn and melancholy opinion, that, if you marry a

Mrs. Malone taking Neal to bed.

John W. Hurley

Neal Malone shadow boxing.

wife, you will, before three months pass over your concatenated state,(31) not have a single complaint to make touching a superabundance of peace and tranquility, or a love of fighting."

"Do you mane to say that any woman would make me afeard?" said the tailor, deliberately rising up and getting his cudgel. "I'll thank you merely to go over the words agin, till I thrash you widin an inch o' your life. That's all."

"Neal," said the schoolmaster, meekly, "I won't fight; I have been too often subdued ever to presume on the hope of a single victory. My spirit is long since evaporated; I am like one of your own shreds, a mere selvage. Do you not know how much my habilaments(32) have shrunk in, even within the last five years? Hear me, Neal; and venerate my words as if they proceeded from the lips of a prophet. If you wish to taste the luxury of being subdued—if you are, as you say, blue-moulded for want of a beating, and sick at heart of a peaceful existence—why, MARRY A WIFE. Neal, send my breeches home with all haste, for they are wanted, you understand. Farewell!"

Mr. O'Connor, having thus expressed himself, departed, and Neal stood, with the cudgel in his hand, looking at the door out of which be passed, with an expression of fierceness, contempt, and reflection, strongly blended on the ruins of his once heroic visage. Many a man has happiness within his reach if he but knew it. The tailor bad been, hitherto, miserable because be pursued a wrong object. The schoolmaster, however, suggested a train of thought upon which Neal now fastened with all the ardour of a chivalrous temperament. Nay, he wondered that the family spirit should have so completely seized upon the fighting side of his heart, as to preclude all thoughts of matrimony; for he could not but remember that his relations were as ready for marriage as for fighting. To doubt this, would have been to throw a blot upon his own escutcheon.(33) He, therefore, very prudently asked himself, to whom, if he did not marry, should he transmit his courage. He was a single man, and, dying as such, he would be the sole depository of his own valour, which, like Junius's secret,(34) must perish with him. If he could have left it, as a legacy, to such of his friends as were most remarkable for cowardice, why the case would be altered; but this was impossible—and he had now no other means of preserving it to posterity than by creating a posterity

John W. Hurley

to inherit it. He saw, too, that the world was likely to become convulsed. Wars, as every body knew, were certainly to break out; and would it not be an excellent opportunity for being father to a colonel, or, perhaps, a general, that might astonish the world. The change visible in Neal, after the schoolmaster's last visit, absolutely thunderstruck all who knew him. The clothes, which he had rashly taken in to fit his shrivelled limbs, were once more let out. The tailor expanded with a new spirit; his joints ceased to be supple, as in the days of his valour; his eye became less fiery, but more brilliant. From being martial, he got desperately gallant; but, somehow, he could not afford to act the hero and lover both at the same time. This, perhaps, would be too much to expect from a tailor. His policy was better. He resolved to bring all his available energy to bear upon the charms of whatever fair nymph he should select for the honour of matrimony; to waste his spirit in fighting would, therefore, be a deduction from the single purpose in view. The transition from war to love is by no means so remarkable as we might at first imagine. We quote Jack Falstaff in proof of this, or, if the reader be disposed to reject our authority, then we quote Ancient Pistol himself—both of whom we consider as the most finished specimens of heroism that ever carried a safe skin. Acres would have been a hero had he worn gloves to prevent the courage from oozing out at his palms, or not felt such an unlucky antipathy to the "snug lying in the Abbey;" and as for Captain Bobadil,(35) he never had an opportunity of putting his plan, for vanquishing an army, into practice. We fear, indeed, that neither his character, nor Ben Johnson's knowledge of human nature, is properly understood; for it certainly could not be expected that a man, whose spirit glowed to encounter a whole host, could, without tarnishing his dignity, if closely pressed, condescend to fight an individual. But as these remarks on courage may be felt by the reader as an invidious introduction of a subject disagreeable to him, we beg to hush it for the present and return to the tailor. No sooner had Neal begun to feel an inclination to matrimony, than his friends knew that his principles had veered, by the change now visible in his person and deportment. They saw he had ratted from courage, and joined love. Heretofore his life had been all winter, darkened by storm and hurricane. The fiercer virtues had played the devil with him; every word was thunder, every look lightning; but now all that had passed away;— before, lie was the fortiter in re, at present he was the suaviter in modo.(36) His existence was perfect spring—beautifully vernal. All the amiable and softer qualities began to bud about his heart; a genial warmth was diffused over him; his soul got green within him; every day was serene, and if a cloud happened to become visible, there was a roguish rainbow astride of it, on which sat a beautiful Iris(37) that laughed down at him, and seemed to say, "why the dickens, Neal, don't you marry a wife?"

Neal could not resist the afflatus(38) which descended on him; an ethereal light dwelled, he thought, upon the face of nature; the colour of the cloth, which he cut out from day to day, was, to his enraptured eye, like the colour of cupid's wings—all purple; his visions were worth their weight in gold; his dreams, a credit to the bed he slept on; and his feelings, like blind puppies, young and alive to the milk of love and kindness which they drew from his heart. Most of this delight escaped the observation of the world, for Neal, like your true lover, became shy and mysterious. It is difficult to say what he resembled; no dark lantern ever had more light shut up within itself, than Neal had in his soul, although his friends were not aware of it. They knew, indeed, that he had turned his back upon valour; but beyond this their knowledge did not extend.

Neal was shrewd enough to know that what he felt must be love;— nothing else could distend him with happiness, until his soul felt light and bladder-like, but love. As an oyster opens, when expecting the tide, so did his soul expand at the contemplation of matrimony. Labour ceased to be a trouble to him; he sang and sewed from morning to night; his hot goose no longer burned him, for his heart was as hot as his goose; the vibrations of his head, at each successive stitch, were no longer sad and melancholy. There was a buoyant shake of exultation in them which showed that his soul was placid and happy within him. Endless honour be to Neal Malone for the originality with which be managed the tender sentiment! He did not, like your common-place lovers, first discover a pretty girl, and afterwards become enamoured of her. No such thing, he had the passion prepared beforehand—cut out and made-up as it were, ready for any girl whom it might fit. This was falling in love in the abstract, and let no man

John W. Hurley

condemn it without a trial; for many a long-winded argument could be urged in its defence. It is always wrong to commence business without capital, and Neal had a good stock to begin with. All we beg is, that the reader will not confound it with Platonism, which never marries; but he is at full liberty to call it Socratism,(39) which takes unto itself a wife, and suffers accordingly. Let no one suppose that Neal forgot the schoolmaster's kindness, or failed to be duly grateful for it. Mr. O'Connor was the first person whom he consulted touching his passion. With a cheerful soul he waited on that melancholy and gentleman-like man, and in the very luxury of his heart told him that he was in love.

"In love, Neal!" said the schoolmaster. "May I inquire with whom?"

"Wid nobody in particular, yet," replied Neal; "but of late I'm got divilish fond o' the girls in general."

"And do you call that being in love, Neal?" said Mr. O'Connor.

"Why, what else would I call it?" returned the tailor. "Amn't I fond of them?"

"Then it must be what is termed the Universal Passion, Neal;" observed Mr. O'Connor, "although it is the first time I have seen such an illustration of it as you present in your own person."

"I wish you would advise me how to act," said Neal; "I'm as happy as a prince since I began to get fond o' them, an' to think of marriage."

The schoolmaster shook his head again, and looked rather miserable. Neal rubbed his hands with glee, and looked perfectly happy. The schoolmaster shook his head again, and looked more miserable than before. Neal's happiness also increased on the second rubbing. Now, to tell the secret at once, Mr. O'Connor would not have appeared so miserable, were it not for Neal's happiness; nor Neal so happy, were it not for Mr. O'Connor's misery. It was all the result of contrast; but this you will not understand unless you be deeply read in modern novels.(40) Mr. O'Connor, however, was a man of sense, who knew, upon this principle, that the longer he continued to shake his head, the more miserable he must become, and the more also would he increase Neal's happiness; but he had no intention of increasing Neal's happiness at his own expense—for, upon the same hypothesis, it would have been for Neal's interest had he remained shaking his head there, and getting miserable until the day of judgment. He consequently declined giving the third shake, for he thought that plain conversation was, after all, more significant and forcible than the most eloquent nod, however ably translated.

"Neal," said he, "could you, by stretching your imagination, contrive to rest contented with nursing your passion in solitude, and love the sex at a distance?"

"How could I nurse and mind my business?" replied the tailor.

"I'll never nurse so long as I'll have the wife; and as for 'magination it depends upon the grain of it, whether I can stretch it or not. I don't know that I ever made a coat of it in my life."

"You don't understand me, Neal," said the schoolmaster. "In recommending marriage, I was only driving one evil out of you by introducing another. Do you think that, if you abandoned all thoughts of a wife, you would get heroic again?—that is, would you take once more to the love of fighting?"

"There is no doubt but I would," said the tailor: "if I miss the wife, I'll kick up such a dust as never was seen in the parish, an' you're the first man that I'll lick. But now that I'm in love," he continued, "sure, I ought to look out for the wife."

"Ah! Neal," said the schoolmaster, "you are tempting destiny: your temerity be, with all its melancholy consequences, upon your own head."

"Come," said the tailor, "it wasn't to hear you groaning to the tune of 'Dhrimmindhoo,' or 'The 'ould woman rockin' her cradle,' that I came; but to know if you could help me in makin' out the wife. That's the discoorse."

"Look at me, Neal," said the schoolmaster, solemnly; "I am at this moment, and have been any time for the last fifteen years, a living caveto(41) against matrimony. I do not think that earth possesses such a luxury as a single solitary life. Neal, the monks of old were happy men: they were all fat and had double chins; and, Neal, I tell you, that all fat men are in general happy. Care cannot come at them so readily as at a thin man; before it gets through the strong outworks of flesh and blood with which they are surrounded, it becomes treacherous to its original purpose, joins the cheerful spirits it meets in the system, and dances about the heart in all the madness of mirth; just like a

John W. Hurley

sincere ecclesiastic, who comes to lecture a good fellow against drinking, but who forgets his lecture over his cups,(42) and is laid under the table with such success, that he either never comes to finish his lecture, or comes often to be laid, under the table. Look at me, Neal, how wasted, fleshless, and miserable, I stand before you. You know how my garments have shrunk in, and what a solid man I was before marriage. Neal, pause, I beseech you: otherwise you stand a strong chance of becoming a nonentity like myself."

"I don't care what I become," said the tailor; "I can't think that you'd be so unrasonable as to expect that any of the Malones should pass out of the world widout either bein' bate or marrid. Have reason, Mr. O'Connor, an' if you can help me to the wife, I promise to take in your coat the next time for nothin'."

"Well, then," said Mr. O'Connor, "what would you think of the butcher's daughter, Biddy Neil? You have always had a thirst for blood, and here you may have it gratified in an innocent manner, should you ever become sanguinary again. 'Tis true, Neal, she is twice your size, and possesses three times your strength; but for that very reason, Neal, marry her if you can. Large animals are placid; and heaven preserve those bachelors, whom I wish well, from a small wife: 'tis such who always wield the sceptre of domestic life, and rule their husbands with a rod of iron."

"Say no more, Mr. O'Connor," replied the tailor, "she's the very girl I'm in love wid, an' never fear, but I'll overcome her heart if it can be done by man. Now, step over the way to my house, an' we'll have a sup on the head of it. Who's that calling?"

"Ah! Neal, I know the tones—there's a shrillness in them not to be mistaken. Farewell! I must depart; you have heard the proverb, 'those who are bound must obey.' Young Jack, I presume is squalling, and I must either nurse him, rock the cradle, or sing comic tunes for him, though heaven knows with what a disastrous heart I often sing 'Begone dull care,' the 'Rakes of Newcastle,' or, 'Peas upon a trencher.' Neal, I say again, pause before you take this leap in the dark. Pause, Neal, I entreat you. Farewell!"

Neal, however, was gifted with the heart of an Irishman, and scorned caution as the characteristic of a coward; lie had, as it appeared, abandoned all design of fighting, but the courage still adhered to him even in making love. He consequently conducted the siege of Biddy Neil's heart with a degree of skill and valour which would not have come amiss to Marshal Gerald at the siege of Antwerp, Locke or Dugald Stewart,(43) indeed, had they been cognizant of the tailor's triumph, might have illustrated the principle on which he succeeded—as to ourselves, we can only conjecture it. Our own opinion is, that they were both animated with a congenial spirit. Biddy was the very pink of pugnacity, and could throw in a body blow, or plant a facer, with singular energy and science.(44) Her prowess hitherto had, we confess, been displayed only within the limited range of domestic life; but should she ever find it necessary to exercise it upon a larger scale, there was no doubt whatsoever, in the opinion of her mother, brothers, and sisters, every one of whom she had successively subdued, that she must undoubtedly distinguish herself. There was certainly one difficulty which the tailor had not to encounter in the progress of his courtship; the field was his own; he had not a rival to dispute his claim. Neither was there any opposition given by her friends; they were, on the contrary, all anxious for the match; and when the arrangements were concluded, Neal felt his hand squeezed by them in succession, with an expression more resembling condolence than joy. Neal, however, had been bred to tailoring, and not to metaphysics; he could cut out a coat very well, but we do not say that lie could trace a principle—as what tailor, except Jeremy Taylor,(45) could? There was nothing particular in the wedding. Mr. O'Connor was asked by Neal to be present at it: but he shook his head, and told him that he had not courage to attend it, or inclination to witness any man's sorrows but his own. He met the wedding party by accident, and was heard to exclaim with a sigh, as they flaunted past him in gay exuberance of spirits—"Ah, poor Neal! he is going like one of her father's cattle to the shambles! Woe is me for having suggested matrimony to the tailor! He will not long be under the necessity of saying that he 'is blue-moulded for want of a beating.' The butcheress will fell him like a Kerry ox, and I may have his blood to answer for, and his discomfiture to feel for, in addition to my own miseries." On the evening of the wedding-day, about the hour of ten o'clock, Neal—whose spirits were uncommonly exalted, for his heart luxuriated within him—danced with his bride's maid; after the dance he sat beside her, and got eloquent in praise of her beauty; and it is said too, that he whispered to her, and chucked her chin with considerable gallantry. The tête-a-téte(46) continued for some time without exciting particular attention, with one exception; but that exception was worth a whole chapter of general rules. Mrs. Malone rose up, then sat down again, and took off a glass of the native; she got up a second time—all the wife rushed upon her heart—she approached them, and in a fit of the most exquisite sensibility, knocked the bride's maid down, and gave the tailor a kick of affecting pathos upon the inexpressibles. The whole scene was a touching one on both sides. The tailor was sent on all-fours to the floor; but Mrs. Malone took him quietly up, put him under her arm, as one would a lap dog, and with stately step marched away to the connubial apartment, in which everything remained very quiet for the rest of the night. The next morning Mr. O'Connor presented himself to congratulate the tailor on his happiness. Neal, as his friend shook hands with him, gave the schoolmaster's fingers a slight squeeze, such as a man gives who would gently intreat your sympathy. The schoolmaster looked at him, and thought he shook his head. Of this, however, he could not be certain ; for, as he shook his own during the moment of observation, he concluded that it might be a mere mistake of the eye, or, perhaps, the result of a mind predisposed to be credulous on the subject of shaking heads. We wish it were in our power to draw a veil, or curtain, or blind of some description, over the remnant of the tailor's narrative that is to follow; but as it is the duty of every faithful historian to give the secret causes of appearances which the world in general do not understand, so we think it but honest to go on, impartially and faithfully, without shrinking from the responsibility that is frequently annexed to truth. For the first three days after matrimony, Neal felt like a man who had been translated to a new and more lively state of existence. He had expected, and flattered himself, that, the moment this event should take place, he would once more resume his heroism, and experience the pleasure of a drubbing. This determination he kept a profound secret—nor was it known until a future period, when he disclosed it to Mr. O'Connor. He intended, therefore, that marriage should be nothing more than a mere parenthesis in his life—a kind of asterisk, pointing, in a note at the bottom, to this single exception in his general conduct—a nota bene(47) to the spirit of a martial man, intimating that he had been peaceful only for a while. In truth, he was, during the influence of love over him, and up to the very day of his marriage, secretly as blue-moulded as ever for want of a beating. The heroic penchant lay snugly latent in his heart, unchecked and unmodified. He flattered himself that he was achieving a capital imposition upon the world at large—that he was actually hoaxing mankind in general—and that such an excellent piece of knavish tranquility had never been perpetrated before his time. On the first week after his marriage, there chanced to be a fair in the next market-town. Neal, after breakfast, brought forward a bunch of shillelahs,(48) in order to select the best; the wife inquired the purpose of the selection, and Neal declared that he was resolved to have a fight that day, if it were to be had, he said, for "love or money."

"The thruth is," he exclaimed, strutting with fortitude about the house, "the thruth is, that I've done the whole of yez—I'm blue-mowlded as ever for want of a batin'."

"Don't go," said the wife.

"I will go," said Neal, with vehemence; "I'll go if the whole parish was to go to prevint me."

In about another half-hour Neal sat down quietly to his business, instead of going to the fair! Much ingenious speculation might be indulged in, upon this abrupt termination to the tailor's most formidable resolution; but, for our own part, we will prefer going on with the narrative, leaving the reader at liberty to solve the mystery as he pleases. In the mean time, we say this much—let those who cannot make it out, carry it to their tailor; it is a tailor's mystery, and no one has so good a right to understand it—except perhaps, a tailor's wife. At the period of his matrimony, Neal had become as plump and as stout as he ever was known to be in his plumpest and stoutest days. He and the schoolmaster had been very intimate about this time; but we know not how it happened that soon afterwards he felt a modest bridelike reluctance in meeting with that afflicted gentleman. As the eve of his union approached, he was in the habit, during the schoolmaster's visits to his workshop, of alluding, in rather a sarcastic tone, considering the unthriving appearance of his friend, to the increasing lustiness of his person. Nay, he has often leaped up from

John W. Hurley

his lap-board, and, in the strong spirit of exultation, thrust out his leg in attestation of his assertion, slapping it, moreover, with a loud laugh of triumph, that sounded like a knell to the happiness of his emaciated acquaintance. The schoolmaster's philosophy, however, unlike his flesh, never departed from him; his usual observation was, "Neal, we are both receding from the same point; you increase in flesh, whilst I, heaven help me, am fast diminishing."

The tailor received these remarks with very boisterous mirth, whilst Mr. O'Connor simply shook his head, and looked sadly upon his limbs, now shrouded in a superfluity of garments, some what resembling a slender thread of water in a shallow summer stream, nearly wasted away, and surrounded by an unproportionate extent of channel. The fourth month after the marriage arrived. Neal, one day, near its close, began to dress himself in his best apparel. Even then, when buttoning his waistcoat, he shook his head after the manner of Mr. O'Connor, and made observations upon the great extent to which it over-folded him.

Well, thought he, with a sigh—this waistcoat certainly did fit me to a T; but it's wondherful to think how—cloth stretches!

"Neal," said the wife, on perceiving him drest, "where are you bound for?"

"Faith, for life," replied Neal, with a mitigated swagger; "and I'd as soon, if it had been the will of Provid—" He paused.

"Where are you going?" asked the wife, a second time.

"Why," he answered, "only to the dance at Jemmy Connolly's; I'll be back early."

"Don't go," said the wife.

"I'll go," said Neal, "if the whole counthry was to prevent me. Thunder an' lightnin', woman, who am I?" he exclaimed, in a loud but rather infirm voice; "amn't I Neal Malone, that never met a man who'd fight him! Neal Malone, that was never beat by man! Why, tare-an-ounze, woman! Whoo! I'll get enraged some time, an' play the divil? Who's afeard, I say?"

"Don't go," added the wife, a third time, giving Neal a significant look in the face. In about another half-hour, Neal sat down quietly to his business, instead of going to the dance! Neal now turned himself, like many a sage in similar circumstances, to philosophy; that is to say—he began to shake his head upon principle, after the manner of the schoolmaster. He would, indeed, have preferred the bottle upon principle; but there was no getting at the bottle, except through the wife; and it so happened that by the time it reached him, there was little consolation left in it. Neal bore all in silence; for silence, his friend had often told him, was a proof of wisdom. Soon after this, Neal, one evening, met Mr. O'Connor by chance upon a plank which crossed a river. This plank was only a foot in breadth, so that no two individuals could pass each other upon it. We cannot find words in which to express the dismay of both, on finding that they absolutely glided past one another without collision. Both paused, and surveyed each other solemnly; but the astonishment was all on the side of Mr. O'Connor.

"Neal," said the schoolmaster, "by all the household gods, I conjure you to speak, that I may be assured you live!" The ghost of a blush crossed the church-yard visage of the tailor.

"Oh!" he exclaimed, "why the devil did you tempt me to marry a wife."

"Neal," said his friend, "answer me in the most solemn manner possible—throw into your countenance all the gravity you can assume; speak as if you were under the hands of the hangman, with the rope about your neck, for the question is, indeed, a trying one which I am about to put. Are you still 'blue-moulded for want of beating?'"

The tailor collected himself to make a reply; he put one leg out—the very leg which he used to show in triumph to his friend; but, alas, how dwindled! He opened his waistcoat, and lapped it round him, until he looked like a weasel on its hind legs. He then raised himself up on his tip toes, and, in an awful whisper, replied, "No ! ! ! the devil a bit I'm blue-mowlded for want of a batin'."

The schoolmaster shook his head in his own miserable manner; but, alas! he soon perceived that the tailor was as great an adept at shaking the head as himself. Nay, he saw that there was a calamitous refinement—a delicacy of shake in the tailor's vibrations, which gave to his own nod a very commonplace character. The next day the tailor took in his clothes; and from time to time continued to adjust them to the dimensions of his shrinking person. The schoolmaster and he, whenever they could steal a moment, met and sympathised together.

John W. Hurley

Mr. O'Connor, however, bore up somewhat better than Neal. The latter was subdued in heart and in spirit; thoroughly, completely, and intensely vanquished. His features became sharpened by misery, for a termagant wife is the whetstone(49) on which all the calamities of a hen-pecked husband are painted by the devil. He no longer strutted as he was wont to do; he no longer carried a cudgel as if he wished to wage a universal battle with mankind. He was now a married man.— Sneakingly, and with a cowardly crawl did he creep along as if every step brought him nearer to the gallows. The schoolmaster's march of misery was far slower than Neal's: the latter distanced him. Before three years passed, he had shrunk up so much, that he could not walk abroad of a windy day without carrying weights in his pockets to keep him firm on the earth, which he once trod with the step of a giant. He again sought the schoolmaster, with whom indeed he associated as much as possible. Here he felt certain of receiving sympathy; nor was he disappointed. That worthy, but miserable man, and Neal, often retired beyond the hearing of their respective wives, and supported each other by every argument in their power. Often have they been heard, in the dusk of evening, singing behind a remote hedge that melancholy ditty, "Let us both be unhappy together;" which rose upon the twilight breeze with a cautious quaver of sorrow truly heart-rending and lugubrious.

"Neal," said Mr. O'Connor, on one of those occasions, "here is a book which I recommend to your perusal; it is called 'The Afflicted Man's Companion;' try, if you cannot glean some consolation out of it."

"Faith," said Neal, "I'm for ever oblaged to you, but I don't want it. I've had 'The Afflicted Man's Companion' too long, and divil an atom of consolation I can get out of it. I have one o' them I tell you; but, be me sowl, I'll not undhertake a pair o' them. The very name's enough for me." They then separated.

The tailor's vis vitae(50) must have been powerful, or he would have died. In two years more his friends could not distinguish him from his own shadow; a circumstance which was of great inconvenience to him. Several grasped at the hand of the shadow instead of his; and one man was near paying it five and sixpence for making a pair of small-clothes. Neal, it is true, undeceived him with some trouble; but candidly admitted that he was not able to carry home the money. It was difficult, indeed, for the poor tailor to bear what he felt; it is true he bore it as long as he could: but at length he became suicidal, and often had thoughts of "making his own quietus with his bare bodkin."(51) After many deliberations and afflictions, he ultimately made the attempt; but, alas! he found that the blood of the Malones refused to flow upon so ignominious an occasion. So he solved the phenomenon; although the truth was, that his blood was not "i' the vein"(52) for it; none was to be had. What then was to be done? He resolved to get rid of life by some process; and the next that occurred to him was hanging. In a solemn spirit he prepared a selvage, and suspended himself from the rafter of his workshop; but here another disappointment awaited him—he would not hang. Such was his want of gravity, that his own weight proved insufficient to occasion his death by mere suspension. His third attempt was at drowning, but he was too light to sink; all the elements—all his own energies joined themselves, he thought, in a wicked conspiracy to save his life. Having thus tried every avenue to destruction, and failed in all, he felt like a man doomed to live for ever. Henceforward he shrunk and shrivelled by slow degrees, until in the course of time he became so attenuated, that the grossness of human vision could no longer reach him. This, however, could not last always. Though still alive, he was to all intents and purposes imperceptible. He could now only be heard; he was reduced to a mere essence—the very echo of human existence, vox et praeterea nihil.(53) It is true the schoolmaster asserted that he occasionally caught passing glimpses of him; but that was because he had been himself nearly spiritualised by affliction, and his visual ray purged in the furnace of domestic tribulation. By and by Neal's voice lessened, got fainter and more indistinct, until at length nothing but a doubtful murmur could be heard, which ultimtately could scarcely be distinguished from a ringing in the ears.

Such was the awful and mysterious fate of the tailor, who, as a hero, could not of course die; he merely dissolved like an icicle, wasted into immateriality, and finally melted away beyond the perception of mortal sense. Mr. O'Connor is still living, and once more in the fullness of perfect health and strength. His wife, however, we may as well hint, has been dead more than two years.

John W. Hurley

Irish Gangs And Stick-Fighting   91

John W. Hurley

Chapter 3: The Party Fight And Funeral

We ought, perhaps, to inform our readers that the connection between a party fight and funeral is sufficiently strong to justify the author in classing them under the title which is prefixed to this story. The one being usually the natural result of the other, is made to proceed from it, as is, unhappily, too often the custom in real life among the Irish.

It has been long laid down as a universal principle, that self-preservation is the first law of nature. An Irishman, however, has nothing to do with this; he disposes of it as he does with the other laws, and washes his hands out of it altogether.But commend him to a fair, dance, funeral, or wedding, or to any other sport where there is a likelihood of getting his head or his bones broken, and if he survive he will remember you, with a kindness peculiar to himself, to the last day of his life—will drub you from head to heel if he finds that any misfortune has kept you out of a row beyond the usual period of three months—will render the same service to any of your friends that stand in need of it; or, in short, will go to the world's end, or fifty miles farther, as he himself would say, to serve you, provided you can procure him a bit of decent fighting. Now, in truth and soberness, it is difficult to account for this propensity, especially when the task of ascertaining it is assigned to those of another country, or even to those Irishmen whose rank in life places them too far from the customs, prejudices, and domestic opinions of their native peasantry, none of which can be properly known without mingling with them. To my own knowledge, however, it proceeds from education. And here I would beg leave to point out an omission of which the several boards of education have been guilty, and which, I believe, no one but myself has yet been sufficiently acute and philosophical to ascertain, as forming a sine qua non(1) in the national instruction of the lower orders of Irishmen.

The cream of the matter is this:—a species of ambition prevails in the Green Isle not known in any other country. It is an ambition of about three miles by four in extent; or, in other words, is bounded by the limits of the parish(2) in which the subject of it may reside. It puts itself forth early in the character, and a hardy perennial it is. In my own case its first development was noticed in the hedge-school(3) which I attended. I had not been long there till I was forced to declare myself either for the Caseys or the Murphys, two tiny factions that had split the school between them. The day on which the ceremony of my declaration took place was a solemn one. After school, we all went to the bottom of a deep valley, a short distance from the school-house; up to the moment of our assembling there, I had not taken my stand under either banner: that of the Caseys was a sod of turf stuck on the end of a broken fishing-rod—the eagle of the Murphys was a Cork red potato hoisted in the same manner. The turf was borne by an urchin who afterwards distinguished himself in fairs and markets as a builla batthah(4) of the first grade, and from this circumstance he was nicknamed Parrah Rackhan.(5) The potato was borne by little Mickle M'Phaudeen Murphy, who afterwards took away Katty Bane Sheridan without asking her own consent or her father's. They were all then boys, it is true, but they gave a tolerable promise of that eminence which they subsequently attained.

When we arrived at the bottom of the glen, the Murphys and the Caseys, including their respective followers, ranged themselves on either side of a long line which was drawn between the belligerent powers with the butt-end of one of the standards. Exactly on this line was I placed. The word was then put to me in full form—"Whether will you side with the decent Caseys or the blackguard Murphys?" "Whether will you side with the decent Murphys or the blackguard Caseys?" "The potato for ever!" said I, throwing up my caubeen,(6) and running over to the Murphy standard. In the twinkling of an eye we were at it; and in a short time the deuce an eye some of us had to twinkle. A battle-royal succeeded that lasted near half an hour, and it would probably have lasted about double the time were it not for the appearance of the "master," who was seen by a little shrivelled vidette, who wanted an arm,(7) and could take no part in the engagement. This was enough—we instantly radiated in all possible directions, so that by the time he had descended through the intricacies of the glen to the field of battle, neither victor nor vanquished was visible, except, perhaps, a straggler or two as they topped the brow of the declivity, looking back over their shoulders to put themselves out of doubt as to their visibility by the master. They seldom looked in vain, however, for there he usually stood, shaking up his rod, silently prophetic of its application on the following day. This threat, for the most part, ended in smoke; for, except he horsed about forty or fifty of us, the infliction of impartial justice was utterly out of his power.

But, besides this, there never was a realm in which the evils of a divided cabinet were more visible: the truth is, the monarch himself was under the influence of female government—an influence which he felt it either contrary to his inclination or beyond his power to throw off. "Poor Norah, long may you reign!" we often used to exclaim, to the visible mortification of the "master," who felt the benevolence of the wish bottomed upon an indirect want of allegiance to himself. Well, it was a touching scene!—how we used to stand with the waistbands of our smallclothes cautiously grasped in our hands, with a timid show of resistance, our brave red faces slobbered over with tears, as we stood naked for execution! Never was there a finer specimen of deprecation in eloquence than we then exhibited— the supplicating look right up into the master's face—the touching modulation of the whine—the additional tightness and caution with which we grasped the waistbands with one hand, when it was necessary to use the other in wiping our eyes and noses with the polished sleeve-cuff—the sincerity and vehemence with which we promised never to be guilty again, still shrewdly including the condition of present impunity for our offence:—"this one—time—master, if ye plaise, sir;" and the utter hopelessness and despair which were legible in the last groan, as we grasped the "master's" leg in utter recklessness of judgment, were all perfect in their way. Reader, have you ever got a reprieve from the gallows? I beg pardon, my dear sir; I only meant to ask, are you capable of entering into what a personage of that description might be supposed to feel, on being informed, after the knot had been neatly tied under the left ear, and the cap drawn over his eyes, that his Majesty had granted him a full pardon? But you remember your own schoolboy days, and that's enough.

The nice discrimination with which Norah used to time her interference was indeed surprising. God help us! limited was our experience, and shallow our little judgments, or we might have known what the master meant when, with the upraised arm hung over us, his eye was fixed upon the door of the kitchen, waiting for Norah's appearance.

Long, my fair and virtuous countrywomen, I repeat it to you all, as I did to Norah—may you reign in the hearts and affections of your husbands (but nowhere else), the grace, ornaments, and happiness of their hearths and lives, you jewels, you! You are paragons of all that's good, and your feelings are highly creditable to yourselves and to humanity.

When Norah advanced, with her brawny uplifted arm (for she was a powerful woman) and forbidding aspect, to interpose between us and the avenging terrors of the birch, do you think that she did not reflect honour on her sex and the national character? I sink the base allusion to the miscaun(8) of fresh butter which we had placed in her hands that morning, or the dish of eggs, or of meal, which we had either begged or stolen at home, as a present for her; disclaiming, at the same time, the rascally idea of giving it from any motive beneath the most lofty-minded and disinterested generosity on our part.

Then, again, never did a forbidding face shine with so winning and amicable an expression as did hers on that merciful occasion. The sun dancing a hornpipe(9) on Easter Sunday morning, or the full moon sailing as proud as a peacock in a new halo head-dress, was a very disrespectable sight, compared to Norah's red beaming face, shrouded in her dowd cap with long ears, that descended to her masculine and substantial neck. Owing to her influence, the whole economy of the school was good; for we were permitted to cuff one another,(10) and do whatever we pleased, with impunity, if we brought the meal, eggs, or butter; except some scapegoat who was not able to accomplish this, and he generally received on his own miserable carcase what was due to us all.

Poor Jack Murray! his last words on the scaffold, for being concerned in the murder of Pierce the gauger(11) were, that he got the first of his bad habits under Pat Mulligan and Norah—that he learned to steal by secreting at home butter and meal to paste up the master's eyes to his bad conduct(12)—and that his fondness for quarrelling arose from being permitted to head a faction at school; a most ungrateful return for the many acts of grace which the indulgence of Norah caused to be issued in his favour.

I was but a short time under Pat, when, after the general example, I had my cudgel, which I used to carry regularly to a certain furze bush within fifty perches of the "seminary,"(13) where I hid it till after "dismiss". I grant it does not look well in me to become my own panegyrist;(14) but I can at least declare that there were few among the Caseys able to resist the prowess of this right arm, puny as it was at the period in question. Our battles were obstinate and frequent; but as the quarrels of the two families and their relations on each side were as bitter and pugnacious in fairs and markets as ours were in school, we hit upon the plan of holding our Lilliputian(15) engagements upon the same days on which our fathers and brothers contested. According to this plan, it very often happened that the corresponding parties were successful, and as frequently that whilst the Caseys were well drubbed in the fair, their sons were victorious at school, and vice versa.

For my part I was early trained to cudgelling, and before I reached my fourteenth year could pronounce as sage and accurate an opinion upon the merits of a shillelagh,(16) as it is called, or cudgel, as a veterinary surgeon of sixty could upon a dead ass at first sight. Our plan of preparing them was this: we sallied out to any place where there was an underwood of blackthorn or oak, and having surveyed the premises with the eye of a connoisseur, we selected the straightest root-growing piece which we could find; for if not root-growing, we did not consider it worth cutting, knowing from experience that a branch, how straight and fair soever it might look, would snap in the twist and tug of war. Having cut it as close to the root as possible, we then lopped off the branches, and put it up in the chimney to season. When seasoned, we took it down, and wrapping it in brown paper, well steeped in hog's lard or oil, we buried it in a horse-dunghill,(17) paying it a daily visit for the purpose of making it straight by doubling back the bends or angles across the knee, in a direction contrary to their natural tendency. Having daily repeated this until we had made it straight, and renewed the oiled wrapping-paper until the staff was perfectly saturated, we then rubbed it well with a woollen cloth containing a little black-lead and grease, to give it a polish. This was the last process; except that if we thought it too light at the top, we used to bore a hole in the lower end with a red-hot iron spindle, into which we poured melted lead, for the purpose of giving it the knock-down weight.

There were very few of Paddy Mulligan's scholars without a choice collection of them, and scarcely one who had not, before his fifteenth year, a just claim to be called the hero of a hundred fights, and the heritor of as many bumps on the cranium as would strike both Gall and Spurzheim(18) speechless.

Now this, be it known, was, and in some districts yet is, an integral part of an Irish peasant's education. In the northern parts of Ireland, where the population of the Catholics on the one side, and of Protestants and Dissenters on the other, is nearly equal, I have known the respective scholars of Catholic and Protestant schools to challenge each other, and meet half-way to do battle, in vindication of their respective creeds; or for the purpose of establishing the character of their respective masters as the more learned man; for if we were to judge by the nature of the education then received, we would be led to conclude that a more commercial nation than Ireland was not on the face of the earth, it being the indispensable part of every scholar's business to become acquainted with the three sets of Book-keeping.(19)

The boy who was the handiest and the most daring with the cudgel at Paddy Mulligan's school was Denis Kelly, the son of a wealthy farmer(20) in the neighbourhood. He was a rash, hottempered, good-natured lad, possessing a more than common share of this blackthorn ambition; on which account he was cherished by his relations as a boy that was likely at a future period to be able to walk over the course of the parish in fair, market, or patron.(21)

He certainly grew up a stout, able young fellow, and before he reached nineteen years was unrivalled at the popular exercises of the peasantry. Shortly after that time he made his debut in a party quarrel,(22) which took place in one of the Christmas Margamores,(23) and fully sustained the anticipations which were formed of him by his relations. For a year or two afterwards no quarrel was fought without him; and his prowess rose until he had gained the very pinnacle of that ambition which he had determined to reach. About this time I was separated from him, having found it necessary, in order to accomplish my objects in life, to reside with a relation in another part of the country.

The period of my absence, I believe, was about fourteen years, during which space I heard no account of him whatsoever. At length, however, that inextinguishable attachment which turns the affections and memory to the friends of our early days—to those scenes which we traversed when the heart was light and the spirits buoyant—determined me to make a visit to my native place, that I might witness the progress of time and care upon those faces that were once so familiar to me; that I might once more look upon the meadows, and valleys, and groves, and mountains where I had so often played, and to which I still found myself bound by a tie that a more enlightened view of life and nature only made stronger and more enduring. I accordingly set off, and arrived, late in the evening of a December day, at a little town within a few miles of my native home. On alighting from the coach, and dining, I determined to walk home, as it was a fine frosty night. The full moon hung in the blue unclouded firmament in all her lustre, and the stars shone out with that tremulous twinkling motion so peculiarly remarkable in frost. I had been absent, I said, about fifteen years, and felt that the enjoyment of this night would form an era in the records of my memory and my feelings. I find myself, indeed, utterly incapable of expressing what I experienced; but those who have ever been in similar circumstances will understand what I mean. A strong spirit of practical poetry and romance was upon me, and I thought that a common-place approach in the open day would have rendered my return to the scenes of my early life a very stale and unedifying matter.

I left the inn at seven o'clock, and as I had only five miles to walk, I would just arrive about nine, allowing myself to saunter on at the rate of two miles and a half per hour. My sensations, indeed, as I went along, were singular; and as I took a solitary road across the mountains, the loneliness of the walk, the deep gloom of the valleys, the towering height of the dark hills, and the pale silvery light of a sleeping lake shining dimly in the distance below, gave me such a distinct notion of the sublime and beautiful as I have seldom since experienced. I recommend every man who has been fifteen years absent from his native fields to return by moonlight.

Well, there is a mystery yet undiscovered in our being, for no man can know his feelings or his capacities. Many a slumbering thought, and sentiment, and association reposes within him of which he is utterly ignorant, and which, except he come in contact with those objects whose influence over his mind can alone call them into being, may never be awakened, or give him one moment of either pleasure or pain. There is, therefore, a great deal in the position which we hold in society, and simply in situation.

I felt this on that night; for the tenor of my reflections was new and original, and my feelings had a warmth and freshness in them which nothing but the situation in which I then found myself could give them. The force of association, too, was powerful; for, as I advanced nearer home, the names of hills, and lakes, and mountains that I had utterly forgotten, as I thought, were distinctly revived in my memory, and a crowd of youthful thoughts and feelings that I imagined my intercourse with the world and the finger of time had blotted out of my being began to crowd afresh on my fancy. The name of a townland would instantly return with its appearance; and I could now remember the history of families and individuals that had long been effaced from my recollection.

But what is even more singular is, that the superstitious terrors of my boyhood began to come over me as formerly, whenever a spot noted for supernatural appearances met my eye. It was in vain that I exerted myself to expel them, by throwing the barrier of philosophic reasoning in their way; they still clung to me, in spite of every effort to the contrary. But the fact is that I was for the moment the slave of a morbid and feverish sentiment, that left me completely at the mercy of the dark and fleeting images that passed over my fancy. I now came to a turn where the road began to slope down into the depths of a valley that ran across it. When I looked forward into the bottom, all was darkness impenetrable, for the moon-beams were thrown off by the height of the mountains that rose on each side of it. I felt an indefinite sensation of fear, because at that moment I recollected that it had been, in my younger days, notorious as the scene of an apparition, where the spirit of a murdered pedlar had never been known to permit a solitary traveller to pass without appearing to him, and walk-

John W. Hurley

ing cheek-by-jowl along with him to the next house on the way, at which spot he usually vanished. The influence of my feelings, or, I should rather say, the physical excitement of my nerves, was by no means slight, as these old traditions recurred to me; although, at the same time, my moral courage was perfectly unimpaired, so that, notwithstanding this involuntary apprehension, I felt a degree of novelty and curiosity in descending the valley: "If it appear," said I, "I shall at least satisfy myself as to the truth of apparitions."

My dress consisted of a long, dark surtout,(24) the collar of which, as the night was keen, I had turned up about my ears, and the corners of it met round my face. In addition to this I had a black silk handkerchief tied across my mouth to keep out the night air, so that, as my dark fur travelling cap came down over my face, there was very little of my countenance visible. I now had advanced half way into the valley, and all about me was dark and still: the moonlight was not nearer than the top of the hill which I was descending; and I often turned round to look upon it, so silvery and beautiful it appeared at a distance. Sometimes I stood for a few moments admiring its effect, and contemplating the dark mountains as they stood out against the firmament, then kindled into magnificent grandeur by the myriads of stars that glowed in its expanse. There was perfect silence and solitude around me; and as I stood alone in the dark chamber of the mountains I felt the impressiveness of the situation gradually supersede my terrors. A sublime sense of religious awe descended on me; my soul kindled into a glow of solemn and elevated devotion, which gave me a more intense perception of the presence of God than I had ever before experienced. "How sacred—how awful," thought I, "is this place!—how impressive is this hour!—surely I feel myself at the footstool of God! The voice of worship is in this deep, soul-thrilling silence; and the tongue of praise speaks, as it were, from the very solitude of the mountains!" I then thought of Him who went up into a mountain-top to pray, and felt the majesty of those admirable descriptions of the Almighty, given in the Old Testament blend in delightful harmony with the beauty and fitness of the Christian dispensation, that brought life and immortality to light. "Here," said I, "do I feel that I am indeed immortal, and destined for scenes of a more exalted and comprehensive existence!"(25) I then proceeded further into the valley, completely freed from the influence of old and super-stitious associations. A few perches below me a small river crossed the road, over which was thrown a little stone bridge of rude work-manship. This bridge was the spot on which the apparition was said to appear; and as I approached it I felt the folly of those terrors which had only a few minutes before beset me so strongly. I found my moral energies recruited, and the dark phantasms of my imagination dis-pelled by the light of religion, which had refreshed me with a deep sense of the Almighty presence. I accordingly walked forward, scarcely bestowing a thought upon the history of the place, and had got within a few yards of the bridge, when, on resting my eye accidentally upon the little elevation formed by its rude arch, I perceived a black coffin placed at the edge of the road, exactly upon the bridge itself!

It may be evident to the reader that, however satisfactory the force of philosophical reasoning might have been upon the subject of the solitude, I was too much the creature of sensation for an hour before to look on such a startling object with firm nerves. For the first two or three minutes, therefore, I exhibited as finished a specimen of the dastardly as could be imagined. My hair absolutely raised my cap some inches off my head; my mouth opened to an extent which I did not conceive it could possibly reach; I thought my eyes shot out from their sockets; and my fingers spread out and became stiff, though powerless. The "obstupui"(26) was perfectly realised in me, for, with the exception of a single groan which I gave on first seeing the ob-ject, I found that if one word would save my life or transport me to my own fire-side, I could not utter it. I was also rooted to the earth, as if by magic; and although instant tergiversation(27) and flight had my most hearty concurrence, I could not move a limb, nor even raise my eyes off the sepulchral-looking object which lay before me. I now felt the perspiration fall from my face in torrents, and the strokes of my heart fell audibly on my ear. I even attempted to say, "God pre-serve me!" but my tongue was dumb and powerless, and could not move. My eye was still upon the coffin, when I perceived that, from being motionless, it instantly began to swing,—first in a lateral, then in a longitudinal direction, although it was perfectly evident that no human hand was nearer it than my own. At length I raised my eyes off it, for my vision was strained to an aching intensity, which I thought

John W. Hurley

must have occasioned my eye-strings to crack. I looked instinctively about me for assistance—but all was dismal, silent, and solitary: even the moon had disappeared among a few clouds that I had not noticed in the sky.

As I stood in this state of indescribable horror I saw the light gradually fade away from the tops of the mountains, giving the scene around me a dim and spectral ghastliness, which to those who were never in such a situation is altogether inconceivable.

At length I thought I heard a noise as it were of a rushing tempest sweeping from the hills down into the valley; but on looking up I could perceive nothing but the dusky desolation that brooded over the place. Still the noise continued; again I saw the coffin move; I then felt the motion communicated to myself, and found my body borne and swung backwards and forwards, precisely according to the motion of the coffin. I again attempted to utter a cry for assistance, but could not: the motion of my body still continued, as did the approaching noise in the hills. I looked up a second time in the direction in which the valley wound off between them, but judge of what I must have suffered when I beheld one of the mountains moving, as it were, from its base, and tumbling down towards the spot on which I stood! In the twinkling of an eye the whole scene, hills and all, began to tremble, to vibrate, and to fly round me, with a rapid, delirious motion; the stars shot back into the depths of heaven, and disappeared; the ground on which I stood began to pass from beneath my feet; a noise like the breaking of a thousand gigantic billows again burst from every direction, and I found myself instantly overwhelmed by some deadly weight, which prostrated me on the earth, and deprived me of sense and motion.

I know not how long I continued in this state; but I remember that, on opening my eyes, the first object that presented itself to me, was the sky glowing as before with ten thousand stars, and the moon walking in her unclouded brightness through the heavens.
The whole circumstance then rushed back upon my mind, but with a sense of horror very much diminished; I arose, and on looking towards the spot, perceived the coffin in the same place. I then stood, and endeavouring to collect myself, viewed it as calmly as possible; it was, however, as motionless and distinct as when I first saw it. I

now began to reason upon the matter, and to consider that it was pusillanimous(28) in me to give way to such boyish terrors. The confidence, also, which my heart, only a short time before this, had experienced in the presence and protection of the Almighty, again returned, and, along with it, a degree of religious fortitude which invigorated my whole system. "Well," thought I, "in the name of God I shall ascertain what you are, let the consequence be what it may." I then advanced until I stood exactly over it, and raising my foot, gave it a slight kick. "Now," said I, "nothing remains but to ascertain whether it contains a dead body or not," but on raising the end of it I perceived by its lightness that it was empty. To investigate the cause of its being left in this solitary spot was, however, not within the compass of my philosophy, so I gave that up. On looking at it more closely I noticed a plate, marked with the name and age of the person for whom it was intended, and on bringing my eye near the letters, I was able, between fingering and reading, to make out the name of my old cudgel-fighting school-fellow, Denis Kelly.

This discovery threw a partial light upon the business; but I now remembered to have heard of individuals who had seen black, unearthly coffins, inscribed with the names of certain living persons; and that these were considered as ominous of the death of those persons.(29) I accordingly determined to be certain that this was a real coffin; and as Denis's house was not more than a mile before me, I decided on carrying it that far: "If he be dead," thought I, "it will be all right, and if not, we will see more about it." My mind, in fact, was diseased by terror. I instantly raised the coffin, and as I found a rope lying on the ground under it, I strapped it about my shoulders and proceeded: nor could I help smiling when I reflected upon the singular transition which the man of sentiment and sensation so strangely underwent;—from the sublime contemplation of the silent mountain solitude and the spangled heavens to the task of carrying a coffin! It was an adventure, however, and I was resolved to see how it would terminate.

There was from the bridge an ascent in the road, not so gradual as that by which I descended on the other side; and as the coffin was rather heavy, I began to repent of having anything to do with it; for I was by no means experienced in carrying coffins. The carriage of it

John W. Hurley

was, indeed, altogether an irksome and unpleasant concern; for owing to my ignorance of using the rope that tied it skilfully, it was every moment sliding down my back, dragging along the stones, or bumping against my heels: besides, I saw no sufficient grounds I had for entering upon the ludicrous and odd employment of carrying another man's coffin, and was several times upon the point of washing my hands out of it altogether. But the novelty of the incident, and the mystery in which it was involved, decided me in bringing it as far as Kelly's house, which was exactly on my way home.

I had yet half a mile to go; but I thought it would be best to strap it more firmly about my body before I could start again: I therefore set it standing on its end, just at the turn of the road, until I should breathe a little, for I was rather exhausted by a trudge under it of half a mile and upwards. Whilst the coffin was in this position, I standing exactly behind it (Kelly had been a tall man, consequently it was somewhat higher than I was), a crowd of people bearing lights advanced round the corner; and the first object which presented itself to their vision was the coffin in that position, whilst I was totally invisible behind it. As soon as they saw it there was an involuntary cry of consternation from the whole crowd; at this time I had the coffin once more strapped firmly by a running knot to my shoulders, so that I could loose it whenever I pleased. On seeing the party, and hearing certain expressions which dropped from them, I knew at once that there had been some unlucky blunder in the business on their part; and I would have given a good deal to be out of the circumstances in which I then stood. I felt that I could not possibly have accounted for my situation, without bringing myself in for as respectable a portion of rank cowardice as those who ran away from the coffin; for that it was left behind in a fit of terror I now entertained no doubt whatever, particularly when I remembered the traditions connected with the spot in which I found it.

"Manim a Yea agus a wurrah!"(30) exclaimed one of them, "if the black man hasn't brought it up from the bridge! Dher a larna heena,(31) he did; for it was above the bridge we first seen him: jist for all the world—the Lord be about us—as Antony and me war coming out on the road at the bridge, there he was standing—a headless man, all black, widout face or eyes upon him—and then we cut acrass the fields home."(32)

"But where is he now, Eman?" said one of them. "Are you sure you seen him?"

"Seen him!" both exclaimed; "do ye think we'd take to our scrapers like two hares, only we did; arrah,(33) bad manners to you, do you think the coffin could walk up wid itself from the bridge to this, only he brought it?—isn't that enough?"

"Thrue for yees," the rest exclaimed; "but what's to be done?"

"Why, to bring the coffin home, now that we're all together," another observed; "they say he never appears to more than two at wanst, so he won't be apt to show himself now, when we're together."

"Well, boys, let two of you go down to it," said one of them, "and we'll wait here till yees bring it up."

"Yes," said Eman Dhu,(34) "do you go down, Owen, as you have the Scapular(35) on you, and the jug of holy water in your hand, and let Billy M'Shane, here, repate the confeethur(36) along wid you."

"Isn't it the same thing, Eman, replied Owen, "if I shake the holy water on you and whoever goes wid you? sure, you know that if only one dhrop of it touched you, the divil himself couldn't harm you!"

"And what needs yourself be afraid, then," retorted Eman, "and you has the Scapular on you to the back of that? Didn't you say, as you war coming out, that if it was the divil you'd disperse him?"

"You had bedther not be mintioning his name, you omadhaun,"(37) replied the other; "If I was your age, and hadn't a wife and childre on my hands, it's myself that would trust in God, and go down manfully; but the people are hen-hearted now besides what they used to be in my time."

During this conversation I had resolved, if possible, to keep up the delusion, until I could get myself extricated with due secrecy out of this ridiculous situation; and I was glad to find that, owing to their cowardice, there was some likelihood of effecting my design.

"Ned," said one of them to a little man, "go down and speak to it, as it can't harm you."

"Why, sure," said Ned, with a tremor in his voice, "I can speak to it where I am, widout going within rache of it. Boys, stay close to me: hem—In the name of—but don't you think I had bedther spake to it in the Latin I sarve mass(38) wid; it can't but answer that, for the sowl

John W. Hurley

of it, seeing it's a blest language."

"Very well," the rest replied; "try that, Ned; give it the best and ginteelest grammar you have, and maybe it may thrate us dacent."

Now it so happened that, in my schoolboy days, I had joined, a class of young fellows who were learning what is called the "Sarvin' of Mass," and had impressed it so accurately on a pretty retentive memory, that I never forgot it. At length, Ned pulled out his beads, and bedewed(39) himself most copiously with the holy water. He then shouted out, with a voice which resembled that of a man in an ague fit,(40) "Dom-i-n-us vo-bis-cum?" "Et cum spiritu tuo,"(41) I replied, in a husky, sepulchral tone, from behind the coffin. As soon as I uttered these words, the whole crowd ran back instinctively with fright; and Ned got so weak, that they were obliged to support him.

"Lord have mercy on us!" said Ned; "boys, isn't it an awful thing to speak to a spirit? my hair is like I dunna what, it's sticking up so stiff upon my head."

"Spake to it in English, Ned," said they, "till we hear what it will say. Ax it does anything trouble it, or whether its sowl's in Purgatory."

"Wouldn't it be better," observed another, "to ax it who murdhered it; maybe it wants to discover that?"

"In the—na-me of Go-o-d-ness," said Ned, down to me, "what are you?"

"I'm the soul," I replied, in the same voice, "of the pedlar that was murdered on the bridge below."

"And—who was it, sur, wid—submission, that—murdhered—you?" To this I made no reply.

"I say," continued Ned, "in—the—name—of—G-o-o-dness—who was it—that took the liberty of murdhering you, decent man?"

"Ned Corrigan," I answered, giving his own name.

"Hem! God preserve us! Ned Corrigan!" he exclaimed, "What Ned, for there's two of them—Is it myself, or the other vagabone?"

"Yourself, you murderer!" I replied.

"Ho!" said Ned, getting quite stout, "is that you, neighbour? Come, now, walk out wid yourself out of that coffin, you vagabond you, whoever you are."

"What do you mane, Ned, by spaking to it that a-away?" the rest inquired.

"Hut," said Ned, "it's some fellow or other that's playing a thrick upon us. Sure, I never knew neither act nor part of the murdher, nor of the murdherers; and you know, if it was anything of that nature, it couldn't tell me a lie, and me a Scapularian,(42) along wid axing it in God's name, wid Father Feasthalagh's(43) Latin."

"Big tare-an'-ouns!"(44) said the rest; "if we thought it was any man making fun of us, but we'd crop the ears off his head,(45) to tache him to be joking!"

To tell the truth, when I heard this suggestion, I began to repent of my frolic; but I was determined to make another effort to finish the adventure creditably.

"Ned," said they, "throw some of the holy water on us all, and in the name of St. Pether and the Blessed Virgin, we'll go down and examine it in a body."

This they considered a good thought, and Ned was sprinkling the water about him in all directions, whilst he repeated some jargon which was completely unintelligible. They then began to approach the coffin at dead-march time, and I felt that this was the only moment in which my plan could succeed; for had I waited until they came down, all would have been discovered. As soon, therefore, as they began to move towards me, I also began, with equal solemnity, to retrograde towards them; so that, as the coffin was between us, it seemed to move without human means.

"Stop, for God's sake, stop!" shouted Ned; "it's movin'! It has made the coffin alive; don't you see it thravelling this way widout hand or foot, barring the boords?"

There was now a halt to ascertain the fact: but I still retrograded. This was sufficient; a cry of terror broke from the whole group, and, without waiting for further evidence, they set off in the direction they came from, at full speed, Ned flinging the jug of holy water at the coffin, lest the latter should follow, or the former encumber him in his flight. Never was there so complete a discomfiture; and so eager were they to escape, that several of them came down on the stones; and I could hear them shouting, with desperation, and imploring the more advanced not to leave them behind. I instantly disentangled myself from the coffin, and left it standing exactly in the middle of

John W. Hurley

the road, for the next passenger to give it a lift as far as Denis Kelly's, if he felt so disposed. I lost no time in making the best of my way home; and on passing poor Denis's house, I perceived, by the bustle and noise within, that he was dead.

I had given my friends no notice of this visit; my reception was consequently the warmer, as I was not expected. That evening, was a happy one, which I shall long remember. At supper I alluded to Kelly, and received from my brother a full account, as given in the following, narrative, of the circumstances which caused his death.

"I need not remind you, Toby, of our schoolboy days, nor of the principles usually imbibed at such schools as that in which the two tiny factions of the Caseys and the Murphys qualified themselves, among the latter of whom you cut so distinguished a figure. You will not, therefore, be surprised to hear that these two factions are as bitter as ever; and that the boys who at Pat Mulligan's school belaboured each other, in imitation of their brothers and fathers, continue to set the same iniquitous example to their children; so that this groundless and hereditary enmity is likely to descend to future generations; unless, indeed, the influence of a more enlightened system of education may check it. But, unhappily, there is a strong suspicion of the object proposed by such a system; so that the advantages likely to result from it to the lower orders of the people will be slow and distant."

"But, John," said I, "now that we are upon that subject, let me ask what really is the bone of contention between Irish factions?"

"I assure you," he replied, "I am almost as much at a loss, Toby, to give you a satisfactory answer, as if you asked me the elevation of the highest mountain on the moon; and I believe you would find equal difficulty in ascertaining the cause of their feuds from the factions themselves. I really am convinced they know not, nor, if I rightly understand them, do they much care. Their object is to fight, and the turning of a straw will at any time furnish them with sufficient grounds for that. I do not think, after all, that the enmity between them is purely personal: they do not hate each other individually; but having originally had one quarrel upon some trifling occasion, the beaten party cannot bear the stigma of defeat without another trial of strength. Then if they succeed, the onus of retrieving lost credit is thrown upon the party that was formerly victorious. If they fail a second time, the double triumph of their conquerors excites them to a greater determination to throw off the additional disgrace; and this species of alternation perpetuates the evil.

"These habits, however, familiarise our peasantry to acts of outrage and violence—the bad passions are cultivated and nourished, until crimes, which peaceable men look upon with fear and horror, lose their real magnitude and deformity in the eyes of Irishmen. I believe this kind of undefined hatred between either parties or nations, is the most dangerous and fatal spirit which could pervade any portion of society. If you hate a man for an obvious and palpable injury, it is likely that when he cancels that injury by an act of subsequent kindness, accompanied by an exhibition of sincere sorrow, you will cease to look upon him as your enemy; but where the hatred is such that, while feeling it, you cannot, on a sober examination of your heart, account for it, there is little hope that you will ever be able to stifle the enmity which you entertain against him. This, however, in politics and religion, is what is frequently designated as principle— a word on which men, possessing higher and greater advantages than the poor ignorant peasantry of Ireland, pride themselves. In sects and parties, we may mark its effects among all ranks and nations. I, therefore, seldom wish, Toby, to hear a man assert that he is of this party or that, from principle; for I am usually inclincd to suspect that he is not in this case, influenced by conviction.

"Kelly was a man who, but for these scandalous proceedings among us, might have been now alive and happy. Although his temperament was warm, yet that warmth communicated itself to his good as well as to his evil qualities. In the beginning his family were not attached to any faction—and when I use the word faction, it is in contradistinction to the word party—for faction, you know, is applied to a feud or grudge between Roman Catholics exclusively. But when he was young, he ardently attached himself to the Murphys; and having continued among them until manhood, he could not abandon them, consistently with that sense of mistaken honour which forms so prominent a feature in the character of Irish peasantry. But although the Kellys were not factionmen, they were bitter party-men, being the ringleaders of every quarrel which took place between the Catholics and Protestants, or, I should rather say, between the Orangemen and

John W. Hurley

Whiteboys.(46)

"From the moment when Denis attached himself to the Murphys, until the day he received the beating which subsequently occasioned his death, he never withdrew from them. He was in all their battles; and in course of time, induced his relations to follow his example; so that, by general consent, they were nicknamed 'the Errigle Slashers.'(47) Soon after you left the country, and went to reside with my uncle, Denis married a daughter of little Dick Magrath's, from the Race-road, with whom he got a little money. She proved a kind, affectionate wife; and, to do him justice, I believe he was an excellent husband. Shortly after his marriage his father died, and Denis succeeded him in his farm; for you know that, among the peasantry, the youngest usually gets the landed property—the elder children being obliged to provide for themselves according to their ability, or otherwise a population would multiply upon a portion of land inadequate to its support.

"It was supposed that Kelly's marriage would have been the means of producing a change in him for the better, but it did not.
He was, in fact, the slave of a low, vain ambition which constantly occasioned him to have some quarrel or other on his hands; and as he possessed great physical courage and strength he became the champion of the parish. It was in vain that his wife used every argument to induce him to relinquish such practices; the only reply he was in the habit of making, was a good-humoured slap on the back and a laugh, saying,

"'That's it, Honor; sure and isn't that the Magraths all over, that would let the manest spalpeen(48) that ever chewed cheese thramp upon them, without raising a hand in their own defence; and I don't blame you for being a coward, seeing that you have their blood in your veins—not but that there ought to be something betther in you, afther all, for it's the M'Karrons, by your mother's side, that had the good dhrop of their own in them, anyhow—but you're a Magrath, out and out.'

"'And, Denis,' Honor would reply, 'it would be a blessed day for the parish if all in it were as peaceable as the same Magraths. There would be no sore heads, nor broken bones, nor fighting, nor slashing of one another in fairs and markets, when people ought to be mind-ing their business. You're ever and always at the Magraths, bekase they don't join you agin the Caseys or the Orangemen, and more fools they'd be to make or meddle between you, having no spite agin either of them; and it would be wiser for you to be sed by the Magraths, and red your hands out of sich ways altogether. What did ever the Murphys do to sarve you or any of your family, that you'd go to make a great man of yourself fighting for them? Or what did the poor Caseys do to make you go agin the honest people? Arrah, bad manners to me, if you know what you're about, or if sonse,(49) or grace can ever come of it; and mind my words, Denis, if God hasn't sed it, you'll live to rue your folly for the same work.'

"At this Denis would laugh heartily. 'Well said, Honor Magrath, but not Kelly. Well, it's one comfort that our childher aren't likely to follow your side of the house, any way. Come here, Lanty; come over, acushla,(50) to your father! Lanty, ma bouchal,(51) what 'ill you do when you grow a man?'

"'I'll buy a horse of my own to ride on, daddy.'

"'A horse, Lanty!—and so you will, ma bouchal; but that's not it—sure, that's not what I mane, Lanty. What 'ill you do to the Caseys?'

"'Ho, ho! the Caseys! I'll bate the blackguards wid your black-thorn, daddy!'

"'Ha, ha, ha!—that's my stout man, my brave little soger! Wus dha lamh, avick!—give me your hand, my son!'(52) 'Here, Nelly,' he would say to the child's eldest sister, 'give him a brave whang of bread, to make him able to bate the Caseys. Well, Lanty, who more will you leather, a-hagur?'(53)

"'All the Orangemen; I'll kill all the Orangemen!'

"This would produce another laugh from the father; who would again kiss and shake hands with his son for these early manifestations of his own spirit.

"'Lanty, ma bouchal,' he would say, 'thank God you're not a Magrath; 'tis you that's a Kelly, every blessed inch of you! and if you turn out as good a buillagh batthah(54) as your father afore you, I'll be contint, avourneen!'(55)

"'God forgive you, Denis,' the wife would reply, 'it's long before you'd think of larning him his prayers, or his catechiz,(56) or any-thing that's good! Lanty, agra,(57) come over to myself, and never

John W. Hurley

heed what that man says; for, except you have some poor body's blessing, he'll bring you to no good.'

"Sometimes, however, Kelly's own natural good sense, joined with the remonstrances of his wife, prevailed for a short time, and he would withdraw himself from the connecxion altogether; but the force of habit and of circumstances was too strong in him, to hope that he could ever overcome it by his own firmness, for he was totally destitute of religion. The peaceable intervals of his life were therefore very short.

"One summer evening I was standing in my own garden, when I saw a man galloping up towards me at full speed. When he approached I recognised him as one of the Murphy faction, and perceived that he was cut and bleeding.

"'Murphy,' said I, 'what's the matter?'

"'Hard fighting, sir,' said he, 'is the matter. The Caseys gathered all their faction, bekase they heard that Denis Kelly has given us up, and they're sweeping the street wid us. I'm going hot foot for Kelly, sir, for even the very name of him will turn the tide in our favour. Along wid that, I have sint in a score of the Duggans, and, if I get in Denis, plase God, we'll clear the town of them!'

"He then set off, but pulled up abruptly, and said,

"'Arrah, Mr. Darcy, maybe you'd be civil enough to lind me the loan of a sword, or bagnet,(58) or gun, or anything that way, that would be sarviceable to a body on a pinch?'

"'Yes!' said I, 'and enable you to commit murder? No, no, Murphy! I'm sorry it's not in my power to put a final stop to such dangerous quarrels!'

"He then dashed off, and in the course of a short time I saw him and Kelly, both on horseback, hurrying into the town in all possible haste, armed with their cudgels. The following day I got my dog and gun, and sauntered about the hills, making a point to call upon Kelly. I found him with his head tied up, and his arm in a sling.

"'Well, Denis,' said I, 'I find you have kept your promise of giving up quarrels!'

"'And so I did, sir,' said Denis; 'but, sure, you wouldn't have me go for to desert them, when the Caseys war three to one over them? No; God be thanked, I'm not so mane as that, anyhow. Besides' they welted both my brothers within an inch of their lives.'

"I think they didn't miss yourself,' said I.

"'You may well say they did not, sir,' he replied; 'and, to tell God's thruth, they thrashed us right and left out of the town, although we rallied three times and came in again. At any rate, it's the first time for the last five years that they dare go up and down the street, calling out for the face of a Murphy or a Kelly; for they're as bitter now agin us as agin the Murphys themselves.'

"'Well, I hope, Denis,' I observed, 'that what occurred yesterday will prevent you from entering into their quarrels in future. Indeed, I shall not give over,(59) until I prevail on you to lead a quiet and peaceable life, as the father of a rising family ought to do.'

"'Denis,' said the wife, when I alluded to the children, looking at him with a reproachful and significant expression—'Denis, do you hear that!—the father of a family, Denis! Oh, then, God look down on that family; but it's—Musha,(60) God bless you and yours, sir,' said she to me, dropping that part of the subject abruptly; 'it's kind of you to trouble yourself about him, at all at all; it's what them that has a betther right to do it, doesn't do.'

"'I hope,' said I, 'that Denis's own good sense will show him the folly and guilt of his conduct, and that he will not, under any circumstances, enter into their battles in future. Come, Denis, will you promise me this?'

"'If any man,' replied Denis, 'could make me do it, it's yourself, sir, or any one of your family; but if the priest of the parish was to go down on his two knees before me, I wouldn't give it up till we give them vagabone Caseys one glorious battherin', which, plase God, we'll do, and are well able to do, before a month of Sundays goes over us. Now, sir, you needn't say another word,' said he, seeing me about to speak, 'for, by Him that made me, we'll do it! If any man, I say, could persuade me agin it, you could; but if we don't pay them full interest for what we got, why, my name's not Denis Kelly—ay, sweep them like varmint out of the town, body and sleeves!'

"I saw argument would be lost on him, so I only observed that I feared it would eventually end badly.

"'Och,(61) many and many's the time, Mr. Darcy,' said Honor, "I prophesied the same thing; and if God hasn't said it, he'll be coming

John W. Hurley

home a corpse to me some day or other; for he got as much bating, sir, as would be enough to kill a horse; and to tell you God's truth, sir, he's breeding up his childher—'

"'Honor,' said Kelly, irritated, 'whatever I do, do I lave it in your power to say that I'm a bad husband? so don't rise me by your talk, for I don't like to be provoked. I know it's wrong, but what can I do? Would you have me for to show the Garran-bane,(62) and lave them like a cowardly thraitor, now that the other faction is coming up to be their match?(63) No; let what will come of it, I'll never do the mane thing—death before dishonour!'

"In this manner Kelly went on for years; sometimes, indeed, keeping quiet for a short period, but eventually drawn in, from the apprehension of being reproached with want of honour and truth to his connexion. This, truly, is an imputation which no peasant could endure; nor, were he thought capable of treachery, would he be safe from the vengeance of his own party. Many a time have I seen Kelly reeling home, his head and face sadly cut, the blood streaming from him, and his wife and some neighbour on each side of him—the poor woman weeping, and deploring the senseless and sanguinary feuds(64) in which her husband took so active a part.

"About three miles from this, down at the Long Ridge, where the Shannons live, dwelt a family of the Grogans, cousins to Denis. They were anything but industrious, although they might have lived very independently, having held a farm on what they call an old take, which means a long lease taken out when the lands were cheap. It so happened, however, that, like too many of their countrymen, they paid little attention to the cultivation of their farm; the consequence of which neglect was, that they became embarrassed, and overburdened with arrears. Their landlord was old Sam Simmons, whose only fault to his tenants was an excess of indulgence, and a generous disposition wherever he could possibly get an opportunity, to scatter his money about him, upon the spur of a benevolence which, it would seem, never ceased goading him to acts of the most Christian liberality and kindness. Along with these excellent qualities, he was remarkable for a most rooted aversion to law and lawyers; for he would lose one hundred pounds rather than recover that sum by legal proceedings, even when certain that five pounds would effect it; but he seldom or never was known to pardon a breach of the peace.

"I have always found that an excess of indulgence in a landlord never fails ultimately to injure and relax the industry of the tenant; at least, this was the effect which his forbearance produced on them. But the most extraordinary good-nature has its limits, and so had his; after repeated warning, and the most unparalleled patience on his part, he was at length compelled to determine on at once removing them from his estate, and letting his land to some more efficient and deserving tenant. He accordingly desired them to remove their property from the premises, as he did not wish, he said, to leave them without the means of entering upon another farm, if they felt so disposed. This they refused to do; adding, that they would at least put him to the expense of ejecting them. He then gave orders to his agent to seize; but they, in the meantime, had secreted their effects by night among their friends and relations, sending a cow to this one, and a horse to that; so that when the bailiff came to levy his execution, he found very little except the empty walls. They were, however, ejected without ceremony, and driven altogether off the farm, for which they had actually paid nothing for the three preceding years. In the mean time the farm was advertised to be let, and several persons had offered themselves as tenants; but what appeared very remarkable was, that the Roman Catholics seldom came a second time to make any further inquiry about it; or, if they did, Simmons observed that they were sure to withdraw their proposals, and ultimately decline having anything to do with it.

"This was a circumstance which he could not properly understand; but the fact was, that the peasantry were almost to a man members of a widely-extending system of agrarian combination, (Whiteboyism), the secret influence of which intimidated such of their own religion as intended to take it, and prevented them from exposing themselves to the penalty which they knew those who should dare to occupy it must pay. In a short time, however, the matter began to be whispered about, until it spread gradually, day after day, through the parish, that those who already had proposed, or intended to propose, were afraid to enter upon the land on any terms. Hitherto, it is true, these threats floated about only in the invisible form of rumour.

"The farm had been now unoccupied for about a year; party spirit ran very high among the peasantry, and no proposals came in, or were at all likely to come. Simmons then got advertisements printed, and had them posted up in the most conspicuous parts of this and the neighbouring parishes. It was expected, however, that they would be torn down; but, instead of that, there was a written notice posted up immediately under each, which ran in the following words:—

"'TAKE NOTESS.
"'Any man that'll dare to take the farm belonging to smooth, Sam Simmons, and sitiuated at the long ridge, will be flayed alive.
"'MAT MIDNIGHT.
"'B.N.—It's it that was latterrally occupied by the Grogans.'

"This occasioned Simmons and the other magistrates(65) of the barony to hold a meeting, at which they subscribed to the amount of fifty pounds as a reward for discovering the author or authors of the threatening notice;(66) but the advertisement containing the reward, which was posted in the usual places through the parish, was torn down on the first night after it was put up. In the meantime a man nicknamed Vengeance—Vesey Vengeance, in consequence of his daring and fearless spirit, and his bitterness in retaliating injury—came to Simmons, and proposed for the farm. The latter candidly mentioned the circumstances of the notice, and fairly told him that he was running a personal risk in taking it.

"'Leave that to me, sir,' said Vengeance; 'if you will set me the farm at the terms I offer, I am willing to become your tenant; and let them that posted up the notices go to old Nick,(67) or, if they annoy me, let them take care I don't send them there. I am a trueblue, sir—a purple man(68)—have lots of fire-arms, and plenty of stout fellows in the parish ready and willing to back me; and, by the light of day! if they make or meddle with me or mine, we will hunt them in the face of the world, like so many mad dogs, out of the country: what are they but a pack of ribles,(69) that would cut our throats, if they dared?'

"'I have no objection; said Simmons, "that you should express a firm determination to defend your life and protect your property; but I utterly condemn the spirit with which you seem to be animated. Be temperate and sober, but be firm. I will afford you every assistance and protection in my power, both as a magistrate and a landlord; but if you speak so incautiously, the result may be serious, if not fatal, to yourself.'

"'Instead of that,' said Vengeance, 'the more a man appears to be afeard, the more danger he is in, as I know by what I have seen; but, at any rate, if they injure me, I wouldn't ask better sport than taking down the ribles—the bloody-minded villains! Isn't it a purty thing that a man darn's put one foot past the other, only as they wish? By the light o' day, I'll pepper them!'(70)

Shortly after this, Vengeance, braving all their threats, removed to the farm, and set about its cultivation with skill and vigour. He had not been long there, however, when a notice was posted one night on his door, giving him ten days to clear off from this interdicted spot, threatening, in case of non-compliance, to make a bonfire of the house and offices, inmates included. The reply which Vengeance made to this was fearless and characteristic. He wrote another notice which he posted on the chapel-door,(71) stating that he would not budge an inch—recommending, at the same time, such as intended paying him a nightly visit to be careful that they might not chance to go home with their heels foremost.(72)

This, indeed, was setting them completely at defiance, and would, no doubt, have been fatal to Vesey, were it not for a circumstance which I will now relate:—In a little dell, below Vesey's house, lived a poor woman, called Doran, a widow; she inhabited a small hut, and was principally supported by her two sons, who were servants, one to a neighbouring farmer, a Roman Catholic, and the other to Dr. Ableson, rector of the parish. He who had been with the rector lost his health shortly before Vengeance succeeded the Grogans as occupier of the land in question, and was obliged to come home to his mother. He was then confined to his bed, from which, indeed, he never rose.

"This boy had been his mother's principal support—for the other was unsettled, and paid her but little attention, being, like most of those in his situation, fond of drinking, dancing, and attending fairs. In short, he became a Ribbonman, and consequently was obliged to attend their nightly meetings.

Now it so happened that for a considerable time after the threaten-

John W. Hurley

ing notice had been posted on Vengeance's door, he received no annoyance, although the period allowed for his departure had been long past, and the purport of the paper uncomplied with. Whether this proceeded from an apprehension on the part of the Ribbonmen of receiving a warmer welcome than they might wish, or whether they deferred the execution of their threat until Vengeance might be off his guard, I cannot determine; but the fact is that some months had elapsed and Vengeance remained hitherto unmolested.

"During this interval the distress of Widow Doran had become known to the inmates of his family, and his mother—for she lived with him—used to bring down each day some nourishing food to the sick boy. In these kind offices she was very punctual; and so great was the poverty of the poor widow, and so destitute the situation of her sick son, that, in fact, the burden of their support lay principally upon Vengeance's family.

"Vengeance was a small, thin man, with fair hair, and fiery eyes; his voice was loud and shrill, his utterance rapid, and the general expression of his countenance irritable. His motions were so quick, that he rather seemed to run than walk. He was a civil, obliging neighbour, but performed his best actions with a bad grace; a firm, unflinching friend, but a bitter and implacable enemy.

Upon the whole, he was generally esteemed and respected—though considered as an eccentric character, for such, indeed, he was. On hearing of Widow Doran's distress, he gave orders that a portion of each meal should be regularly sent down to her and her son; and from that period forward they were both supported principally from his table.

"In this way some months had passed, and still Vengeance was undisturbed in his farm. It often happened, however, that Doran's other son came to see his brother; and during these visits it was but natural that his mother and brother should allude to the kindness which they daily experienced from Vesey.

"One night, about twelve o'clock, a tap came to Widow Doran's door, who happened to be attending the invalid, as he was then nearly in the last stage of his illness. When she opened it, the other son entered, in an evident hurry, having the appearance of a man who felt deep and serious anxiety.

Irish Gangs And Stick-Fighting   119

"'Mother,' said he, 'I was very uneasy entirely about Mick, and just started over to see him, although they don't know at home that I'm out, so I can't stay a crack; but I wish you would go to the door for two minutes, as I have something to say to him.'

"'Why, thin, Holy Mother!—Jack, a-hagur, is there anything the matter, for you look as if you had seen something?'(73)

"'Nothing worse than myself, mother,' he replied; 'nor there's nothing the matter at all—only I have a few words to say to Mick here, that's all.

"The mother accordingly removed herself out of hearing.

"'Mick,' says the boy, 'this is a bad business—I wish to God I was clear and clane out of it.

"'What is it?' said Mick, alarmed.

"'Murther, I'm afeard, if God doesn't turn it off of them, somehow.'

"'What do you mane, man, at all?' said the invalid, raising himself, in deep emotion, on his elbow, from his poor straw bed.

"'Vengeance,' said he—'Vengeance, man—he's going to get it. I was out with the boys on Sunday evening, and at last it's agreed on to visit him to-morrow night. I'm sure and sartin he'll never escape, for there's more in for him than taking the farm, and daring them so often as he did—he shot two fingers off a brother in-law of Jem Reilly's one night that they war on for threshing him, and that's coming home to him along with the rest.'

"'In the name of God, Jack,' inquired Mick, 'what do they intend to do to him?'

"'Why,' replied Jack, 'it's agreed to put a coal in the thatch, in the first place; and although they were afeard to his name, what he's to get besides, I doubt they'll make a spatch-cock of himself. They won't meddle with any other family though—but he's down for it."(74)

"'Are you to be one of the them?' asked Mick.

"'I was the third man named,' replied the other, 'bekase, they said, I knew the place.'

"'Jack,' said his emaciated brother, with much solemnity, raising himself up in the bed—'Jack, if you have act or part in that bloody business, God in his glory you'll never see. Fly the country—cut off a finger or toe—break your arm—or do something that may prevent

John W. Hurley

you from being there. Oh, my God!' he exclaimed, whilst the tears fell fast down his pale cheeks—'to go to murder the man, and lave his little family without a head or a father over them, and his wife a widow! To burn his place, widout rhime, or rason, or offince! Jack, if you go, I'll die cursing you. I'll appear to you—I'll let you rest neither night nor day, sleeping nor waking, in bed or out of bed. I'll haunt you, till you'll curse the very hours
you war born.'

"'Whist,(75) Micky,' said Jack, 'you're frightening me: I'll not go—will that satisfy you?'

"'Well, dhrop down on your two knees, there,' said Mickey, 'and swear before the God that has his eye upon you this minute, that you'll have no hand in injuring him or his, while you live. If you don't do this, I'll not rest in my grave, and maybe I'll be a corpse before mornin'.'

"'Well, Micky,' said Jack, who, though wild and unthinking, was a lad whose heart and affections were good, 'it would be hard for me to refuse you that much, and you not likely to be long wid me—I will;' and he accordingly knelt down and swore solemnly, in words which his brother dictated to him, that he would not be concerned in the intended murder.

"'Now, give me your hand, Jack,' said the invalid; 'God bless you—and so he will. Jack, if I depart before I see you again, I'll die happy. That man has supported me and my mother, for near the last three months, bad as you all think him. Why, Jack, we would both be dead of hunger long ago, only for his family; and, my God! To think of such a murdhering intention makes my blood run cowld'—

"'You had better give him a hint then,' said Jack, 'some way, or he'll be done for, as sure as you're stretched on that bed; but don't mintion names, if you wish to keep me from being murdhered for what I did. I must be off now, for I stole out of the barn;(76) and only that Atty Laghy's gone along wid the master to the—fair, to help him to sell the two coults, I couldn't get over at all.'

"'Well, go home, Jack, and God bless you, and so he will, for what you did this night.'

"Jack accordingly departed, after bidding his mother and brother farewell.

"When the old woman came in, she asked her son if there was anything wrong with his brother, but he replied that there was not.

"'Nothing at all,' said he—'but will you go up airly in the morning, plase God, and tell Vesey Johnston that I want to see him; and—that—I have a great dale to say to him.'

"'To be sure I will, Micky; but, Lord guard us, what ails you, avourneen, you look so frightened?'

"'Nothing at all, at all, mother; but will you go where I say airly to-morrow, for me?'

"'It's the first thing I'll do, God willin',' replied the mother. And the next morning Vesey was down with the invalid very early, for the old woman kept her word, and paid him a timely visit.

"'Well, Micky, my boy,' said Vengeance, as he entered the hut, 'I hope you're no worse this morning.'

"'Not worse, Sir,' replied Mick; 'nor, indeed, am I anything better either, but much the same way. Sure it's I that knows very well that my time here is but short.'

"'Well, Mick, my boy,' said Vengeance, 'I hope you're prepared for death—and that you expect forgiveness, like a Christian. Look up, my boy, to God at once, and pitch the priests and their craft to ould Nick, where they'll all go at the long run.'

"'I b'lieve,' said Mick, with a faint smile, 'that you're not very fond of the priests, Mr. Johnston; but if you knew the power they possess as well as I do, you wouldn't spake of them so bad, anyhow.'

"'Me fond of them!' replied the other; 'why, man, they're a set of the most gluttonous, black-looking hypocrites, that ever walked on neat's leather; and ought to be hunted out of the country—hunted out of the country, by the light of day! Every one of them; for they do nothing but egg the people against the Protestants.'

"'God help you, Mr. Johnston,' replied the invalid, 'I pity you from my heart for the opinion you hould about them. I suppose if you were sthruck dead on the spot wid a blast from the fairies,(77) that you think a priest couldn't cure you by one word's spaking?'

"'Cure me!' said Vengeance, with a laugh of disdain; 'by the light of day! If I caught one of them curing me, I'd give him the purtiest chase you ever saw in your life, across the hills.'

"'Don't you know,' said Mick, 'that priest Dannelly cured Bob

John W. Hurley

Beaty of the falling sickness—until he broke the vow that was laid upon him, of not going into a church, and the minute he crosses the church-door, didn't he dhrop down as bad as ever—and what could the minister do for him?'

"'And don't you know,' rejoined Vengeance, 'that that's all a parcel of the most lying stuff possible; lies—lies—all lies—and vagabondism? Why, Mick, you Papishes worship the priests; you think they can bring you to heaven at a word. By the light of day they must have good sport laughing at you, when they get among one another. Why don't they teach you and give you the Bible to read, the ribelly rascals? But they're afraid you'd know too much then.'

"'Well, Mr. Johnston,' said Mick, 'I b'lieve you'll never have a good opinion of them, at any rate.'

"'Ay, when the sky falls,' replied Vengeance; 'but you're now on your death-bed, and why don't you pitch them to ould Nick, and get a Bible? Get a Bible, man; there's a pair of them in my house, that's never used at all—except my mother's, and she's at it night and day. I'll send one of them down to you: turn yourself to God—to your Redeemer, that died on the mount of Jehoshaphat, or somewhere about Jerusalem, for your sins—and don't go out of the world from the hand of a rascally priest, with a band about your eyes, as if you were at blind-man'sbluff; for, by the light of day you're as blind as a bat in a religious way.'

"'There's no use in sending me a Bible,' replied the invalid, 'for I can't read it: but, whatever you may think, I'm very willing to lave my salvation with my priest.'

"'Why, man,' observed Vengeance, 'I thought you were going to have some sense at last, and that you sent for me to give you some spiritual consolation.'

"'No, Sir,' replied Mick; 'I have two or three words to spake to you.'

"'Come, come, Mick, now that we're on a spiritual subject, I'll hear nothing from you till I try whether it's possible to give you a true insight into religion. Stop, now, and let us lay our heads together, that we may make out something of a dacenter creed for you to believe in than the one you profess. Tell me the truth, do you believe in the priests?'

"'How?' replied Mick; 'I believe that they're holy men—but I know they can't save me without the Redeemer, and his blessed mother.'

"'By the light above us, you're shuffling,(78) Mick—I say you do believe in them—now, don't tell me to the contrary—I say you're shuffling as fast as possible.'

"'I tould you truth, Sir,' replied Mick; 'and if you don't believe me, I can't help it.'

"'Don't trust in the priests, Mick; that's the main point to secure your salvation.'

"Mick, who knew his prejudices against the priests, smiled faintly, and replied—

"'Why, Sir, I trust in them as bein' able to make inthercession wid God for me, that's all.'

"'They make intercession! By the stool I'm on, a single word from one of them would ruin you. They, a set of ribles, to make interest for you in heaven! Didn't they rise the rebellion in Ireland?—answer me that.'

"'This is a subject, Sir, we would never agree on,' replied Mick.

"'Have you the Ten Commandments?' inquired Vesey.

"'I doubt my mimory's not clear enough to have them in my mind,' said the lad, feeling keenly the imputation of ignorance, which he apprehended from Vesey's blunt observations.

"Vesey, however, had penetration enough to perceive his feelings, and, with more delicacy than could be expected from him, immediately moved the question.

"'No matter, Mick,' said he, 'if you would give up the priests, we would get over that point: as it is, I will give you a lift in the Commandments; and, as I said a while ago, if you take my advice, I'll work up a creed for you that you may depend upon. But now for the Commandments—let me see.

"'First: Thou shalt have no other gods but me. Don't you see, man, how that peppers the priests?

"'Second: Remember that thou keep holy the Sabbath-day.

"'Third: Though shalt not make to thyself—no, hang it no!—I'm out—that's the Second—very right. Third: Honour thy father and thy mother—you understand that, Mick? It means that you are bound to—to—just so—to honour thy father and your mother, poor woman.'

"My father—God be good to him!—is dead near fourteen years, sir,' replied Mick.

"'Well, in that case, Mick, you see all that's left for you is to honour your mother—although I'm not certain of that either; the Commandments make no allowance at all for death, and in that case why, living or dead, the surest way is to respect and obey them—that is, if the thing wern't impossible. I wish we had blind George M'Girr here, Mick; although he's as great a rogue as ever escaped hemp,(79) yet he'd beat the devil himself at a knotty point.'

"'His breath would be bad about a dying man,' observed Mick.

"'Ay, or a living one,' said Vesey; 'however, let us get on—we were at the Third. Fourth: Thou shalt do no murder.'

"At the word murder, Mick started, and gave a deep groan, whilst his eyes and features assumed a gaunt and hollow expression, resembling that of a man struck with an immediate sense of horror and affright.

"'Oh! For heaven's sake, sir, stop there,' said Doran; 'that brings to my mind the business I had with you, Mr Johnston.'

"'What is it about?' inquired Vengeance, in his usual eager manner.

"'Do you mind,'(80) said Mick, 'that a paper was stuck one night upon your door, threatening you, if you wouldn't lave that farm you're in?'

"'I do, the blood-thirsty villains! But they knew a trick worth two of coming near me.'

"'Well,' said Mick, 'a strange man, that I never seen before, came into me last night, and tould me, if I'd see you, to say that you would get a visit from the boys(81) this night, and to take care of yourself.'

"'Give me the hand, Mick,' said Vengeance—'give me the hand; in spite of the priests, by the light of day you're an honest fellow. This night, you say, they're to come? And what are the bloody wrethces to do, Mick? But I needn't ask that, for I suppose it's to murder myself, and to burn my place.'

"'I'm afeard, sir, you're not far from the truth,' replied Mick; 'but, Mr. Johnston, for God's sake, don't mintion my name; for, if you do, I'll get myself what they war laying out for you—be burned in my bed, maybe.'

"'Never fear, Mick.' replied Vengeance; 'your name will never cross my lips.'

"'It's a great thing,' said Mick, 'that would make me turn informer; but sure, only for your kindness and the goodness of your family, the Lord spare you to one another! Mightn't I be dead long ago? I couldn't have one minute's peace if you or yours came to any harm when I could prevint it.'

"'Say no more, Mick,' said Vengeance, taking his hand again; 'I know that, leave the rest to me; but how do you find yourself, my poor fellow? You look weaker than you did, a good deal.'

"'Indeed I'm going very fast, Sir,' replied Mick; 'I know it'll soon be over with me.'

"'Hut, no, man,' said Vengeance, drawing his hand rapidly across his eyes, and clearing his voice, 'not at all—don't say so: would a little broth serve you? Or a bit of fresh meat?—or would you have a fancy for anything that I could make out for you? I'll get you wine, if you think it would do you good.'

"'God reward you,' said Mick feebly—'God reward you, and open your eyes to the truth. Is my mother likely to come in, do you think?'

"'She must be here in a few minutes,' the other replied; 'she was waiting till they'd churn, that she might bring you down a little fresh milk and butter.'

"'I wish she was wid me,' said the poor lad, 'for I'm lonely wantin' her—her voice and the very touch of her hands goes to my heart. Mother, come to me, and let me lay my head upon your breast, agra machree,(82) for I think it will be for the last time: we lived lonely, avourneen, wid none but ourselves—sometimes in happiness, when the nabours 'ud be kind to us—and sometimes in sorrow, when there 'ud be none to help us. It's over now, mother, and I'm lavin' you for ever!'

"Vengeance wiped his eyes—'Rouse yourself, Mick,' said he, 'rouse yourself.'

"'Who is that sitting along with you on the stool?' said Mick.

"'No one, replied his neighbour; 'but what's the matter with you, Mick?—your face is changed.'

"Mick, however, made no reply; but after a few slight struggles, in

John W. Hurley

which he attempted to call upon his mother's name, he breathed his last. When Vengeance saw that he was dead—looked upon the cold, miserable hut in which this grateful and affectionate young man was stretched—and then reflected on the important service he had just rendered him, he could not suppress his tears.

"After sending down some of the females to assist his poor mother in laying him out, Vengeance went among his friends and acquaintances, informing them of the intelligence he had received, without mentioning the source from which he had it.

After dusk that evening, they all flocked, as privately as possible, to his house, to the number of thirty or forty, well provided with arms and ammunition. Some of them stationed themselves in the outhouses, some behind the garden-hedge, and others in the dwelling-house."

When my brother had got thus far in his narrative, a tap came to the parlour-door, and immediately a stout-looking man, having the appearance of a labourer, entered the room.

"Well, Lachlin," said my brother, "what's the matter?"

"Why, Sir," said Lachlin, scratching his head, "I had a bit of a favour to ax, if it would be plasin' you to grant it to me."

"What is that?" said my brother.

"Do you know, Sir," said he, "I haven't been at a wake—let us see—this two or three years, anyhow; and, if you'd have no objection, why, I'd slip up awhile to Denis Kelly's; he's a distant relation of my own, Sir; and blood's thicker that wather, you know."

"I'm just glad you came in, Lachlin," said my brother; "I didn't think of you; take a chair here, and never heed the wake to-night, but sit down and tell us about the attack on Vesey Vengeance, long ago. I'll get you a tumbler of punch; and, instead of going to the wake, I will allow you to go to the funeral to-morrow."

"Ah, Sir," said Lachlin, "you know whenever the punch is consarned, I'm aisily persuaded; but not making little of your tumbler, Sir," said the shrewd fellow, "I would get two or three of them if I went to the wake."

"Well, sit down," said my brother, handing him one, "and we won't permit you to get thirsty while you're talking, at all events."

"In troth,(83) you haven't your heart in the likes of it," said Lachlin.

"Gintlemen, your healths—your health, Sir, and we're happy to see you wanst more. Why, this, I remember you, Sir, when you were a gorsoon,(84) passing to school wid your satchell on your back; but, I'll be bound you're by no means as soople now as you were thin. Why, Sir." turning to my brother, "he could fly or kick football wid the rabbits.—Well, this is raal stuff!"

"Now, Lachlin," said my brother, "give us an account of the attack you made on Vesey Vengeance's house, at the Long Ridge, when all his party were chased out of the town."

"Why, thin, Sir, I ought to be ashamed to mintion it; but you see, gintlemen, there was no getting over being connected wid them; but I hope your brother's safe, Sir!"(85)

"Oh, perfectly safe, Lachlin; you may rest assured he'll never mention it."

"Well, Sir," said Lachlin, addressing himself to me, "Vesey Vengeance was—."

"Lachlin," said my brother, "he knows all about Vesey; just give him an account of the attack."

"The attack, Sir! No, but the chivey(86) we got over the mountains. Why, Sir, we met in an ould empty house, you see, that belonged to the Farrells of Ballyboulteen, that went over to America that spring. There war none wid us, you may be sure, but them that war up;(87) and in all we might be about sixty or seventy. The Grogans, one way or another, got it up first among them, bekase they expected that Mr. Simmons would take them back when he'd find that no one else dare venthur upon their land. There war at that time two fellows down from the county Longford in their neighbourhood, of the name of Collier—although that wasn't their right name—they were here upon their keeping, for the murder of a proctor(88) in their own part of the country. One of them was a tall, powerful fellow, with sandy hair, and red brows; the other was a slender chap, that must have been drawn into it by his brother—for he was very mild and innocent, and always persuaded us agin evil. The Grogans brought lashings of whiskey, and made them that war to go foremost amost drunk—these war the two Colliers, some of the strangers from behind the mountains, and a son of Widdy Doran's, that knew every inch about the place, for he was bred and born jist below the house a bit. He wasn't wid us, however, in regard of his brother being under boord(89) that night; but, instid of him, Tim Grogan went to show the way up the little glin to the house, though, for that matther, the most of us knew it as well as he did; but we didn't like to be the first to put a hand to it, if we could help it.

"At any rate, we sot in Farrell's empty house, drinking whiskey, till they war all gathered, when about two dozen of them got the damp soot from the chimley, and rubbed it over their faces, making them so black, that their own relations couldn't know them. We then went across the country in little lots, of about six or ten, or a score, and we war glad that the wake was in Widdy Doran's, seeing that, if any would meet us, we war going to it you know, and the blackening of the faces would pass for a frolic;(90) but there was no great danger of being met, for it was now long beyant midnight.

"Well, gintlemen, it puts me into a tremble, even at this time, to think of how little we cared about what we were bent upon. Them that had to manage the business war more than half drunk; and, hard fortune to me! But you would think it was to a wedding they went— some of them singing songs against the law—some of them quite merry, and laughing as if they had found a mare's nest. The big fellow, Collier, had a dark landthern wid a half-burned turf in it to light the bonfire,(91) as they said; others had guns and pistols—some of them charges, and some of them not; some had bagnets,(92) and ould rusty swords, pitchforks, and so on.

Myself had nothing in my hand but the flail(93) I was thrashing wid that day; and to tell the thruth, the divil a step I would have gone with them, only for fraid of my health: for, as I said awhile gone, them that promised to go, and turned tail, would be marked as the informers. Neither was I so blind, but I could see that there war plenty there that would stay away if they durst.

"Well, we went on till we came to a little dark corner below the house, where we met and held a council of war upon what we should do. Collier and the other strangers from behind the mountains war to go first, and the rest war to stand round the house at a distance—he carried the lanthern, a bagnet, and a horse pistol; and half-a-dozen more war to bring over bottles of straw from Vengeance's own haggard,(94) to hould up to the thatch. It's all past and gone now—but three of the Reillys were desperate against Vesey that night, particularly one of them that he had shot about a year and a half before—that is, peppered two of the right-hand fingers off of him, one night in a scuffle, as Vesey came home from an Orange-lodge. Well, all went on purty fair; we had got as far as the out-houses, where we stopped, to see if we could hear any noise; but all was quiet as you plase.

"'Now, Vengeance,' says Reilly, swearing a terrible oath out of him—'you murdering Orange villain, you're going to get your pay,' says he.

"'Ay,' says Grogan, 'what he often threatened to others he'll soon meet himself, plase God!—come boys,' says he, 'bring the straw and light it, and just lay it up, my darlings, nicely to the thatch here, and ye'll see what a glorious bonfire we'll have of the black orange villain's blankets in less than no time.'

"Some of us could hardly stand this: 'Stop, boys,' cried one of Dan Slevin's sons—'stop, Vengeance is bad enough, but his wife and children never offinded us—we'll not burn the place.'

"'No,' said others, spaking out when they heard any body at all having courage to do so—'it's too bad, boys, to burn the place; for if we do,' says they, 'some of the innocent may be burned before they get from the house, or even before they waken out of their sleep.'

"'Knock at the door first,' says Slevin, 'and bring Vengenace out; let us cut the ears off his head and lave him.'

"'Damn him!' says another, 'let us not take the vagabone's like; it's enough to take the ears from him, and to give him a prod or two of a bagnet on the ribs; but don't kill him.'

"'Well, well,' says Reilly, 'let us knock at the door, and get himself and the family out,' says he, 'and then we'll see what can be done wid him.'

"'Tattheration(95) to me,' says the big Longford fellow, 'if he had sarved me, Reilly, as he did you, but I'd roast him in the flames of his own house,' says he.

"'I'd have you to know.' says Slevin, 'that you have no command here, Collier. I'm captain at the present time,' says he, 'and more nor what I wish shall not be done. Go over,' says he to the black faces, 'and rap him up.'

"Accordingly they began to knock at the door, commanding Vengeance to get up and come out to them.

John W. Hurley

"'Come, Vengeance,' says Collier, 'put on you,(96) my good fellow, and come out till two or three of your neighours, that wish you well gets a sight of your purty face, you babe of grace!'

"'Who are you that wants me at all?' says Vengeance from within.

"'Come out, first,' says Collier; 'a few friends that has a crow to pluck with you: walk out, avourneen; or if you'd rather be roasted alive, why you may stay where you are,' says he.

"'Gentlemen,' say Vengeance, 'I have never to my knowledge, offinded any of you; and I hope you won't be so cruel as to take an industrious, hard-working man from his family, in the clouds of the night, to do him an injury. Go home, gentlemen, in the name of God, and let me and mine alone. You're all mighty dacent gentlemen, you know, and I'm determined never to make or meddle with any of you. Sure, I know right well it's purtecting me you would be, dacent gentlement. But I don't think there's any of my neighbours there, or they wouldn't stand by and see me injured.'

"'Thrue for you, avick,' says they, giving, at the same time, a terrible patterrara agin the door, with two or three big stones.

"'Stop, stop!' says Vengeance, 'don't break the door, and I'll open it. I know you're merciful, dacent gentlemen—I know you're merciful.'

"So the thief came and unbarred it quietly, and the next minute about a dozen of them that war within the house let slap at us. As God would have had it, the crowd didn't happen to be forenent(97) the door, or numbers of them would have been shot, and the night was dark, too, which was in our favour. The first volley was scarcely over, when there was another slap from the out-houses; and after that another from the gardens; and after that, to be sure, we took to our scrapers. Several of them were very badly wounded; but as for Collier, he was shot dead, and Grogan was taken prisoner, with five more, on the spot. There never was such a chase as we got; and only that they thought there was more of us in it, they might have tuck most of us prisoners.

"'Fly, boys!' says Grogan, as soon as they fired out of the house—'we've been sould,' says be, 'but I'll die game, any how,'—and so he did, poor fellow; for although he and the other four war transported, one of them never sould the pass or stagged.(98) Not but that they might have done it, for all that, only that there was a whisper sent to them, that if they did, a single soul belonging to one of them wouldn't be left living. The Grogans were cousins of Denis Kelly's, that's now laid out there above.

"From the time this tuck place till after the 'sizes, there wasn't a stir among them on any side; but when that war over, the boys began to prepare. Denis, heavens be his bed, was there in his glory. This was in the spring 'sizes, and the May fair(99) soon followed. Ah! that was the bloody sight, I'm tould—for I wasn't at it—atween the Orangemen and them. The Ribbonmen war bate, though, but not till after there was a desperate fight on both sides. I was tould that Denis Kelly that day knocked down five-and-twenty men in about three-quarters of an hour; and only that long John Grimes hot him a polthoge on the sconce(100) with the butt-end of the gun, it was thought the Orangemen would be beat. That blow broke his skull, and was the manes of his death. He was carried home senseless."

"Well, Lachlin," said my brother, "if you didn't see it, I did. I happened to be looking out of John Carson's upper window—for it wasn't altogether safe to contemplate it within reach of the missiles. It was certainly a dreadful and a barbarous sight. You have often observed the calm, gloomy silence that precedes a thunderstorm; and had you been there that day you might have seen its illustration in a scene much more awful. The thick living mass of people extended from the corner-house, nearly a quarter of a mile, at this end of the town, up to the parsonage on the other side. During the early part of the day, every kind of business was carried on in a hurry and an impatience, which denoted the little chance they knew there would be for transacting it in the evening.

"Up to the hour of four o'clock the fair was unusually quiet, and, on the whole, presented nothing in any way remarkable; but after that hour you might observe the busy stir and hum of the mass settling down into a deep, brooding, portentous silence, that was absolutely fearful. The females, with dismay and terror pictured in their faces, hurried home; and in various instances you might see mothers, and wives, and sisters, clinging about the sons, husbands, and brothers, attempting to drag them by main force from the danger which they knew impended over them. In this they seldom succeeded; for the

John W. Hurley

person so urged was usually compelled to tear himself from them by superior strength.

"The pedlars, and basket-women, and such as had tables and standings(101) erected in the streets, commenced removing them with all possible haste. The shopkeepers, and other inhabitants of the town, put up their shutters, in order to secure their windows from being shattered. Strangers, who were compelled to stop in town that night, took shelter in the inns and other houses of entertainment where they lodged: so that about five o'clock the street was completely clear and free for action.

"Hitherto there was not a stroke—the scene became even more silent and gloomy, although the moral darkness of their ill-suppressed passions was strongly contrasted with the splendour of the sun, that poured down a tide of golden light upon the multitude. This contrast between the natural brightness of the evening, and the internal gloom of their hearts, as the beams of the sun rested upon the ever-moving crowd, would, to any man who knew the impetuosity with which the spirit of religious hatred was soon to rage among them, produce novel and singular sensations. For, after all, Toby, there is a mysterious connection between natural and moral things, which often invests both nature and sentiment with a feeling that certainly would not come home to our hearts, if such a connection did not exist. A rose-tree beside a grave will lead us from sentiment to reflection; and any other association, where a painful or melancholy thought is clothed with a garb of joy or pleasure, will strike us more deeply in proportion as the contrast is strong. On seeing the sun or moon struggling through the darkness of surrounding clouds, I confess, although you may smile, that I feel for the moment a diminution of enjoyment—something taken, as it were, from the sum of my happiness.

"Ere the quarrel commenced, you might see a dark and hateful glare scowling from the countenances of the two parties, as they viewed and approached each other in the street—the eye was set in deadly animosity, and the face marked with an ireful paleness, occasioned at once by revenge and apprehension. Groups were silently hurrying with an eager and energetic step to their places of rendez-vous, grasping their weapons more closely, or grinding their teeth in the impatience of their fury. The veterans on each side were surrounded

Pat Mulligan the schoolmaster.

John W. Hurley

Kelly standing arms akimbo.

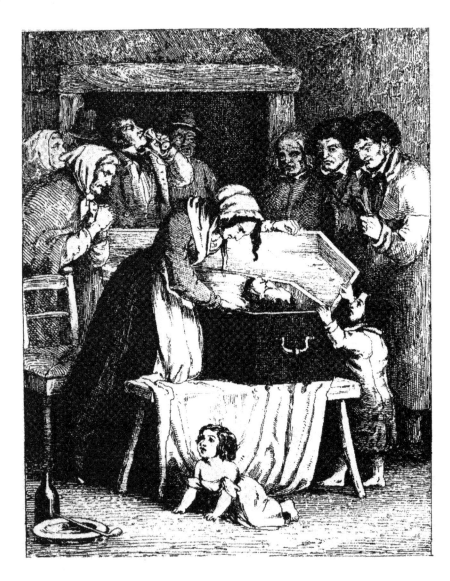

Mrs. Kelly lamenting over the coffin of her husband.

136   John W. Hurley

Denis Kelly's casket in the grave.

by their respective followers, anxious to act under their direction; and the very boys seemed to be animated with a martial spirit, much more eager than that of those who had greater experience in party quarrels.

"Jem Finigan's public-house was the head-quarters and rallying-point of the Ribbonmen; the Orangemen assembled in that of Joe Sherlock, the master of an Orange lodge. About six o'clock the crowd in the street began gradually to fall off to the opposite ends of the town—the Roman Catholics towards the north, the Protestants towards the south. Carson's window, from which I was observing their motions, was exactly half-way between them, so that I had a distinct view of both. At this moment I noticed Denis Kelly coming forward from the closely condensed mass formed by the Ribbonmen: he advanced with his cravat(102) off, to the middle of the vacant space between the parties, holding a fine oak cudgel in his hand. He then stopped, and addressing the Orangemen, said,

"'Where's Vengeance and his crew now? Is there any single Orange villain among you that dare come down and meet me here, like a man? Is John Grimes there? for if he is, before we begin to take you out of a face,(103) to hunt you altogether out of the town, ye Orange villains, I would be glad that he'd step down to Denis Kelly here for two or three minutes; I'll not keep him longer.

"There was now a stir and a murmur among the Orange-men, as if a rush was about to take place towards Denis; but Grimes, whom I saw endeavouring to curb them in, left the crowd and advanced towards him.

"At this moment an instinctive movement among both masses took place; so that when Grimes had come within a few yards of Kelly, both parties were within two or three perches of them. Kelly was standing, apparently off his guard, with one hand thrust carelessly into the breast of his waistcoat, and the cudgel in the other; but his eye was fixed calmly upon Grimes as he approached. They were both powerful, fine men—brawny, vigorous, and active. Grimes had somewhat the advantage of the other in height; he also fought with his left hand, from which circumstance he was nicknamed Kitthogue.(104) He was a man of a dark, stern-looking countenance; and the tones of his voice were deep, sullen, and of appalling strength.

John W. Hurley

"As they approached each other, the windows on each side of the street were crowded; but there was not a breath to be heard in any direction, nor from either party. As for myself, my heart palpitated with anxiety. What they might have felt, I do not know: but they must both have experienced considerable apprehension; for as they were the champions of their respective parties, and had never before met in single encounter, their characters depended on the issue of the contest.

"'Well, Grimes,' said Denis, 'sure, I've often wished for this same meetin', man, betune myself and you; I have what you're goin' to get in for you this long time; but you'll get it now, avick,(105) plase God——'

"'It was not to scould I came, you Popish, ribly rascal,'(106) replied Grimes, 'but to give you what you're long——'

"'Ere the word had been out of his mouth, however, Kelly sprung over to him; and making a feint, as if he intended to lay the stick on his ribs, he swung it past without touching him, and, bringing it round his own head like lightning, made it tell with a powerful back-stroke, right on Grimes's temple, and in an instant his own face was sprinkled with the blood which sprung from the wound. Grimes staggered forward towards his antagonist, seeing which, Kelly sprung back, and was again meeting him with full force, when Grimes, turning a little, clutched Kelly's stick in his right hand, and being left-handed himself, ere the other could wrench the cudgel from him, he gave him a terrible blow upon the back part of the head, which laid Kelly in the dust.

"'There was then a deafening shout from the Orange party; and Grimes stood until Kelly should be in the act of rising, ready then to give him another blow. The coolness and generalship of Kelly, however, were here very remarkable; for, when he was just getting to his feet, 'Look at your party coming down upon me!' he exclaimed to Grimes, who turned round to order them back, and in the interim Kelly was upon his legs.

"'I was surprised at the coolness of both men; for Grimes was by no means inflated with the boisterous triumph of his party,—nor did Denis get into a blind rage on being knocked down. They approached again, their eyes kindled into savage fury, tamed down into the wariness of experienced combatants; for a short time they stood eyeing each other, as if calculating upon the contingent advantages of attack or defence. This was a moment of great interest; for, as their huge and powerful frames stood out in opposition, strung and dilated by passion and the energy of contest, no judgment, however experienced, could venture to anticipate the result of the battle, or name the person likely to be victorious. Indeed, it was surprising how the natural sagacity of these men threw their movements into scientific form and elegance. Kelly raised his cudgel, and placed it transversely in the air between himself and his opponent; Grimes instantly placed his against it—both weapons thus forming a St. Andrew's cross—whilst the men themselves stood foot to foot, calm and collected. Nothing could be finer than their proportions, nor superior to their respective attitudes; their broad chests were in a line; their thick, well set necks laid a little back, as were their bodies, without, however, losing their balance; and their fierce but calm features grimly but placidly scowling, at each other, like men who were prepared for the onset.

"At length Kelly made an attempt to repeat his former feint with variations; for, whereas he had sent the first blow to Grimes's right temple, he took measures now to reach the left. His action was rapid, but equally quick was the eye of his antagonist, whose cudgel was up in ready guard to meet the blow. It met it; and with such surprising power was it sent and opposed, that both cudgels, on meeting, bent across each other into curves. An involuntary huzza followed this from their respective parties—not so much on account of the skill displayed by the combatants as in admiration of their cudgels, and of the judgment with which they must have been selected. In fact, it was the staves, rather than the men, that were praised; and certainly the former did their duty. In a moment their shillelaghs were across each other once more, and the men resumed their former attitudes; their savage determination, their kindled eyes, the blood which disfigured the face of Grimes, and begrimed also the countenance of his antagonist into a deeper expression of ferocity, occasioned many a cowardly heart to shrink from the sight. There they stood, gory and stern, ready for the next onset; it was first made by Grimes, who tried to practise on Kelly the feint which Kelly had before practised on him. Denis, after his usual manner, caught the blow in his open hand, and

John W. Hurley

clutched the staff with an intention of holding it until he might visit Grimes, now apparently unguarded, with a levelling blow; but Grimes's effort to wrest the cudgel from his grasp, drew all Kelly's strength to that quarter, and prevented him from availing himself of the other's defenceless attitude.

A trial of muscular power ensued, and their enormous bodily strength was exhibited in the stiff tug for victory. Kelly's address prevailed; for while Grimes pulled against him with all his collected vigour, the former suddenly let go his hold, and the latter, having lost his balance, staggered back: lightning could not be more quick than the action of Kelly, as, with tremendous force, his cudgel rung on the unprotected head of Grimes, who fell, or rather was shot to the ground, as if some superior power had dashed him against it; and there he lay for a short time, quivering under the blow he had received.

"A peal of triumph now arose from Kelly's party; but Kelly himself, placing his arms a-kimbo,(107) stood calmly over his enemy, awaiting his return to the conflict. For nearly five minutes he stood in this attitude, during which time Grimes did not stir; at length Kelly stooped a little, and peering closely into his face, exclaimed—

"'Why, then, is it acting you are?—any how, I wouldn't put it past you, you cunning vagabone; 'tis lying to take breath he is—get up, man, I'd scorn to touch you till you're on your legs—not all as one, for sure, it's yourself would show me no such forbearance. Up with you, man alive; I've none of your own thrachery in me. I'll not rise my cudgel till you're on your guard.'

"There was an expression of disdain, mingled with a glow of honest, manly generosity on his countenance, as he spoke, which made him at once the favourite with such spectators as were not connected with cither of the parties. Grimes arose, and it was evident that Kelly's generosity deepened his resentment more than the blow which had sent him so rapidly to the ground ; however, he was still cool, but his brows knit, his eye flashed with double fierceness, and his complexion settled into a dark blue shade, which gave to his whole visage an expression fearfully ferocious. Kelly hailed this as the first appearance of passion; *his* brow expanded as the other approached, and a dash of confidence, if not of triumph, softened in some degree the sternness of his features.

"With caution they encountered again, each collected for a spring, their eyes gleaming at each other like those of tigers. Grimes made a motion as if he would have struck Kelly with his fist; and as the latter threw up his guard against the blow, he received a stroke from Grimes's cudgel on the under part of the right arm. This had been directed at his elbow, with an intention of rendering the arm powerless: it fell short, however, yet was sufficient to relax the grasp which Kelly had of his weapon. Had Kelly been a novice, this stratagem alone would have soon vanquished him; his address, however, was fully equal to that of his antagonist. The staff dropped instantly from his grasp, but a stout thong of black polished leather, with a shining tassel at the end of it, had bound it securely to his massive wrist; the cudgel, therefore, only dangled from his arm, and did not, as the other expected, fall to the ground, or put Denis to the necessity of stooping for it—Grimes's object being to have struck him in that attitude.

"A flash of indignation now shot from Kelly's eye, and with the speed of lightning he sprung within Grimes's weapon, determined to wrest it from him. The grapple that ensued was gigantic. In a moment Grimes's staff was parallel with the horizon between them, clutched in the powerful grasp of both. They stood exactly opposite, and rather close to each other; their arms sometimes stretched out stiff and at full length, again contracted, until their faces, glowing and distorted by the energy of the contest, were drawn almost together. Sometimes the prevailing strength of one would raise the staff slowly, and with gradually developed power, up in a perpendicular position: again, the reaction of opposing strength would strain it back, and sway the weighty frame of the antagonist, crouched and set into desperate resistance, along with it; whilst the hard pebbles under their feet were crumbled into powder, and the very street itself furrowed into gravel by the shock of their opposing strength. Indeed, so well matched a pair never met in contest; their strength, their wind, their activity, and their natural science appeared to be perfectly equal.

"At length, by a tremendous effort, Kelly got the staff twisted nearly out of Grime's hand, and a short shout, half encouraging, half indignant, came from Grimes's party. This added shame to his other passions, and threw all impulse of almost superhuman strength into him: he recovered his advantage, but nothing more; they twisted—they heaved their great frames against each other—they struggled—their action became rapid—they swayed each other this way and that—their eyes like fire, their teeth locked, and their nostrils dilated. Sometimes they twined about each other like serpents, and twirled round with such rapidity, that it was impossible to distinguish them—sometimes, when a pull of more than ordinary power took place, they seemed to cling together almost without motion, bending down until their heads nearly touched the ground, their cracking joints seeming to stretch by the effort, and the muscles of their limbs standing out from the flesh, strung in amazing tension.

"In this attitude were they, when Denis, with the eye of a hawk, spied a disadvantage in Grimes's position; he wheeled round, placed his broad shoulder against the shaggy breast of the other, and giving him what is called an 'inside crook,'(108) strained him, despite of every effort, until he fairly got him on his shoulder, and off the point of resistance. There was a cry of alarm from the windows, particularly from the females, as Grimes's huge body was swung over Kelly's shoulder, until it came down in a crash upon the hard gravel of the street, while Denis stood in triumph, with his enemy's staff in his hand. A loud huzza followed this from all present, except the Orangemen, who stood bristling with fury and shame for the temporary defeat of their champion.

"Denis again had his enemy at his mercy, but he scorned to use his advantage ungenerously; he went over, and placing the staff in his hands—for the other had got to his legs—retrograded to his place, and desired Grimes to defend himself.

"After considerable manoeuvring on both sides, Denis, who appeared to be the more active of the two, got an open on his antagonist, and by a powerful blow upon Grimes's ear sent him to the ground with amazing force. I never saw such a blow given by mortal: the end of the cudgel came exactly upon the ear, and as Grimes went down, the blood spurted out of his mouth and nostrils; he then kicked convulsively several times as he lay upon the ground, and that moment I really thought he would never have breathed more.

"The shout was again raised by the Ribbonmen, who threw up their hats, and bounded from the ground with the most vehement exultation. Both parties then waited to give Grimes time to rise and renew the battle; but he appeared perfectly contented to remain where he was: for there appeared no signs of life or motion in him.

"'Have you got your gruel,(109) boy?' said Kelly, going over to where he lay;—'Well, you met Denis Kelly, at last, didn't you? and there you lie; but plase God, the most of your sort will soon lie in the same state. Come, boys,' said Kelly, addressing his own party, 'now for bloody Vengeance and his crew, that thransported the Grogans and the Caffries, and murdered Collier. Now, boys, have at the murderers, and let us have satisfaction for all!'

"A mutual rush instantly took place; but, ere the Orangemen came down to where Grimes lay, Kelly had taken his staff, and handed it to one of his own party. It is impossible to describe the scene that ensued. The noise of the blows, the shouting, the yelling, the groans, the scalped heads and gory visages gave both to the eye and the ear an impression that could not easily be forgotten. The battle was obstinately maintained on both sides for nearly an hour, and with a skill of manoeuvring, attack, and retreat that was astonishing.

"Both parties arranged themselves against each other, forming something like two lines of battle, and these extended along the town nearly from one end to the other. It was curious to remark the difference in the persons and appearances of the combatants. In the Orange line the men were taller and of more powerful frames; but the Ribbonmen were more hardy, active, and courageous. Man to man, notwithstanding their superior bodily strength, the Orangemen could never fight the others; the former depend too much upon their fire and side-arms, but they are by no means so well trained to the use of the cudgel as their enemies. In the district where the scene of this fight is laid, the Catholics generally inhabit the mountainous part of the country, to which, when the civil feuds of worse times prevailed, they had been driven at the point of the bayonet; the Protestants and Presbyterians, on the other hand, who came in upon their possessions, occupy the richer and more fertile tracts of the land; being more wealthy, they live with less labour, and on better food. The characteristic features produced by these causes are such as might be expected—the Catholic being, like his soil, hardy, thin, and capable of bearing all weathers; and the Protestants, larger, softer, and more inactive.

John W. Hurley

"Their advance to the first onset was far different from a faction fight. There existed a silence here, that powerfully evinced the inextinguishable animosity with which they encountered. For some time they fought in two compact bodies, that remained unbroken so long as the chances of victory were doubtful. Men went down, and were up, and went down in all directions, with uncommon rapidity; and as the weighty phalanx of Orangemen stood out against the nimble line of their mountain adversaries, the intrepid spirit of the latter, and their surprising skill and activity, soon gave symptoms of a gradual superiority in the conflict. In the course of about half an hour, the Orange party began to give way in the northern end of the town; and, as their opponents pressed them warmly and with unsparing hand, the heavy mass formed by their numbers began to break, and this decomposition ran up their line, until in a short time they were thrown into utter confusion. They now fought in detached parties; but these subordinate conflicts, though shorter in duration than the shock of the general battle, were much more inhuman and destructive; for whenever any particular gang succeeded in putting their adversaries to flight, they usually ran to the assistance of their friends in the nearest fight—by which means they often fought three to one. In these instances the persons inferior in number suffered such barbarities, as it would be painful to detail.

"There lived a short distance out of the town a man nicknamed Jemsy Boccagh,(110) on account of his lameness—he was also sometimes called 'Hop-an'-go-constant,' who fell the first victim to party spirit. He had got arms on seeing his friends likely to be defeated, and had the hardihood to follow, with charged bayonet, a few Ribbonmen, whom he attempted to intercept as they fled from a large number of their enemies who had got them separated from their comrades. Boccagh ran across a field, in order to get before them in the road, and was in the act of climbing a ditch, when one of them, who carried a spade-shaft, struck him a blow on the head, which put an end to his existence.(111)

"This circumstance imparted, of course, fiercer hatred to both parties—triumph inspiring the one, a thirst for vengeance nerving the other. Kelly inflicted tremendous punishment in every direction; for scarcely a blow fell from him which did not bring a man to the ground.

It absolutely resembled a military engagement, for the number of combatants amounted at least to four thousand men. In many places the street was covered with small pools and clots of blood, which flowed from those who lay insensible—while others were borne away bleeding, groaning, or staggering, having been battered into a total unconsciousness of the scene about them.

"At length the Orangemen gave way, and their enemies, yelling with madness and revenge, began to beat them with unrestrained fury. The former, finding that they could not resist the impetuous tide which burst upon them, fled back past the church, and stopped not until they had reached an elevation, on which lay two or three heaps of stones, that had been collected for the purpose of paving the streets. Here they made a stand, and commenced a vigorous discharge of them against their pursuers. This checked the latter; and the others, seeing them hesitate, and likely to retreat from the missiles, pelted them with such effect, that the tables became turned, and the Ribbonmen made a speedy flight back into the town.

"In the meantime several Orangemen had gone into Sherlock's, where a considerable number of arms had been deposited, with an intention of resorting to them in case of a defeat at the cudgels. These now came out, and met the Ribbonmen on their flight from those who were pelting them with the stones. A dreadful scene ensued. The Ribbonmen, who had the advantage in numbers, finding themselves intercepted before by those who had arms, and pursued behind by those who had recourse to the stones, fought with uncommon bravery and desperation. Kelly, who was furious, but still collected and decisive, shouted out in Irish, lest the opposite party might understand him, 'Let every two men seize upon one of those who have the arms.'

"This was attempted, and effected with partial success; and I have no doubt but the Orangemen would have been ultimately beaten and deprived of their weapons, were it not that many of them who had got their pistols out of Sherlock's, discharged them among their enemies, and wounded several. The Catholics could not stand this; but wishing to retaliate as effectually as possible, lifted stones wherever they could find them, and kept up the fight at a distance, as they retreated. On both sides, wherever a solitary foe was caught strag-

John W. Hurley

gling from the rest, he was instantly punished with a most cruel and blood-thirsty spirit.

"It was just about this time that I saw Kelly engaged with two men, whom he kept at bay with great ease—retrograding, however, as he fought, towards his own party. Grimes, who had some time before this recovered and joined the fight once more, was returning, after having pursued several of the Ribbonmen past the market-house, where he spied Kelly thus engaged. With a Volunteer gun in his hand, and furious with the degradation of his former defeat, he ran over and struck him with the butt-end of it upon the temple—and Denis fell. When the stroke was given, an involuntary cry of 'Murder,—foul, foul!' burst from those who looked on from the windows; and long John Steele, Grimes's father in-law, in indignation, raised his cudgel to knock him down for this treacherous and malignant blow;—but a person out of Neal Cassidy's back-yard hurled a round stone, about six pounds in weight, at Grimes's head, that felled him to the earth, leaving him as insensible, and nearly in as dangerous a state, as Kelly,—for his jaw was broken.

"By this time the Catholics had retreated out of the town, and Denis might probably have received more punishment, had those who were returning from the pursuit recognised him; but James Wilson, seeing the dangerous situation in which he lay, came out, and, with the assistance of his servant-man, brought him into his own house. When the Orangemen had driven their adversaries off the field, they commenced the most hideous yellings through the streets—got music, and played party tunes—offered any money for the face of a Papist; and any of that religion who were so unfortunate as to make their appearance, were beaten in the most relentless manner. It was precisely the same thing on the part of the Ribbonmen; if a Protestant, but, above all, an Orangeman, came in their way, he was sure to be treated with barbarity; for the retaliation on either side was dreadfully unjust—the innocent suffering as well as the guilty. Leaving the window, I found Kelly in a bad state below stairs.

"'What's to be done?' said I to Wilson.

"'I know not,' replied he, 'except I put him between us on my jaunting-car and drive him home.'

"This appeared decidedly the best plan we could adopt; so, after putting to the horse, we placed him on the car, sitting one on side of him, and, in this manner, left him at his own house."

"'Did you run no risk,' said I, "in going among Kelly's friends whilst they were under the influence of party feeling and exasperated passion?'

"'No,' said he; 'we had rendered many of them acts of kindness, and had never exhibited any spirit but a friendly one towards them; and such individuals, but only such, might walk through a crowd of enraged Catholics or Protestants quite unmolested.'

"The next morning Kelly's landlord, Sir W. R ____, and two magistrates, were at his house, but he lay like a log, without sense or motion. Whilst they were there the Surgeon arrived, and, after examining his head, declared that the skull was fractured. During that and the following day, the house was surrounded by crowds, anxious to know his state; and nothing might be heard amongst most of them but loud and undisguised expressions of the most ample revenge. The wife was frantic; and, on seeing me, hid her face in her hands, exclaiming,

"'Ah, Sir, I knew it would come to this; and you, too, tould him the same thing. My curse and God's curse on it for quarrelling! Will it never stop in the country till they rise some time and murdher one another out of the face?'

"As soon as the swelling in his head was reduced, the Surgeon performed the operation of trepanning,(112) and thereby saved his life; but his strength and intellect were gone, and he just lingered for four months, a feeble, drivelling simpleton, until, in consequence of a cold, which produced inflammation in the brain, he died, as hundreds have died before, the victim of party spirit." Such was the account which I heard of my old school-fellow, Denis Kelly; and, indeed, when I reflected upon the nature of the education he received, I could not but admit that the consequences were such as might naturally be expected to result from it. The next morning a relation of Mrs. Kelly's came down to my brother, hoping that, as they wished to have as decent a funeral as possible, he would be so kind as to attend it.

"Musha, God knows, sir," said the man, "it's poor Denis, heavens be his bed! that had the regard and reverence for every one, young and ould, of your father's family; and it's himself that would be the proud man, if he was living, to see you, sir, riding after his coffin."

"Well," said my brother, "let Mrs. Kelly know that I shall certainly attend, and so will my brother, here, who has come to pay me a visit.— Why, I believe, Tom, you forget him!"

"Your brother, sir! Is it Master Toby, that used to cudgel the half of the counthry when he was at school? Gad's my life, Masther Toby, (I was now about thirty-six) but it's your four quarters, sure enough! Arrah, thin, sir, who'd think it—you're grown so full and stout?— but, faix,(113) you'd always the bone in you! Ah, Masther Toby!" said he, "he's lying cowld, this morning, that would be the happy man to lay his eyes wanst more upon you. Many an' many's the winther's evening did he spind, talking about the time when you and he were bouchals togethcr, and of the pranks you played at school, but especially of the time you both leathered the four Grogans, and tuck the apples from them—my poor fellow!—and now to be stretched a corpse, lavin' his poor widdy and child her behind him!"
I accordingly expressed my sorrow for Denis's death, which, indeed, I sincerely regretted, for he possessed materials for an excellent char- acter, had not all that was amiable and good in him been permitted to run wild.

As soon as my trunk and travelling-bag had been brought from the inn, where I had left them the preceding night, we got our horses, and, as we wished to show particular respect to Denis's remains, rode up, with some of our friends, to the house. When we approached, there were large crowds of the country-pcople before the door of his well thatched and respectable-looking dwelling, which had three chim- neys, and a set of sash-windows, clean and well glazed. On our ar- rival, I was soon recognised and surrounded by numbers of those to whom I had formerly been known, who received and welcomed me with a warmth of kindness and sincerity, which it would be in vain to look for among the peasantry of any other nation.

Indeed, I have uniformly observed, that when no religious or po- litical feeling influences the heart and principles of an Irish peasant, he is singularly sincere and faithful in his attachments, and has al- ways a bias to the generous and the disinterested. To my own knowl- edge, circumstances frequently occur, in which the ebullition of party spirit is altogether temporary, subsiding after the cause that produced it has passed away, and leaving the kind peasant to the natural, affectionate, and generous impulses of his character.

But poor Paddy, unfortunately, is as combustible a material in politics or religion, as in fighting—thinking it his duty to take the weak side,(114) without any other consideration, than because it is the weak side.

When we entered the house I was almost suffocated with the strong fumes of tobacco-smoke, snuff, and whiskey; and as I had been an old school-fellow of Denis's, my appearance was the signal for a general burst of grief among his relations, in which the more distant friends and neighbours of the deceased joined, to keep up the keening.(115)

I have often, indeed always, felt that there is something extremely touching in the Irish cry; in fact, that it breathes the very spirit of wild and natural sorrow. The Irish peasantry, whenever a death takes place, are exceedingly happy in seizing upon any contingent circumstances that may occur, and making them subservient to the excitement of grief for the departed, or the exaltation and praise of his character and virtues. My entrance was a proof of this—I had scarcely advanced to the middle of the floor, when my intimacy with the deceased, our boyish sports, and even our quarrels, were adverted to with a natural eloquence and pathos, that, in spite of my firmness, occasioned me to feel the prevailing sorrow. They spoke, or chaunted mournfully, in Irish; but the substance of what they said was as follows:—

"Oh, Denis, Denis, avourneen! you're lying low, this morning of sorrow!—lying low are you, and does not know who it is (alluding to me) that is standing over you, weeping for the days you spent together in your youth! It's yourself, acushla agus asthore machree,(116) that would stretch out the right hand warmly to welcome him to the place of his birth, where you had both been so often happy about the green hills and valleys with each other! He's here now, standing over you; and it's he, of all his family, kind and respectable as they are, that was your own favourite, Denis, avourneen dhelish!(117) He alone was the companion that you loved!—with no other could you be happy!—For him did you fight, when he wanted a friend in your young quarrels! and if you had a dispute with him, were you not sorry

John W. Hurley

for it? Are you not now stretched in death before him, and will he not forgive you?"

All this was uttered, of course, extemporaneously, and without the least preparation. They then passed on to an enumeration of his virtues as a father, husband, son, and brother—specified his worth as he stood related to society in general, and his kindness as a neighbour and a friend.

An occurrence now took place which may serve, in some measure, to throw light upon many of the atrocities and outrages which take place in Ireland. Before I mention it, however, I think it necessary to make a few observations relative to it. I am convinced that those who are intimately acquainted with the Irish peasantry, will grant that there is not on the earth a class of people in whom the domestic affections of blood-relationship are so pure, strong, and sacred. The birth of a child will occasion a poor man to break in upon the money set apart for his landlord, in order to keep the christening, surrounded by his friends and neighbours, with due festivity. A marriage exhibits a spirit of joy, an exuberance of happiness and delight, to be found only in the Green Island; and the death of a member of a family is attended with a sincerity of grief, scarcely to be expected from men so much the creatures of the more mirthful feelings. In fact, their sorrow is a solecism(118) in humanity—at once deep and loud—mingled up, even in its deepest paroxysms, with a laughter-loving spirit. It is impossible that an Irishman, sunk in the lowest depths of affliction, could permit his grief to flow in all its sad solemnity, even for a day, without some glimpse of his natural humour throwing a faint and rapid light over the gloom within him. No: there is an amalgamation of sentiments in his mind which, as I said before, would puzzle any philosopher to account for. Yet it would be wrong to say, though his grief has something of an unsettled and ludicrous character about it, that he is incapable of the most subtle and delicate shades of sentiment, or the deepest and most desolating intensity of sorrow. But he laughs off those heavy vapours which hang about the moral constitution of the people of other nations, giving them a morbid habit, which leaves them neither strength nor firmness to resist calamity—which they feel less keenly than an Irishman, exactly as a healthy man will feel the pangs of death with more acuteness than one who is wasted away by debility and decay. Let any man witness an emigration, and he will satisfy himself that this is true. I am convinced that Goldsmith's(119) inimitable description of one in his "Deserted Village," was a picture drawn from actual observation. Let him observe the emigrant, as he crosses the Atlantic, and he will find, although he joins the jest, and the laugh, and the song, that he will seek a silent corner or a silent hour, to indulge the sorrow which he still feels for the friends, the companions, and the native fields that he has left behind him. This constitution of mind is beneficial: the Irishman seldom or never hangs himself, because he is capable of too much real feeling to permit himself to become the slave of that which is factitious. There is no void in his affections or sentiments, which a morbid and depraved sensibility could occupy; but his feelings, of what character soever they may be, are strong, because they are fresh and healthy. For this reason, I maintain, that when the domestic affections come under the influence of either grief or joy, the peasantry of no nation are capable of feeling so deeply. Even on the ordinary occasions of death, sorrow, though it alternates with mirth and cheerfulness, in a manner peculiar to themselves, lingers long in the unseen recesses of domestic life: any hand therefore, whether by law or violence, that plants a wound HERE, will suffer to the death.

When my brother and I entered the house, the body had just been put into the coffin; and it is usual after this takes place, and before it is nailed down, for the immediate relatives of the family to embrace the deceased, and take their last look and farewell of his remains. In the present instance, the children were brought over, one by one, to perform that trying and melancholy ceremony. The first was an infant on the breast, whose little innocent mouth was held down to that of its dead father; the babe smiled upon his still and solemn features, and would have played with his graveclothes, but that the murmur of unfeigned sorrow, which burst from all present, occasioned it to be removed. The next was a fine little girl, of three or four years, who inquired where they were going to bring her daddy, and asked if he would not soon come back to her.

"My daddy's sleeping a long time," said the child, "but I'll waken him till he sings me 'Peggy Slevin.' I like my daddy best, bekase I sleep wid him—and he brings me good things from the fair; he bought me this ribbon," said she, pointing to a ribbon which he had purchased for her.

The rest of the children were sensible of their loss, and truly it was a distressing scene. His eldest son and daughter, the former about fourteen, the latter about two years older, lay on the coffin, kissing his lips, and were with difficulty torn away from it.

"Oh!" said the boy, "he is going from us, and night or day we will never see him or hear him more! Oh! father—father—is that the last sight we are ever to see of your face? Why, father dear, did you die, and leave us for ever?—for ever—wasn't your heart good to us, and your words kind to us—Oh! your last smile is smiled—your last kiss given—and your last kind word spoken to your childhre that you loved, and that loved you as we did. Father, core of my heart, are you gone for ever, and your voice departed? Oh! the murdherers, oh! the murdherers, the murdherers!" he exclaimed, "that killed my father; for only for them, he would be still wid us: but, by the God that's over me, if I live, night or day I will not rest, till I have blood for blood; nor do I care who hears it, nor if I was hanged the next minute."(120)

As these words escaped him, a deep and awful murmur of suppressed vengeance burst from his relations. At length their sorrow became too strong to be repressed; and as it was the time to take their last embrace and look of him, they came up, and after fixing their eyes on his face in deep affliction, their lips began to quiver, and their countenances became convulsed. They then burst out simultaneously into a tide of violent grief, which, after having indulged in it for some time, they checked. But the resolution of revenge was stronger than their grief, for, standing over his dead body, they repeated, almost word for word, the vow of vengeance which the son had just sworn. It was really a scene dreadfully and terribly solemn; and I could not avoid reflecting upon the mystery of nature, which can, from the deep power of domestic affection, cause to spring a determination to crime of so black a dye. Would to God that our peasantry had a clearer sense of moral and religious duties, and were not left so much as they are to the headlong impulse of an ardent temperament, and an impetuous character; and would to God that the clergy who superintend their morals, had a better knowledge of human nature, and a more liberal education! During all this time the heart-broken widow sat beyond the coffin, looking upon what passed with a stupid sense of bereavement, and when they had all performed this last ceremony, it was found necessary to tell her that the time was come for the procession of the funeral, and that they only waited for her to take, as the rest did, her last look and embrace of her husband. When she heard this, it pierced her like an arrow: she became instantly collected, and her complexion assumed a dark shade of despairing anguish, which it was an affliction even to look upon. She then stooped over the coffin, and kissed him several times, after which she ceased sobbing, and lay silently with her mouth to his.

The character of a faithful wife sorrowing for a beloved husband has that in it which compels both respect and sympathy. There was not at this moment a dry eye in the house. She still lay silent on the coffin; but, as I observed that her bosom seemed not to heave as it did a little before, I was convinced that she had become insensible. I accordingly beckoned to Kelly's brother, to whom I mentioned what I had suspected; and, on his going over to ascertain the truth, he found her as I had said. She was then brought to the air, and after some trouble recovered; but I recommended them to put her to bed, and not to subject her to any unnecessary anguish, by a custom which was really too soul-piercing to endure. This, however, was, in her opinion, the violation of an old rite, sacred to her heart and affections—she would not hear of it for an instant. Again she was helped out between her brother and brother-inlaw, and after stooping down, and doing as the others had done—

"Now," said she, "I will sit here and keep him under my eye as long as I can—surely you won't blame me for it; you all know the kind of husband he was to me, and the good right I have to be sorry for him! Oh!" she added, "is it thrue at all?—is he, my own Denis, the young husband of my early—and my first love, in good airnest, dead, and going to leave me here—me, Denis, that you loved so tindherly, and our childher, that your brow was never clouded aginst? Can I believe myself, or is it a dhrame? Denis, avick machree! avick machree!(121) your hand was dreaded, and a good right it had, for it was the manly hand, that was ever and always raised in defense of them that wanted a friend; abroad, in the faction-fight, against the

John W. Hurley

oppressor, your name was ever feared, achusla?—but at home—
AT HOME—where was your fellow? Denis aghra, do you know the
lips that's spaking to you?—your young bride—your heart's light—
Oh! I remimber the day you war married to me like yesterday. Oh!
avourneen, then and since wasn't the heart of your own Honor bound
up in you—yet not a word even to me. Well, agrah machree, 'tisn't
your fault, it's the first time you ever refused to spake to your own
Honor. But you're dead, avourneen, or it wouldn't be so—you're
dead before my eyes—husband of my heart, and all my hopes and
happiness goes into the coffin and the grave along wid you, for ever!"

All this time she was rocking herself from side to side, her complexion pale and ghastly as could be conceived, and the tears streaming from her eyes. When the coffin was about to be closed, she retired until it Wis nailed down, after which she returned with her bonnet and cloak on her, ready to accompany it to the grave. I was aston-
ished—for I thought she could not have walked two steps without
assistance; but it was the custom, and to neglect it. I fonnd, would
have thrown the imputation of insincerity upon her grief. While they
were preparing to bring the coffin out, I could hear the chat and conversation of those who were standing in crowds before the door, and
occasionally a loud, vacant laugh, and sometimes a volley of them,
responsive to the jokes of some rustic wit, probably the same person
who acted master of the revels(122) at the wake.

Before the coffin was finally closed, Ned Corrigan, whom I had
put to fight the preceding night, came up, and repeated the De
Profundis,(123) in very strange Latin, over the corpse. When this,
was finished, he got a jug of holy water, and after dipping his thumb
in it, first made the sign of the cross upon his own forehead, and
afterwards sprinkled it upon all present, giving my brother and myself an extra compliment, supposing, probably, that we stood most in
need of it. When this was over, he sprinkled the corpse and the coffin
in particular most profusely. He then placed two pebbles from Lough
Derg,(124) and a bit of holy candle, upon the breast of the corpse,
and having said a Pater and Ave,(125) in which he was joined by the
people, he closed the lid, and nailed it down.

"Ned," said his brother, "are his feet and toes loose?"

"Musha, but that's more than myself knows," replied Ned—

"Are they, Katty?" said he, inquiring from the sister of the deceased.

"Arrah, to be sure, avourneen!" answered Katty—"do you think we would lave him to be tied that way, when he'd be risin' out of his last bed at the day of judgment? Wouldn't it be too bad to have his toes tied then, avourneen?"

The coffin was then brought out and placed upon four chairs before the door, to be keened; and, in the mean time, the friends and well-wishers of the deceased were brought into the room to get each a glass of whiskey, as a token of respect. I observed also, that such as had not seen any of Kelly's relations until then, came up, and shaking hands with them, said—"I'm sorry for your loss!"

This expression of condolence was uniform, and the usual reply was,—"Thank you, Mat, or Jim!" with a pluck of the skirt accompanied by a significant nod, to follow. They then got a due share of whiskey; and it was curious, after they came out, their faces a little flushed, and their eyes watery with the strong, ardent spirits, to hear with what heartiness and alacrity they entered into Denis's praises. When he had been keened in the street, there being no hearse, the coffin was placed upon two handspikes which were fixed across, but parallel to each other under it. These were borne by four men, one at the end of each, with the point of it crossing his body a little below his stomach; in other parts of Ireland, the coffin is borne upon a bier on the shoulders, but this is more convenient and less distressing.

When we got out upon the road, the funeral was of great extent—for Kelly had been highly respected. On arriving at the merin(126) which bounded the land he had owned, the coffin was laid down, and a loud and wailing keene took place over it. It was again raised, and the funeral proceeded in a direction which I was surprised to see it take, and it was not until an acquaintance of my brother's had explained the matter that I understood the cause of it. In Ireland when a murder is perpetrated, it is sometimes usual, as the funeral proceeds to the grave-yard, to bring the corpse to the house of him who committed the crime, and lay it down at his door, while the relations of the deceased kneel down, and, with an appalling solemnity, utter the deepest imprecations, and invoke the justice of heaven on the head of the murderer. This, however, is generally omitted if the residence of

John W. Hurley

the criminal be completely out of the line of the funeral, but if it be possible, by any circuit, to approach it, this dark ceremony is never omitted. In cases where the crime is doubtful, or unjustly imputed, those who are thus visited come out, and laying their right hand upon the coffin, protest their innocence of the blood of the deceased, calling God to witness the truth of their asseverations; but, in cases where the crime is clearly proved against the murderer, the door is either closed, the ceremony repelled by violence, or the house abandoned by the inmates until the funeral passes.(127)

The death of Kelly, however, could not be actually, or, at least, directly, considered a murder, for it was probable that Grimes did not inflict the stroke with an intention of taking away his life, and, besides, Kelly survived it four months. Grimes's house was not more than fifteen perches from the road: and when the corpse was opposite the little bridle-way that led up to it, they laid it down for a moment, and the relations of Kelly surrounded it, offering up a short prayer, with uncovered heads. It was then borne toward the house, whilst the keening commenced in a fond and wailing cry, accompanied with clapping of hands, and every other symptom of external sorrow. But, independent of their compliance with this ceremony, as an old usage, there is little doubt that the appearance of any thing connected with the man who certainly occasioned Kelly's death, awoke a keener and more intense sorrow for his loss. The wailing was thus continued until the coffin was laid opposite Grimes's door; nor did it cease then, but, on the contrary, was renewed with louder and more bitter lamentations.

As the multitude stood compassionating the affliction of the widow and orphans, it was the most impressive and solemn spectacle that could be witnessed. The very house seemed to have a condemned look; and, as a single wintry breeze waved a tuft of long grass that grew on a seat of turf at the side of the door, it brought the vanity of human enmity before my mind with melancholy force. When the keening ceased, Kelly's wife, with her children, knelt, their faces towards the house of their enemy, and invoked, in the strong language of excited passion, the justice of heaven upon the head of the man who had left her a widow, and her children fatherless. I was anxious to know if Grimes would appear to disclaim the intention of murder;

but I understood that he was at market—for it happened to be market-day.

"Come out!" said the widow—"come out, and look at the sight that's here before you! Come and view your own work! Lay but your hand upon the coffin, and the blood of him you murdhered will spout, before God and these Christian people, in your guilty face!

But, oh! may the Almighty God bring this home to you!(128)—May you never lave this life, John Grimes, till worse nor has overtaken me and mine falls upon you and yours! May our curse light upon you this day!—the curse, I say, of the widow and the orphans, that your bloody hand has made us, may it blast you! May you, and all belonging to you wither off of the 'airth! Night and day, sleeping and waking—like snow off the ditch may you melt, until your name and your place be disremimbered, except to be cursed by them that will hear of you and your hand of murdher! Amin, we pray God this day!—and the widow and orphan's prayer will not fall to the ground while your guilty head is above it! Childhre, did you all say it?"

At this moment a deep, terrific murmur, or rather ejaculation, corroborative of assent to this dreadful imprecation, pervaded the crowd in a fearful manner; their countenances darkened, their eyes gleamed, and their scowling visages stiffened into an expression of determined vengeance.

When these awful words were uttered, Grimes's wife and daughters approached the window in tears, sobbing, at the same time, loudly and bitterly.

"You're wrong," said the wife—"you're wrong, Widow Kelly, in saying that my husband murdhered him!—he did not murdher him; for, when you and yours were far from him, I heard John Grimes declare before the God who's to judge him, that he had no thought or intention of taking his life; he struck him in anger, and the blow did him an injury that was not intended. Don't curse him, Honor Kelly," said she, "don't curse him so fearfully; but, above all, don't curse me and my innocent childher, for we never harmed you, nor wished you ill! But it was this party work did it! Oh, my God!" she exclaimed, wringing her hands in utter bitterness of spirit, "when will it be ended between friends and neighbours, that ought to live in love and kindness together, instead of fighting in this blood-thirsty manner!"

John W. Hurley

She then wept more violently, as did her daughters.

"May God give me mercy in the last day, Mrs. Kelly, as I pity from my heart and soul you and your orphans," she continued; "but don't curse us, for the love of God—for you know we should forgive our enemies, as we ourselves, that are the enemies of God, hope to be forgiven."

"May God forgive me, then, if I have wronged you or your husband," said the widow, softened by their distress; "but you know, that whether he intended his life or not, the stroke he gave him has left my childher without a father, and myself dissolate. Oh, heavens above me!" she exclaimed, in a scream of distraction and despair, "is it possible—is it thrue—that my manly husband—the best father that ever breathed the breath of life—my own Denis, is lying dead—murdhered before my eyes? Put your hands on my head, some of you—put your hands on my head, or it will go to pieces. Where are you, Denis—where are you, the strong of hand, and the tender of heart? Come to me, darling, I want you in my distress. I want comfort, Denis; and I'll take it from none but yourself, for kind was your word to me in all my afflictions!"

All present were affected; and, indeed, it was difficult to say, whether Kelly's wife or Grimes's was more to be pitied at the moment.

The affliction of the latter and of her daughters was really pitiable; their sobs were loud, and the tears streamed down their cheeks like rain. When the widow's exclamations had ceased, or rather were lost in the loud cry of sorrow which were uttered by the keeners and friends of the deceased—they, too, standing somewhat apart from the rest, joined in it bitterly; and the solitary wail of Mrs. Grimes differing in character from that of those who had been trained to modulate the most profound grief into strains of a melancholy nature, was particularly wild and impressive. At all events, her Christian demeanour, joined to the sincerity of her grief, appeased the enmity of many; so true is it that a soft answer turneth away wrath. I could perceive, however, that the resentment of Kelly's male relations did not appear to be in any degree moderated.

The funeral again proceeded, and I remarked(129) that whenever a strange passenger happened to meet it, he always turned back, and accompanied it for a short distance, after which he resumed his journey, it being considered unlucky to omit this usage on meeting a funeral. Denis's residence was not more than two miles from the churchyard, which was situated in the town where he had received the fatal blow. As soon as we had got on about the half of this way, the priest of the parish met us, and the funeral, after proceeding a few perches more, turned into a green field, in the corner of which stood a table with the apparatus for saying mass spread upon it.

The coffin was then laid down once more, immediately before this temporary altar; and the priest, after having robed himself, the wrong or sable side(130) of the vestments out, as is usual in the case of death, began to celebrate mass for the dead, the congregation all kneeling. When this was finished, the friends of the deceased approached the altar, and after some private conversation,
the priest turned round, and inquired aloud—

"Who will give Offerings?"

The people were acquainted with the manner in which this matter is conducted, and accordingly knew what to do. When the priest put the question, Denis's brother, who was a wealthy man, came forward, and laid down two guineas on the altar; the priest took this up, and putting it on a plate, set out among the multitude, accompanied by two or three of those who were best acquainted with the inhabitants of the parish. He thus continued putting the question, distinctly, after each man had paid; and according as the money was laid down, those who accompanied the priest pronounced the name of the person who gave it, so that all present might hear it. This is also done to enable the friends of the deceased to know not only those who show them this mark of respect, but those who neglect it, in order that they may treat them in the same manner on similar occasions. The amount of money so received is very great; for there is a kind of emulation among the people, as to who will act with most decency and spirit, that is exceedingly beneficial to the priest. In such instances the difference of religion is judiciously over-looked; for although the prayers of Protestants are declined on those occasions, yet it seems the same objection does not hold good against their money, and accordingly they pay as well as the rest. When the priest came round to where I stood, he shook hands with my brother, with whom he appeared to be on very friendly and familiar terms; he and I were then introduced to

John W. Hurley

each other.

"Come," said he, with a very droll(131) expression of countenance, shaking the plate at the same time up near my brother's nose—"Come, Mr. D'Arcy, down with your offerings, if you wish to have a friend with St. Peter when you go as far as the gates; down with your money, sir, and you shall be remembered, depend upon it."

"Ah!" said my brother, pulling out a guinea, "I would with the greatest pleasure; but I fear this guinea is not orthodox. I'm afraid it has the heretical mark upon it."

"In that case," replied his reverence laughing heartily, "your only plan is to return it to the bosom of the church, by laying it on the plate here—it will then be within the pale,(132) you know."
This reply produced a great deal of good-humour among that part of the crowd which immediately surrounded them—not excepting his nearest relations, who laughed heartily.

"Well," said my brother, as he laid it on the plate, "how many prayers will you offer up in my favour for this?"

"Leave that to myself," said his Reverence, looking at the money; "it will be before you, I say, when you go to St. Peter."

He then held the plate over to me in a droll manner; and I added another guinea to my brother's gift; for which I had the satisfaction of having my name called out so loud, that it might be heard a quarter of a mile off.

"God bless you, sir," said the priest, "and I thank you."

"John," said I, when he left us, "I think that is a pleasant, and rather a sensible man?"

"He's as jovial a soul," replied my brother, "as ever gave birth to a jest, and he sings a right good song. Many a convivial hour have he and I spent together; and a more hospitable man besides, never yet existed. Although firmly attached to his own religion, he is no bigot; but, on the contrary, an excellent, liberal, and benevolent man."

When the offerings were all collected, he returned to the altar, repeated a few additional prayers in prime style—as rapid as lightning; and after hastily shaking the holy water on the crowd, the funeral moved on. It was now two o'clock, the day clear and frosty, and the sun unusually bright for the season. During mass, many were added to those who formed the funeral train at the outset; so that, when we got out upon the road, the procession appeared very large. After this, few or none joined it; for it is esteemed by no means "dacent" to do so after mass, because, in that case, the matter is ascribed to an evasion of the offerings; but those whose delay has not really been occasioned by this motive, make it a point to pay them at the grave-yard, or after the interment, and sometimes even on the following day—so jealous are the peasantry of having any degrading suspicion attached to their generosity.

The order of the funeral now was as follows:—Foremost the women—next to them the corpse, surrounded by the relations—the eldest son, in deep affliction, "led the coffin," as chief mourner, holding in his hand the corner of a sheet or piece of linen, fastened to the mort-cloth,(133) called moor-cloth. After the coffin came those who were on foot, and in the rear were the equestrians.(134) When we were a quarter of a mile from the churchyard, the funeral was met by a dozen of singing-boys, belonging to a chapel choir, which the priest, who was fond of music, had some time before formed. They fell in, two by two, immediately behind the corpse, and commenced singing the Requiem, or Latin hymn for the dead.

The scene through which we passed at this time, though not clothed with the verdure and luxuriant beauty of summer, was, nevertheless, marked by that solemn and decaying splendour which characterises a fine country, lit up by the melancholy light of a winter setting sun. It was, therefore, much more in character with the occasion. Indeed I felt it altogether beautiful; and, as the "dying day-hymn stole aloft," the dim sun-beams fell, through a vista of naked motionless trees, upon the coffin, which was borne with a slower and more funereal pace than before, in a manner that threw a solemn and visionary light upon the whole procession. This, however, was raised to something dreadfully impressive, when the long train, thus proceeding with a motion so mournful, was seen, each, or at least the majority of them, covered with a profusion of crimson ribbons, to indicate that the corpse they bore owed his death to a deed of murder.(135) The circumstance of the sun glancing his rays upon the coffin was not unobserved by the peasantry, who considered it as a good omen to the spirit of the departed.

As we went up the street which had been the scene of the quarrel that proved so fatal to Kelly, the coffin was again laid down on the spot where he received his death-blow; and, as was usual, the wild and melancholy keene was raised. My brother saw many of Grime's friends among the spectators, but he himself was not visible. Whether Kelly's party saw them or not, we could not say; if they did, they seemed not to notice them, for no expression of revenge or indignation escaped them.

At length, we entered the last receptacle of the dead. The coffin was now placed upon the shoulders of the son and brothers of the deceased, and borne round the churchyard; whilst the priest, with his stole upon him, preceded it, reading prayers for the eternal repose of the soul. Being then laid beside the grave, a "De profundis" was repeated by the priest and the mass-server; after which a portion of fresh clay, carried from the fields, was brought to his Reverence, who read a prayer over it, and consecrated it.

This is a ceremony which is never omitted at the interment of a Roman Catholic. When it was over, the coffin was lowered into the grave, and the blessed clay shaken over it. The priest now took the shovel in his own hands, and threw in the three first shovelsful—one in the name of the Father, one in the name of the Son, and one in the name of the Holy Ghost. The sexton then took it, and in a short time Denis Kelly was fixed for ever in his narrow bed. While these ceremonies were going forward, the churchyard presented a characteristic picture. Beside the usual groups who straggle through the place, to amuse themselves by reading the inscriptions on the tombs, you might see many individuals kneeling on particular graves, where some relation lay—for the benefit of whose soul they offered up their prayers with an attachment and devotion which one cannot but admire. Sometimes all the surviving members of the family would assemble, and repeat a Rosary for the same purpose.

Again, you might see an unhappy woman beside a newly-made grave, giving way to lamentation and sorrow for the loss of a husband, or of some beloved child. Here, you might observe the "last bed" ornamented with hoops, decked in white paper, emblematic of the virgin innocence of the individual who slept below;—there, a little board-cross informing you that "this monument was erected by a disconsolate husband to the memory of his beloved wife." But that which excited greatest curiosity was a sycamore tree, which grew in the middle of the burying-ground.

It is necessary to inform the reader, that in Ireland many of the churchyards are exclusively appropriated to the interment of Roman Catholics, and, consequently, the corpse of no one who had been a Protestant would be permitted to pollute or desecrate them. This was one of them: but it appears that, by some means or other, the body of a Protestant had been interred in it—and hear the consequence! The next morning heaven marked its disapprobation of this awful visitation by a miracle; for, ere the sun rose from the east, a full-grown sycamore had shot up out of the heretical grave, and stands there to this day, a monument at once of the profanation and its consequence. Crowds were looking at this tree, feeling a kind of awe, mingled with wonder, at the deed which drew down such a visible and lasting mark of God's displeasure. On the tombstones near Kelly's grave, men and women were seated, smoking tobacco to their very heart's content; for, with that profusion which characterises the Irish in everything, they had brought out large quantities of tobacco, whiskey, and bunches of pipes. On such occasions it is the custom for those who attend the wake or the funeral to bring a full pipe home with them; and it is expected that, as often as it is used, they will remember to say, "God be merciful to the soul of him that this pipe was over."

The crowd, however, now began to disperse; and the immediate friends of the deceased sent the priest, accompanied by Kelly's brother, to request that we would come in, as the last mark of respect to poor Denis's memory, and take a glass of wine and a cake.

"Come, Toby," said my brother, " we may as well go in, as it will gratify them ; we need not make much delay, and we will still be at home in sufficient time for dinner."

"Certainly you will," said the Priest; " for you shall both come and dine with me to-day."

"With all my heart," said my brother; "I have no objection, for I know you give it good."

When we went in, the punch was already reeking from immense white jugs, that couldn't hold less than a gallon each.

" Now," said his Reverence, very properly, " you have had a decent and creditable funeral, and have managed every thing with great pro-

John W. Hurley

priety; let me request, therefore, that you will not get drunk, nor permit yourselves to enter into any disputes or quarrels; but be moderate in what you take, and go home peaceably."

"Why, thin, your Reverence," replied the widow, "he's now in his grave, and, thank God, it's he that had the decent funeral all out—ten good gallons did we put over you, astore,(136) and it's yourself that liked the decent thing, any how—but sure, Sir, it would shame him where he's lyin', if we disregarded him so far as to go home widout bringing in our friends, that didn't desert us in our throuble, an' thratin' them for their kindness."

While Kelly's brother was filling out all their glasses, the priest, my brother, and I, were taking a little refreshment. When the glasses were filled, the deceased's brother raised his in his hand, and said,—

"Well, gintlemen," addressing us, "I hope you'll pardon me for not dhrinking your healths first; but people, you know, can't break through an ould custom, at any rate—so I give poor Denis's health that's in his warm grave, and God be marciful to his sowl."(137)

The priest now winked at me to give them their own way; so we filled our glasses, and joined the rest in drinking "Poor Denis's health, that's now in his warm grave, and God be merciful to his soul."
When this was finished, they then drank ours, and thanked us for our kindness in attending the funeral. It was now past five o'clock; and we left them just setting into a hard bout of drinking, and rode down to his Reverence's residence.

"I saw you smile," said he, on our way, "at the blundering toast of Mat Kelly; but it would be labour in vain to attempt setting them right. What do they know about the distinctions of more refined life? Besides, I maintain, that what they said was as well calculated to express their affection, as if they had drunk honest Denis's memory. It is, at least, unsophisticated. But did you hear," said he, "of the apparition that was seen last night, on the mountain road above Denis's?"

"I did not hear of it," I replied, equivocating a little.

"Why," said he, "it is currently reported that the spirit of a murdered pedlar, which haunts the hollow of the road at Drumfurrar bridge,(138) chased away the two servant men as they were bringing home the coffin, and that finding it a good fit, he got into it, and walked half a mile along the road, with the wooden surtout upon him; and, finally, that to wind up the frolic, he left it on one end half-way between the bridge and Denis's house, after putting a crowd of the countrymen to flight. I suspect some droll knave has played them a trick. I assure you, that a deputation of them, who declared that they saw the coffin move along of itself, waited upon me this morning, to know whether they ought to have put him into the coffin, or gotten another."

"Well," said my brother, in reply to him, "after dinner we will probably throw some light upon that circumstance; for I believe my brother here knows something about it."

"So, sir," said the priest, "I perceive you have been amusing yourself at their expense?"

I seldom spent a pleasanter evening than I did with Father Molloy (so he was called), who was, as my brother said, a shrewd, sensible man, possessed of convivial powers of the first order. He sang us several good songs; and, to do him justice, he had an excellent voice. He regretted very much the state of party and religious feeling, which be did every thing in his power to suppress.

"But," said he, "I have little co-operation in my efforts to communicate knowledge to my flock, and implant better feelings among them. You must know," he added, "that I am no great favourite with them. On being appointed to this parish by my bishop, I found that the young man who was curate to my predecessor, had formed a party against me, thinking, by that means, eventually to get the parish himself. Accordingly, on coming here, I found the chapel doors closed on me; so that a single individual among them would not recognise me as their proper pastor. By firmness and spirit, however, I at length succeeded, after a long struggle against the influence of the curate, in gaining admission to the altar; and, by a proper representation of his conduct to the bishop, I soon made my gentleman knock under.(139) Although beginning to gain ground in the good opinion of the people, I am by no means yet a favourite. The curate and I scarcely speak; but I hope that in the course of time, both he and they will begin to find, that by kindness and a sincere love for their welfare on my part, good-will and affection will ultimately be established among us. At least, there shall be nothing left undone so far as I am concerned to effect

John W. Hurley

it."

It was now near nine o'clock, and my brother was beginning to relate an anecdote concerning the clergyman who had preceded Father Molloy in the parish, when a messenger from Mr. Wilson, already alluded to, came up in breathless haste, requesting the priest, for God's sake, to go down into town instantly, as the Kellys and the Grimeses were engaged in a fresh quarrel.

"My God!" he exclaimed—"when will this work have an end? But, to tell you the truth, gentlemen, I apprehended it; and I fear that something still more fatal to the parties will yet be the consequence. Mr. D'Arcy, you must try what you can do with the Grimeses, and I will manage the Kellys."

We then proceeded to the town, which was but a very short distance from the Priest's house; and, on arriving, found a large crowd before the door of the house in which the Kellys had been drinking, engaged in hard conflict. The priest was on foot, and had brought his whip with him, it being an argument, in the hands of a Roman Catholic pastor, which tells so home that it is seldom gainsaid.(140) Mr. Molloy and my brother now dashed in amongst them; and by remonstrance, abuse, blows, and entreaty, they with difficulty succeeded in terminating the fight. They were also assisted by Mr. Wilson and other persons, who dared not, until their appearance, run the risk of interfering between them. Wilson's servant, who had come for the priest, was still standing beside me, looking on; and, while my brother and Mr. Molloy were separating the parties, I asked him how the fray commenced.

"Why, Sir," said he, "it bein' market-day, the Grimeses chanced to be in town, and this came to the ears of the Kellys, who were drinking in Cassidy's here, till they got tipsy; some of them then broke out, and began to go up and down the street, shouting for the face of a murdhering Grimes. The Grimeses, Sir, happened at the time to be drinking with a parcel of their friends in Joe Sherlock's, and hearing the Kellys calling out for them, why, as the dhrop,Sir, was in on both sides,(141) they were soon at it. Grimes has given one of the Kellys a great bating; but Tom Grogan, Kelly's cousin, a little before we came down, I'm tould, has knocked the seven senses out of him, with a pelt of a brick-bat(142) in the stomach."

Soon after this, however, the quarrel was got under; and, in order to prevent any more bloodshed that night, my brother and I got the Kellys together, and brought them as far as our residence, on their way home. As they went along, they uttered awful vows, and determinations of the deepest revenge, swearing repeatedly, that they would shoot Grimes from behind a ditch, if they could not in any other manner have his blood. They seemed highly intoxicated; and several of them were cut and abused in a dreadful manner; even the women were in such a state of excitement and alarm, that grief for the deceased was, in many instances, forgotten. Several of both sexes were singing; some laughing with triumph at the punishment they had inflicted on the enemy; others of them, softened by what they had drunk, were weeping in tones of sorrow that might be heard a couple of miles off. Among the latter were many of the men, some of whom, as they staggered along, with their frieze big-coats hanging off one shoulder, clapped their hands, and roared like bulls, as if they intended, by the loudness of their grief then, to compensate for their silence when sober.

It was also quite ludicrous to see the men kissing each other, sometimes in this maudlin(143) sorrow, and at others when exalted into the very madness of mirth. Such as had been cut in the scuffle, on finding the blood trickle down their faces, would wipe it off—then look at it, and break out into a parenthetical volley of curses against the Grimeses; after which, they would resume their grief, hug each other in mutual sorrow, and clap their hands as before. In short, such a group could be seen no where but in Ireland. When my brother and I had separated from them. I asked him what had become of Vengeance, and if he were still in the country.

"No," said he; "with all his courage and watchfulness, he found that his life was not safe; he, accordingly, sold off his property, and collecting all his ready cash, emigrated to America, where, I hear, he is doing well."

"God knows," I replied, "I shouldn't be surprised if one half of the population were to follow his example, for the state of society here, among the lower orders, is truly deplorable." "Ay, but you are to consider now," he replied, "that you have been looking at the worst of it. If you pass an unfavourable opinion upon our countrymen when in

John W. Hurley

the public-house or the quarrel, you ought to remember what they are under their own roofs, and in all the relations of private life."

The "Party Fight," described in the foregoing sketch, is unhappily no fiction, and it is certain that there are thousands still alive who have good reason to remember it. Such a fight, or I should rather say battle—for such in fact it was—did not take place in a state of civil society, if I can say so, within the last half century in this country. The preparations for it were secretly being made for two or three months previous to its occurrence, and however it came to light, it so happened that each party became cognizant of the designs of the other. This tremendous conflict, of which I was an eye-witness,—being then but about twelve years of age—took place in the town, or rather city, of Clogher, in my native county of Tyrone. The reader may form an opinion of the bitterness and ferocity with which it was fought on both sides when he is informed that the Orangemen on the one side, and the Ribbonmen on the other, had called in aid from the surrounding counties of Monaghan, Cavan, Fermanagh, and Derry; and, if I mistake not, also from Louth. In numbers, the belligerents could not have been less than from four to five thousand men. The fair day on which it occurred is known simply as "the Day of the great Fight."

The cemetary.

John W. Hurley

ENDNOTES

Chapter 1: The Battle Of The Factions

(1) keep him in wind—Keep his mouth from drying out so that he can keeptalking.

(2) Ciceronian—Cicero was a famous Latin orator whom even the Irish school children of Carleton's generation would have been familiar with.

(3) Cork-red phatie—A kind of potato common in Ireland, which has a red skin.

(4) bulliah battha—Carleton says: "Literally, a stroke of cudgel; put for cudgel-player." From Irish "bualadh-bata" or "buillebata", literally a fight with sticks; it also means, (as here), a "cudgel-player". From Irish "bualadh", "striking" and "bata", a "stick".

(5) the hard frost—The hard frost was a very bad winter storm which was famous throughout Ireland in the 19th century. In Ireland, country people often used to reckon historical events in relation to famous and unusual meteorological events.

(6) lost a grinder—Lost a tooth.

(7) a tip—A strike.

(8) phaties—"Praties" or "potatoes", from Irish "práta".

(9) Pastorini nor Columbkill—In 19th century Ireland various prophesies circulated among the people which claimed to foretell the resurrection of the Irish people and the downfall of the English. These prophesies were attributed to St. Columbkill and a man named Pastorini.

(10) Brehon Code—From Irish "breitheamh" for "judge". The old Irish law code which had its origins in the pre-Christian law code of the Druidic Order. Carleton says: "this was the old code of law peculiar to Ireland before the introduction of English legislation into it."

(11) Psalters—Carleton says: "There were probably only two Psalters, those of Tara and Cashel. The Psalters were collections of genealogical history, partly in verse; from which latter circumstance they had their name."

(12) the Flood—As with the hard frost, the Flood was a great torrent of rain which wreaked havoc in the Irish countryside, and was remembered 200 years after.

(13) berrin—A "burying" or funeral.

(14) striking their heels against their hams—The Irish had a way of jumping high up in the air and hitting their thighs with their heels; in the stage Irishman stereotype, this evolved into the Irishman "clicking his heels". In the phrase used here by Carleton, their "hams" are their thighs.

(15) timourous—Fearful. Bailiffs, proctors and stewards collected rents for the landlords. If a bailiff, proctor or steward tried to collect rents from the O'Hallaghans, he was likely to get his house burned down and himself killed.

(16) matrimonial concatenation—Matrimonial link. The kidnapping of girls for marriage was a common practice of the Whiteboys, and Carleton's mention of this means in effect, that the O'Hallaghans were Whiteboys or possibly Caravats.

(17) the bad drop—A "drop" was a strain of any kind 'running in the blood'. A man inclined to evil ways 'has a bad drop' or 'a black drop' in him; a miser 'has a hard drop'. The expression carries an idea of heredity.

(18) disembogued—Poured.

(19) the march ditch, or merin—The border. This may come from the fact that in ancient times, ditches which were created as defensive borders were patrolled or "marched" along, hence a "march ditch".

(20) gorsoons—A young boy, possibly from French "garçon", but also from Irish "gas" a stem or stalk.

(21) vagating—Wandering.

(22) pastured—Grazed.

(23) houghed and mutilated each other's cattle—To hough cattle meant to cut the ligaments of the cow so that they could no longer stand. Destroying property and killing and mutilating cattle in such a way was usually how Whiteboys delivered warnings to their enemies.

(24) stultity—Craziness or foolishness.

(25) retrograde—They were somewhat opposed to using the law and would also have rather fought it out.

(26) horpus corpus—Latin "habeas corpus", but "horpus corpus" was the common pronunciation amongst the Irish peasantry in Carleton's time.

(27) potation—A friendly drink between us.

John W. Hurley

(28) afflatus—In this instance "afflatus" means a breath.

(29) seriatim—In a series. The Stations of the Cross are laid out in a series.

(30) Fourteen—These are called the "Fourteen Stations of the Cross".

(31) Stentorian lungs, some melodia sacra—Stentor was a Greek herald in the Trojan War. He had a loud voice, and a "stentorian" voice, would be a loud one. A "melodia sacra" is a "sacred melody" or song.

(32) paudareens—Rosary beads. From Irish "paidrín", the Rosary. In this case Carleton mentions how a man might tie an amber bead to his rosary, and lift a light bit of straw by the alleged force of its attraction, as if the bead were a sacred or magical relic. As Carleton says: "Pilgrims and other impostors pass these things upon the people as miracles upon a small scale."

(33) Nosegays—A small bunch of flowers.

(34) heusteron proteron—An Hiberno-Latin term similar to our modern term "cruisin' for a bruisin'". Literally it means something like "hello there destruction".

(35) you persave—You understand.

(36) out—This expression in remote parts of the country was understood to mean being at mass.

(37) troth—Truth.

(38) Paddy Mellon—According to Carleton: "Paddy Mellon—a short, thickset man, with grey hair, which he always kept cropped close—was the most famous shoemaker in the parish; in fact, the Drummond of a large district. No shoes were considered worth wearing if he did not make them. But, having admitted this, I am bound in common justice and honesty to say that so big a liar never put an awl into leather. No language could describe his iniquity in this respect. I myself am a living witness of this. Many a trudge has the villain taken out of me in my boyhood, and as sure as I went on the appointed day—which was always Saturday—so surely did he swear that they would be ready for me on that day week. He was, as a tradesman, the most multifarious and barefaced liar I ever met, and what was the most rascally trait about him, was the faculty he possessed of making you believe the lie as readily after the fifteenth repetition of it, as when it was uttered fresh from his lips."

(39) duck-nebs—Wide in the front of the shoe.

(40) a-hagur—Or "ahaygar" from Irish "a théagair" meaning "my friend" or "my dear". The vocative of Irish "téagur", "love", "a dear person".

(41) Arrah—An Irish language expression used like our "now": "Now how could I guess, woman alive?"

(42) musha—Sometimes spelt "mossa". This is a sort of assertive particle used at the opening of a sentence, like the English "well, indeed" and carrying little or no meaning. 'Do you like your new house?' 'Mossa I don't like it much.' Another form of "wisha", and both anglicized from the Irish "má'seadh", or "muise" used in Irish in much the same sense.

(43) flipe—One who is "flippant", or disrespectful.

(44) a shift on a Maypowl—A woman's slip tied on a Maypole. On May 1st, Irish Mayday celebrations included raising the Maypole and tying various ribbons to it. A shift would not sit well on a Maypole and would look ridiculous.

(45) Manwill—"Manual", a Catholic prayer book.

(46) Purcession—According to Carleton: "The Procession of the Host. A Catholic tradition where the Consecrated Host, enshrined in a silver vessel formed like a chalice, was borne by a priest under a silken canopy; and to this the other clergymen present offered up incense from a censer, while they circumambulated the chapel inside and out, (if the weather was good)."

(47) confabulation—Conversation.

(48) antipodial—Directly opposite.

(49) gingham—Clothing fabric of yarn-dyed cotton in plain weave.

(50) bad cess—Bad luck.

(51) Ay, faix—"Yes, fách" or "Faith", a 19th century Hiberno-Irish expression close to our modern "Well now", as in "Well now, I wouldn't agree with that". In Irish "fách" literally means "in favor of ".

(52) scroodgin—Also "skroodging"; the pressure in a crowd.

(53) Moroky blacks—This seems to be another type of potato.

(54) Authorised Version—This is short for "the Authorized Version of the Bible".

(55) megrim—Vertigo or dizziness.

(56) terra firma—Latin for "solid ground".

John W. Hurley

(57) slipped the knot of his cravat—He untied his "cravat" or necktie. John O'Callaghan seems to have anticipated someone falling in the river and was preparing for that when Rose fell in.

(58) engulphed—Engulfed.

(59) ma bouchal—From Irish "mo buachaill", "my boy".

(60) Colleen Galh—From Irish "Cailín Geal" or "fair girl".

(61) penultimately amalgamated—Finally united as one.

(62) pell-mell—Fighting in disordered confusion.

(63) when the drop was in, and the spirits up—When a drop of alcohol was taken in, the spirits of the fighters were up.

(64) apt to fly—Likely to break.

(65) kippeen—Any little bit of a stick; often used as a sort of pet name for a formidable cudgel or shillelagh for fighting. From Irish "cip", a stake or stock, with the diminutive.

(66) scythe, flail, spade—The scythe, flail and spade were common farm implements also used as weaponry by the Irish. The spade is a particular type of Irish shovel with a long shaft and a thin blade. The flail was used for threshing and is longer than but similar to the Okinawan nunchaku. The scythe was used for harvesting crops but is best known today as the weapon of the "Grim Reaper".

(67) desultory skrimmages—Fights not connected with the main fight.

(68) Orangemen and Ribbonmen—Those Irish secret societies of the 19th century which were sectarian in nature, were divided into the two basic polarities of "Na Buachaillín Bána" or Roman Catholic "Whiteboys" and Freemasonic Protestant "Orangemen". While the Whiteboys were never truly sectarian (as there were Protestant members), the "Ribbonmen" were a specifically Catholic organization which evolved out of the Whiteboy movement and which predominated in the north and northwest of Ireland. The Whiteboys have evolved into various non-sectarian but political organizations, and as an Irish military force evolved into the Irish Republican Army. The Orange Order is still in existence as one of the many heavily armed Protestant secret societies. It is alleged by Irish Catholics that many of its members collude with British security forces to rig much of the politics of the Northern Irish State and to orchestrate most of the anti-Catholic terrorist attacks in the Northern Irish State. Despite years of protestations to the contrary, it has become evident in

recent years that many Orangemen are indeed members of the para-military police force, the Royal Ulster Constabulary, and hence are able to carry out sectarian attacks against Catholics without detection, or are able to do so in collusion with Protestant death squads or with any of the death squads which seem to exist among the British security forces. It was actually members of Protestant secret societies who carried out the first sectarian murders against Catholics in 1966 which initiated the current period of "Troubles" in Northern Ireland.

(69) the musket or the bayonet—Party Fighting involved clashes of Catholics against Protestants, often with Protestants owning and using guns in the battles. See Chapter 3, The Party Fight And Funeral.

(70) acumen—In this case the point, apex or height of his enjoyment.

(71) mollify—Soften.

(72) Maybe the songs and the shouting—The factions each had their own slogans and war songs, many of which still exist today.

(73) garran—Irish "garrán", a grove. But according to Carleton: "A horse; but it was always used as meaning a bad one—one without mettle. When figuratively applied to a man, it means a coward." When speaking of the "Garrán bán" Carleton says: "The white horse, i.e. be wanting in mettle. Tradition affirms that James the Second escaped on a white horse from the Battle of the Boyne; and from circumstance a white horse has become the emblem of cowardice."

(74) play a stave—This is a play on words between a stave being a fighting stick and the musical "staves" used to show notes on sheet music.

(75) not up—Not initiated into Whiteboyism.

(76) huzza—"Hurrah!"

(77) caubeens—From Irish "cáibín"; an old Irish shabby cap or hat.

(78) tattered frieze—Irish overcoats were made from frieze which is a heavy wool material. In this case a "tattered frieze" means a ragged, torn coat.

(79) home-made—Irish frieze was mostly manufactured at home, which accounts for the expression here.

(80) shillely—Shillelagh. A handstick of oak, an oaken cudgel for fighting, common all over Ireland. It is mistakenly claimed that the name came from a district in Wicklow called Shillelagh, formerly noted for its oak woods "in which grand shil-

John W. Hurley

lelahs were plentiful". The word actually comes from "Sail-éille", a "thonged cud-gel" or "(Bata) Siúil-éille" a "thonged walking (stick)".

(81) avourneen—"My love"; the vocative case of Irish "muirnín", a sweetheart, a loved person.

(82) avick—From Irish "a mhic" meaning "my son" in the vocative.

(83) Tunder-an'-ouns!—An exclamation in Irish possibly from "teann tar anonnse" meaning literally "strength come over". Elsewhere Carleton uses the exclamation "thunder-an'- lightnin'!" and here "tunder" may simply mean "thunder".

(84) this stick has the lead in it—The stick had had a hole drilled in the end which was filled with molten lead, adding to the force of the blow.

(85) By the powdhers—"By the powers". An oath meaning something like "by the power of God". A Dubliner might say "Be Jaysus" (By Jesus), meaning the same thing.

(86) tare-an-ounty—An exclamation in Irish possibly from "tar anonn te" meaning literally "come over hot", and in context "come on and fight".

(87) four pounder—The first rock weighing four pounds that she finds.

(88) cake—Harden.

(89) spalpeens—From the Irish word "spailpín". Spalpeens were laboring men—reapers, mowers, potato-diggers, etc.—who traveled about in the autumn seeking employment from the farmers, each with his spade, or his scythe, or his reaping hook. They congregated in the towns on market and fair days, where the farmers of the surrounding districts came to hire them. Each farmer brought home his own men, fed them on good potatoes and milk, and sent them to sleep in the barn on dry straw, a bed—as one of them said—'a bed fit for a lord, let alone a spalpeen'. The word "spalpeen" came to be used in the sense of a low rascal.

(90) brick-bat—A piece or chunk of brick, rock or cobblestone.

(91) shillelaghs—Also "shillelahs". A handstick of oak, an oaken cudgel for fight-ing, common all over Ireland. It is mistakenly claimed that the name came from a district in Wicklow called Shillelagh, formerly noted for its oak woods "in which grand shillelahs were plentiful". The word actually comes from "Sailéille", a "thonged cudgel" or "(Bata) Siúil-éille" a "thonged walking (stick)".

(92) videlicet—From French, meaning "that is to say".

(93) asseverated—Asserted.

(94) Neal Malone—Neal Malone is the tailor for the O'Callaghan side, and is the main character of the Carleton story Neal Malone.

(95) good man—A brave man. According to Carleton: "He was a man of huge size and prodigious strength and died in consequence of an injury he received in lifting one of the cathedral bells of Clogher, which is said to be ten hundredweight."

(96) weeshy—Small, little.

(97) the mealy collar of his waistcoat—Mealy can mean both soft or pale in color. A waistcoat is a vest.

(98) gudgeon—A gudgeon is a small fish often used for bait when fishing.

(99) annigulate—Annihilate. According to Carleton: "Many of the jawbreakers— and this was one in a double sense—used by the hedge-schoolmasters, are scattered among the people, by whom they are so twisted that it would be extremely difficult to recognize them."

(100) dhuragh—An Irish expression meaning, according to Carleton: "An additional portion of anything thrown in from a spirit of generosity, after the measure agreed on is given. When the miller, for instance, receives his toll, the country people usually throw in several handsful of meal as Dhuragh."

(101) murther sheery—From "murder síoraí" literally "eternal murders" but in another story Carleton translates it as "murder everlasting".

(102) Murther-an-age—An exclamation in Irish possibly from English "murder" and Irish "an aghaidh", "against" meaning "against murder".

(103) Nebuchodonosor—Nebuchadnezzar is a figure from the Bible who was said to be King of Babylon and conqueror of Jerusalem, and hence a kind of bully.

(104) Sampson—Another biblical giant.

(105) the milling style—This was a common 18th and 19th century pseudonym for boxing, with boxers often being called "millers" as part of the slang of "the Fancy"— the crowd of "fans" (many of whom were Irish stick-fighters and wrestlers) who followed boxing. Probably from Irish "milleadh", "destruction", "to destroy".

(106) dusted—"Knocked out" or "knocked down" and into the "dust".

(107) not pretermitting—"Not to mention".

John W. Hurley

(108) broken-paled—A "pale" is a stick, so "broken-paled" means "those with broken sticks".

(109) trickling sconces—Heads which, having been hit in the fighting, were bleeding or trickling with blood.

Chapter 2: Neal Malone

(1) cross-legged corporation—Tailors often sat with their legs crossed as they worked.

(2) breeches-maker—Pants maker or tailor.

(3) eschewed inexpressibles—Went without underwear.

(4) Jupiter's frieze jocks—The wool underwear of the god Jupiter.

(5) Patagonians—Patagonia is a region of South America mostly in Argentina but partly in Chile.

(6) Con of the Hundred Battles—Conn Cét Chathach, a legendary Irish military hero who was High King at Tara in 122 A.D.

(7) the first cudgel-players and pugilists of the parish—That is, the "best" of the parish.

(8) fourteen stone weight—There are 14 pounds in one "stone", so 14 stone would be 196 pounds. He was trying to provoke men much larger than himself.

(9) cuticle remained undiscoloured—Head remained unbloodied.

(10) Blur-an'-agers—An exclamation in Irish possibly "blúire an aghaidhse" from "blúire" a "bit, fragment, scrap" and "an aghaidh", "against" meaning "against a bit".

(11) spalpeen—From the Irish word "spailpín". Spalpeens were laboring men— reapers, mowers, potato-diggers, etc.—who traveled about in the autumn seeking employment from the farmers, each with his spade, or his scythe, or his reaping hook. They congregated in the towns on market and fair days, where the farmers of the surrounding districts came to hire them. Each farmer brought home his own men, fed them on good potatoes and milk, and sent them to sleep in the barn on dry straw, a bed—as one of them said—'a bed fit for a lord, let alone a spalpeen'. The word "spalpeen" came to be used in the sense of a low rascal.

(12) I'm blue-mowlded for want of a batin'!—"I'm desperate for a fight!"

(13) traneen—A long slender grass-stalk, like knitting-needle. Used here like "I don't give a damn".

(14) Hotspur, and went to buffets one hand against the other—Hotspur was the nickname of Sir Henry Percy, a character from Shakespeare's play Henry IV. A "Hotspur" has since come to mean a hot-headed person. "Went to buffets" means "went to blows" or "went to punching", as a "buffet" is a blow with the fist.

(15) was ready to support him—Ready to fight for him.

(16) a martial tailor—A fighting tailor.

(17) kippeen—Any little bit of a stick; often used as a sort of pet name for a formidable cudgel or shillelagh for fighting. From Irish "cip", a stake or stock, with the diminutive.

(18) warrior—The formidable or intimidating nature of a warrior.

(19) It affected his cutting out!—It affected his ability in cutting out material for clothes.

(20) lap-board—One of the tools of a tailor.

(21) hot goose—The iron of a tailor had a long curved handle which resembled a gooses neck.

(22) pacific state—Peaceful state.

(23) bloodletting—An obsolete medical procedure, where the patient was made to bleed in order to reduce blood pressure and thus balance the "bodily humors".

(24) dastardly phlebotomy—"Evil bloodletting", meaning evil in that it would rob Neal of the chance to bleed as a result of fighting.

(25) Tare-an'-ounze!—An exclamation in Irish possibly from "tar anonnse" meaning literally "come over", and in context "come on and fight".

(26) Skiomachia—In Latin "scio" means "to know" or "to have skill in" and a "machaera" was a single edged sword. A term for a "man to man duel" was a "monomachia" so it's possible that "sciomachia" came to mean training in dueling. In the context of the story it seems to be a 19th century Irish term for "shadowboxing".

(27) come to the scratch—In some older forms of both stick-fighting and boxing, the two fighters would step up to a line where their front foot would be placed, and from which they could not move. The line was called the "scratch" (as in a "scratch" on the ground), and here "come to the scratch" means "come to the fight" or "meet the challenge".

(28) New Burlington-street pathos—This seems to be a reference to a contemporary novel or play of Carleton's day.

(29) affliction of the first water—Normally "first water" would have meant "best" or "purest". In this case it means "greatest" or "biggest"—a really bad affliction.

(30) Are you able to carry a staff still, Neal?—"Are you still able to stick-fight Neal?"

(31) concatenated state—Linked or chained together, as in "ball and chain"

(32) habilaments—Clothes, "habiliments".

(33) escutcheon—Literally a shield with a coat of arms on it. A "blot on his escutcheon" would be a "stain on his honor".

(34) Junius's secret—Junius was a Latin personal name taken from the Roman God "Juno", the sister and wife of Jupiter. She was the goddess of marriage and the Queen of the gods. But Carleton seems to be referring to the unknown writer who penned numerous letters to the papers in the late 18th century which attacked the British government and which were signed "Junius". The identity of the writer was never discovered.

(35) Captain Bobadil—Captain Bobadil is a swashbuckling character in a play called Every Man In His Humour, written by Ben Johnson, a contemporary of Shakespeare. Jack Falstaff and Ensign (or Ancient) Pistol, appear in Shakespeare's Henry IV and The Merry Wives of Windsor.

(36) fortiter in re, at present he was the suaviter in modo—"Really brave, he was lately pleasant."

(37) Iris—Iris was the goddess of the rainbow in Greek mythology.

(38) afflatus—Inspiration; powerful impulse.

(39) Platonism/Socratism—Platonic philosophy is idealistic and somewhat impractical; Socratic philosophy is all practicality and logic.

(40) modern novels—This seems to be a reference to the literary criticism of

Carleton's day.

(41) caveto—Caveat; a warning.

(42) over his cups—Over his drinks, his cups "of alcohol".

(43) Dugald Stewart—The siege of Antwerp took place in 1585. John Locke (1632-1704) was an empirical philosopher and Dugald Stewart (1753-1828) was a philosopher of the Scottish "common sense" school.

(44) science—Biddy was very pugnacious. Throwing in a body blow is just what it says; "plant a facer" is a punch to the face.

(45) Jeremy Taylor—Jeremy Taylor (1613-1667), was a Protestant Anglican bishop and later vice-chancellor of Trinity College Dublin known for his writings on religion, philosophy and ethics.

(46) tête-a-téte—A private conversation. From French "tête-à-tête," literally "head-to-head".

(47) nota bene—"Note well".

(48) shillelahs—Or "shillelaghs". A handstick of oak, an oaken cudgel for fighting, common all over Ireland. It is mistakenly claimed that the name came from a district in Wicklow called Shillelagh, formerly noted for its oak woods "in which grand shillelahs were plentiful". The word actually comes from "Sailéille", a "thonged cudgel" or "(Bata) Siúil-éille" a "thonged walking (stick)".

(49) whetstone—A "whetstone" is the abrasive stone used for sharpening knives. A "termagant" or "quarrelsome" wife is abrasive.

(50) vis vitae—From Latin "life force".

(51) making his own quietus with his bare bodkin—Releasing oneself from life ("committing suicide") by using a pointed tailor's tool usually used for making holes in cloth.

(52) i' the vein—"In the vein". This whole section of the story can be summed up this way: Neal tries to commit suicide but he has such hard luck, that even his body won't help him end his problems. It's meant to be taken comically.

(53) vox et praeterea nihil—From Latin "a voice and henceforth, nothing".

Chapter 3: The Party Fight And Funeral

(1) sine qua non—From Latin "without equal."

(2) parish—A parish is a geographic and organizational district of a church. Under the British government in Ireland, this same area designated a district of the local civil government as well.

(3) hedge-school—Hedgeschools were originally set up as illegal or "underground" schools where the Gaelic-speaking (and Catholic) Irish could get an education. In the 17th century the ancient Irish "Bardic Schools"—in existence as the central institution of Gaelic Irish culture since Druidic, pre-Christian times—were attacked by the English, and the Bardic Scholars persecuted. Just as the Romans had attacked the Druids in Gaul and Britain, so the English attacked the Irish Bards, the remaining vestige of the old Druidic Order in Europe. The Bards took to the hills, continuing to teach their traditional subjects, including a pre-Republican, native Irish Nationalism. In time, these illegal schools came to be known as "hedgeschools" as they often convened out of doors near groves of trees or hidden behind hedges.

(4) builla batthah—From Irish "bualadh-bata" or "buille-bata", literally a fight with sticks; it also means, (as here), a "cudgelplayer". From Irish "bualadh", "striking" and "bata", a "stick".

(5) Parrah Rackhan—"Paddy Riot" or "Paddy the Rioter", from Irish "Pádraig Racán", "Patrick Racket".

(6) caubeen—From Irish "cáibín", an old Irish shabby cap or hat.

(7) vidette, who wanted an arm—I am unable to identify "vidette". "Wanted an arm" means that the little child was missing an arm.

(8) miscaun—A portion of butter, weighing from one pound to six or eight, made in the shape of a prism.

(9) hornpipe—A hornpipe is a kind of Irish dance. Irish folklore taught that on Easter Sunday morning the Sun would dance a hornpipe or jig to celebrate the Resurrection.

(10) cuff one another—Fight one another.

(11) Pierce the gauger—A gauger was an exciseman or sort of tax assessor.

(12) paste up the master's eyes to his bad conduct—"Glue the teacher's eyes shut." The boys in the school were bribing the teacher and the teacher's wife with food

and drink, to avoid getting severe corporal punishment when caught doing something wrong. Those who could not pay were beaten.

(13) seminary—A nickname for a hedge-school.

(14) panegyrist—Poetical praiser.

(15) Lilliputian—From Irish writer Jonathan Swift's Gulliver's Travels; the small (six inches tall) people called the Lilliputs whom Gulliver encounters on an island and are very much like Faction members in disposition and very much like Leprechauns in size. Since his story, the term "Lilliputian" has come to mean a "small person" in the English language.

(16) shillelagh—Or "shillelah". A handstick of oak, an oaken cudgel for fighting, common all over Ireland. It is mistakenly claimed that the name came from a district in Wicklow called Shillelagh, formerly noted for its oak woods "in which grand shillelahs were plentiful". The word actually comes from "Sail-éille", a "thonged cudgel" or "(Bata) Siúil-éille" a "thonged walking (stick)".

(17) horse-dunghill—A mound of horse manure was (and in many places still is) used for fertilizer on farms. The process of wrapping the stick in paper while soaking it in oil and placing it in the dunghill was meant to help make the stick flexible so that it could be shaped. The dunghill actually creates and gives off heat higher than 98 degrees so it was a perfect source for constant, consistent and cost-free heat.

(18) Gall and Spurzheim—This is a reference to the two men who formulated the pseudo-science of phrenology—reading the bumps on a persons skull in order to learn about that person's level of intelligence and personality traits. The theories of Dr. Franz Joseph Gall (1758-1828) and his assistant Dr. Johann Kaspar Spurzheim (1776-1832), became part of the most popular method of the practice of phrenology.

(19) the three sets of Book-keeping—This seems to be a euphemism for a body of stick-fighting techniques. In The Battle of the Factions, and elsewhere in Carleton's literature, he uses mathematical terms to describe specific stick-fighting techniques.

(20) wealthy farmer—Denis Kelly as the son of a wealthy farmer was part of the Catholic middle-class that gravitated towards Irish nationalism. In a generation, men like Kelly became Fenians and abandoned the divisiveness of faction fighting, exchanging the stick for the gun.

(21) fair, market, or patron—Kelly's "blackthorn ambition", (like that of other Irish stick-fighters), was "expressed" at the fairs, markets and patrons where stick-fights most commonly occurred. A "patron" was a religious festival honoring the local

patron saint of the area; these festivals started with religious devotions such as the Rosary, and were followed by a market fair which often ended with a faction fight.

(22) party quarrel—A faction fight between Catholics and Protestants.

(23) Margamores—From Irish "margadh mór", meaning "great" (or big) markets. The Margamores were held just before special days such as Christmas or Easter, and Carleton says: "There are three of these held before Christmas, and one or two before Easter, to enable the country folks to make their markets, and prepare for them more comfortably celebrating those great convivial festivals. They are almost as numerously attended as fairs; for which reason they are termed 'big markets'."

(24) dark surtout—A long, close-fitting overcoat.

(25) existence!—Here the main character, Toby D'Arcy, is overcoming his child-hood fears about the people of the Sídhe and other folk beliefs common to the Gaelic Irish. As a Protestant convert, Toby uses quotations from the Bible to help reinforce his courage. As we see further on in the story, Irish Catholics in the same position tended to intone Latin prayers.

(26) obstupui—Stupefication, amazement, astonishment.

(27) tergiversation—Evasion or flight.

(28) pusillanimous—Lacking courage or resolve; cowardly.

(29) persons—This was part of Irish fairy lore, but it was also a common practice of Whiteboys and other Irish secret societies to post illustrations of coffins on the doors of their enemies. It's possible that in some cases they constructed actual coffins for the same purpose.

(30) Manlm a Yea agus a wurrah!—"M'anam a Dhia agus a Mhuire!"—"My soul to God and the Virgin!"

(31) Dher a larna heena—Carleton says: "By the very book—meaning the bible, which, in 19th century Irish, was not simply called the book, but the very book, or the book itself."

(32) home—Toby D'Arcy mentioned earlier that his coat and hat were black and that they covered him completely. This gave the appearance to those on the bridge that he was a headless spirit.

(33) arrah—An Irish language expression used like our "now": "Now how could I guess, woman alive?"

(34) Eman Dhu—Irish, "Éamann Dubh", "Black Eamann" or "Black Edmund".

(35) Scapular—According to Carleton: "The scapular is one of the highest religious orders, and is worn by both priest and layman. It is considered by the people a safeguard against evil, both spiritual and physical."

(36) confeethur—Carleton says: "The Confiteor is a prayer, or rather a general confession of sin, said by the penitent on going to confess his offences to the priest."

(37) omadhaun—Irish "amádan", a fool.

(38) sarve mass—According to Carleton: "The person who serves Mass, as it is called, is he who makes responses to the priest during that ceremony. As the mass is said in Latin the serving of it must necessarily fall upon many who are ignorant of that language, and whose pronunciation of it is, of course, extremely ludicrous."

(39) bedewed—Covered himself with the holy water as if it were dew.

(40) ague fit—An "ague fit" is a fit of shivering. The character is stuttering his Latin ("Dom-i-n-us vo-bis-cum?") in fear as though he has a chill and is shivering.

(41) "Dom-i-n-us vo-bis-cum?" "Et cum spiritu tuo."—Latin for "Lord be with you?"; "And with your spirit too."

(42) Scapularian—One who wears the Scapular.

(43) Father Feasthalagh's—In another story by Carleton he defines "feasthalagh" as "nonsense".

(44) Big tare-an'-ouns!—An exclamation in Irish possibly from "beag tar anonnse" meaning "come over (here) a little".

(45) we'd crop the ears off his head—This was a punishment which the Whiteboys and other secret societies inflicted on their enemies.

(46) Orangemen and Whiteboys—Those Irish secret societies of the 19th century which were sectarian in nature, were divided into the two basic polarities of "Na Buachaillí Bána" or Roman Catholic "Whiteboys" and Freemasonic Protestant "Orangemen". While the Whiteboys were never truly sectarian (as there were Protestant members), the "Ribbonmen" were a specifically Catholic organization which evolved out of the Whiteboy movement and which predominated in the north and northwest of Ireland. The Whiteboys have evolved into various non-sectarian but political organizations, and as an Irish military force evolved into the Irish Republican Army. The Orange Order is still in existence as one of the many heavily armed

Protestant secret societies. It is alleged by Irish Catholics that many of its members collude with British security forces to rig much of the politics of the Northern Irish State and to orchestrate most of the anti-Catholic terrorist attacks in the Northern Irish State. Despite years of protestations to the contrary, it has become evident in recent years that many Orangemen are indeed members of the para-military police force, the Royal Ulster Constabulary, and hence are able to carry out sectarian attacks against Catholics without detection, or are able to do so in collusion with Protestant death squads or with any of the death squads which seem to exist among the British security forces. It was actually members of Protestant secret societies who carried out the first murders against Catholics in 1966 which initiated the current period of "Troubles" in Northern Ireland. The difference between "faction-men" and "party-men" was that Faction men would fight other Catholics while Party men would fight Protestants. Some gangs did both, but in general Party men had more nationalistic or "patriotic" political motivations for fighting, while Faction men usually fought over issues of land, labor and class, or family or regional rivalries. Ultimately, most of these were usually economic issues.

(47) the Errigle Slashers—Many Factions and Faction leaders had the nickname "slasher". Some forms of Irish stick-fighting utilize fencing techniques including the "Wheel", "Cut" and "Slash".

(48) manest spalpeen—Here "mane" means "cowardly". "Spalpeen" is from the Irish word "spailpín". Spalpeens were laboring men—reapers, mowers, potato-diggers, etc.—who traveled about in the autumn seeking employment from the farmers, each with his spade, or his scythe, or his reaping-hook. They congregated in the towns on market and fair days, where the farmers of the surrounding districts came to hire them. Each farmer brought home his own men, fed them on good potatoes and milk, and sent them to sleep in the barn on dry straw, a bed—as one of them said—'a bed fit for a lord, let alone a spalpeen'. The word "spalpeen" came to be used in the sense of a low rascal.

(49) souse—Good luck.

(50) acushla—From Irish "a chuisle", usually short for "cushlamochree" or "chuisle mo chroí", a term of endearment meaning "pulse of my heart". "A chuisle" would mean "pulse".

(51) ma bouchal—From Irish "mo buachaill", "my boy".

(52) Wus dha lamh, avick!—give me your hand, my son!—Irish, "Thus do lámh, a mhic!" or "Give me your hand, my son!"

(53) a-hagur—Or "ahaygar" from Irish "a théagair" meaning "my friend" or "my dear". The vocative of Irish "téagur", "love", "a dear person".

(54) buillagh batthah—Though the spelling is a bit different, this is the same as note 4, "builla batthah": From Irish "bualadhbata" or "buille-bata", literally a fight with sticks; it also means, (as here), a "cudgel-player". From Irish "bualadh", "striking" and "bata", a "stick".

(55) avourneen—Irish for "my love"; the vocative case of Irish "muirnín", a sweetheart, a loved person.

(56) catechiz—The Roman Catholic catechism.

(57) agra—A term of endearment meaning "my love"; vocative of Irish "grádh", "love".

(58) bagnet—Bayonet.

(59) I shall not give over—I shall not quit or stop, until I convince you to lead a quiet life.

(60) Musha—Sometimes spelt "mossa". This is a sort of assertive particle used at the opening of a sentence, like the English "well, indeed" and carrying little or no meaning. 'Do you like your new house?' 'Mossa I don't like it much.' Another form of "wisha", and both anglicized from the Irish "má'seadh", or "muise" used in Irish in much the same sense.

(61) Och—From Irish "ochone", "alas", but used in a variety of ways.

(62) Garran-bane—From Irish, "garrán bán". Carleton says: "The white horse, i.e. be wanting in mettle. Tradition affirms that James the Second escaped on a white horse from the Battle of the Boyne; and from circumstance a white horse has become the emblem of cowardice."

(63) coming up to be their match?—Now that the other faction is improving in their ability to fight and are nearly able to match or defeat his faction.

(64) sanguinary feuds—Bloody feuds.

(65) magistrates—One type of the local law authority which existed before the establishment of a constabulary or police force.

(66) threatening notice—The threatening "Notess" or "Notice" posted by "Mat Midnight". This was a common practice of the Whiteboys.

(67) old Nick—The devil.

John W. Hurley

(68) true-blue, sir—a purple man—These terms denote certain stages of initiation into the neo-Masonic system of the Orange Order, with orange, blue, purple and black sashes denoting some of the "degrees" of rank.

(69) ribles—Rebels.

(70) pepper them—Shoot them with buckshot.

(71) chapel-door—In the 19th century a Roman Catholic church was called "the chapel" by Roman Catholics, while a Protestant house of worship was called "a church".

(72) heels foremost—A person with their "heels foremost" or "heels forward" could only be someone lying on their back being carried. This is a metaphor for someone who is dead: "that they might not go home dead".

(73) you had seen something—This phrase means "you look as if you had seen a ghost".

(74) he's down for it "He's in for it" or "he's gonna get it".

(75) Whist—"Silence" or "be silent" from Irish "tost" meaning "silence", with the first "t" aspirated ("thost") which gives it the sound of "wh".

(76) I stole out of the barn—I ran out of the barn. Laboring servants in Ireland (such as spalpeens), usually slept in the barns of those who hired them.

(77) a blast from the fairies—It was (and in some places still is) believed that the people of the Sídhe or "fairies" were capable of inflicting pain, disease and death with a special dart or spear, which was felt by mortals as a blast of wind. Such gusts of wind were called the "Gaoithe Sídhe" or "Fairy Blast".

(78) shuffling—Backpedaling, not taking a stance on your argument, or going back on what you just said and contradicting yourself since your argument is not well thought out.

(79) escaped hemp—Escaped a hemp rope; escaped a hanging.

(80) Do you mind—Do you remember.

(81) the boys—The Whiteboys; in later times, the IRA.

(82) agra machree—Irish, "agrádh mo chroí", "love of my heart".

(83) troth—Truth.

Irish Gangs And Stick-Fighting 189

(84) gorsoon—A young boy, possibly from French "garçon", but also from Irish "gas" a stem or stalk.

(85) I hope your brother's safe, Sir!—Lachlin is saying that he didn't want to get caught up in membership in the Whiteboys, but that he was drafted into it. "I hope your brother's safe Sir", means "I hope I can talk freely in front of your (Protestant) brother here without fear of being arrested for admitting my membership in the Whiteboys".

(86) chivey—Hunt, chase or harass.

(87) war up—That is, had been made members of a secret society.

(88) here upon their keeping, for the murder of a proctor—They were here "on the run" and on their own, for killing a tithe proctor. The tithe system was notoriously sectarian, corrupt, unfair and resented by Catholics. As part of the Penal Laws, all Irish Roman Catholics had to pay tithes to support the Protestant Church of Ireland, (the Anglican Church in Ireland). Under English law Roman Catholicism was illegal the official state religion being the Church of Ireland. Many Protestant ministers were also landlords, and tithe proctors were men hired by the local Anglican clergyman to collect the tithes (or taxes) of the Protestant Church for the clergyman. Tithe Proctors were notoriously corrupt and by today's standards would be something between tax collectors, racketeers and loan sharks. The Tithe Proctors often increased the tithes, keeping the extra money for themselves, and often took advantage of those who owed tithe money by loan sharking and then demanding payment when they knew repayment would be impossible. They could then blackmail the tenant for whatever they wanted or evict them. They were deeply hated by the people.

(89) under boord—Technically, the state of a corpse between death and interment. From the board laid across the chest of a corpse, with a plate of snuff and a Bible or Prayerbook laid on it. According to Carleton, in that part of the country where the scene of the story takes place, "the bodies of those who die are not stretched out on a bed, and the face exposed; on the contrary, they are generally placed on the ground, or in a bed, but with a board resting upon two stools or chairs over them. This is covered with a clean sheet, generally borrowed from some wealthier neighbor; so that the person of the deceased is altogether concealed. Over the sheet upon the board, are placed plates of cut tobacco, pipes, snuff, &c. This is what is meant by being 'undher boord'. It is a euphemism for being dead.

(90) the blackening of the faces would pass for a frolic—In many parts of Ireland, mummers and wrenboys would disguise themselves with "blackface"—smearing their faces with black coal dust—as part of the costumes they wore during their performances. The Whiteboys and other secret societies often used this early form

John W. Hurley

of camouflage to pass their activities off as nothing more than a night out performing or partying. Mumming was still very common until the 1960s in particular parts of Ulster, and Wrening is still a tradition throughout Ireland.

(91) bonfire—The Whiteboys always carried a half-burned piece of turf or coal with them in something like a lantern case or tea pot, in order to use when starting fires to burn their enemies out. This piece of smoldering turf or coal was referred to as "the seed of fire".

(92) bagnets—Bayonets.

(93) flail—A flail is a farm tool used for threshing wheat, made of two long sticks connected by a thong. It is similar to the Okinawan nunchaku in its construction and in the way it is used, but it is larger in size. Lachlin states that while others had guns, pistols, bayonets, old rusty swords and pitchforks, he had only the flail he had used all day.

(94) haggard—Bring over pieces of straw from Vengeance's own barn.

(95) Tattheration—A "tat" is a tangled mass of hair.

(96) put on you—This might be from Irish "siúl a thógáil" or "géarú sa siúl" meaning "to put on", "increase" or "pick-up" speed. In the story it would mean "speed it up" or "hurry up".

(97) forenent—Opposite.

(98) sould the pass or stagged—"Sell out" and talk about their fellow Whiteboys to avoid prosecution.

(99) spring 'sizes, and the May fair—The spring "assizes", the seasonal court sessions.

(100) polthoge on the sconce—A blow on the head. From Irish, "paltóg"; a blow, a blow with the fist.

(101) standings—Standings were covered booths or open-air shops, made for selling goods at fairs and markets.

(102) cravat—A cravat is French for a necktie or neckcloth.

(103) out of a face—This means "to drive you out", "to hunt you altogether out of the town".

(104) Kitthogue—A left-handed person. From Irish "ciotóg", "ciotach", same sounds and meaning.

(105) avick—From Irish "a mhic" meaning "my son" in the vocative.

(106) Popish, ribly rascal—To this day members of the Orange Order and other Protestant Loyalist gangs, use the sectarian terms "Popery" when referring to Roman Catholicism and "Papists" when referring to Roman Catholics. "Popery" comes from the role played by the "Pontiff" or "Pope" as leader of the Catholic Church. Because of continued Catholic resistance to the undemocratic forms of British rule in Ireland, the majority of Catholics have consistently fought against the authority of the Crown in Ireland and hence are viewed as being "rebels" by those who are loyal to the Crown and who are mostly Protestant.

(107) a-kimbo—He stood with his hands on his hips, his elbows pointing outwards ("akimbo").

(108) inside crook—This is a technique used in Irish "collar and elbow" wrestling.

(109) gruel—Gruel is a kind of porridge, and this phrase means "have you had your fill?" or "have you had enough?"

(110) Boccagh—Irish "bacach"; a lame person.

(111) existence—According to Carleton: "Fact. The person who killed him escaped to America where he got himself naturalized, and when the British government claimed him, he pleaded his privilege of being an American citizen, and he was consequently not given up. Boccagh was a very violent Orangeman, and a very offensive one."

(112) trepanning—An ancient medical procedure where a hole is bored into the skull to relieve pressure on the brain.

(113) but, faix—"But, fách" or "Faith", a 19th century Hiberno-Irish expression close to our modern "Well now", as in "Well now, I wouldn't agree with that". In Irish "fách" literally means "in favor of" but here it means "now": "but, now, you'd always the (back) bone in you".

(114) weak side—According to Carleton: "A gentleman once told me an anecdote, of which he was an eye-witness. Some peasants, belonging to opposite factions, had met under peculiar circumstances; there were, however two on one side, and four on the other—in this case, there was likely to be no fight, but, in order to balance the number, one of the more numerous party joined the weak side—'bekase, boys, it would be a burnin' shame, so it would, for four to kick two; and, except I join them, by the powers, there's no chance of there being a bit of sport, or a row, at

John W. Hurley

all at all!' Accordingly, he did join them, and the result of it was, that he and his party were victorious; so honestly did he fight!"

(115) keening—"Keen", from Irish "caoineadh" or "caoin", the traditional lament sung by mourners at Irish wakes and funerals.

(116) acushla agus asthore machree—In Irish, "a chuisle agus a stór mo chróí"; "the pulse and beloved of my heart".

(117) avourneen dhelish!—From Irish "a mhuirnín dílis"; "my own sweetheart".

(118) solecism—A breach of good manners.

(119) Goldsmith's—The Irish author Oliver Goldsmith wrote a novel called "The Deserted Village" and this is the story being referred to.

(120) minute—Carleton (as an eyewitness to these events) says simply: "Such were the words."

(121) avick machree!—From Irish "a mhic mo chroí" or "son of my heart!"

(122) master of the revels—At Irish wakes of the 19th century, many "wake games" designed to appease the dead were played, and these were lead by a "master of revels". The playing of these games and the carnival like spirit associated with them was an ancient and likely pre-Christian tradition which thrived in Ireland until the mid-19th century.

(123) De Profundis—The De profundis is the psalm which in the Roman Catholic Church is repeated over the dead.

(124) Lough Derg—Lough Derg is an ancient place of pilgrimage for Irish Catholics. Carleton says: "Those who make a Station at Lough Derg are in the habit of bringing home some of its pebbles, which are considered to be sacred and possessed of many virtues."

(125) Pater and Ave—Literally, Latin for "Father and Hail", but short for "Pater Noster" and "Ave Maria", the Our Father and Hail Mary, the main prayers recited in the Roman Catholic Rosary.

(126) merin—A border.

(127) funeral passes—Carleton says: "Many of these striking and startling old customs have nearly disappeared, and indeed it is better that they should."

(128) this home to you!—Carleton says: "Does not this usage illustrate the proverb of the guilt being brought home to a man, when there be no doubt of his criminality?"

(129) I remarked—I noticed.

(130) sable side—The reverse side of the vestment was black or "sable", and the priest would have turned the vestment around and worn the black side out for funerals.

(131) droll—Humorous.

(132) within the pale—The small area around Dublin controlled by the Anglo-Normans was guarded by a wooden fence or palisade called a "pale". This area became known as "The Pale" and Norman inhabitants in the area spoke of themselves as being "within The Pale" and spoke of the Gaelic Irish who lived outside it as existing "beyond The Pale". Eventually the phrase "beyond the pale" came to be used in a racist way in the English language to describe a person or thing which was beyond the scope of English "civilization" and existed in the realm of alleged Gaelic (and later other) cultural "barbarism". So the priest is turning the phrase on his Protestant friend by saying that the coin is now "within the pale" of the (Irish) Catholic Church.

(133) mort-cloth—Death shroud.

(134) equestrians—Those carrying the coffin were followed by those on foot and then those on horseback or "equestrians".

(135) murder—Carleton says: "Certainly this wearing of red ribbons gives a very dreadful aspect to a funeral procession. It is not many years since it was witnessed in my native parish."

(136) astore—Also "asthore", a term of endearment meaning "my treasure". The vocative of "stór", "treasure".

(137) sowl—According to Carleton: "A fact."

(138) Drumfurrar bridge—In another story Carleton mentions that the Drumfurrar road was a lonely mountain road said to be haunted.

(139) knock under—Give up.

(140) gainsaid—The "argument" is the priests horsewhip, which was often used to break up faction fights.

John W. Hurley

(141) the dhrop, Sir, was in on both sides—People on both sides had been "taking in" a "drop" of liquor. Both sides were drunk.

(142) brick-bat—A piece or chunk of brick, rock or cobblestone.

(143) maudlin—Drunkenly sentimental or melodramatic.

John W. Hurley

Made in the USA
Columbia, SC
20 November 2023

26793051R00109